THE COUNTY GUIDES

DEATH IN DEVON

IAN SANSOM

Fully Illustrated Throughout

FOURTH ESTATE • *London*

Fourth Estate
An imprint of HarperCollins*Publishers*
1 London Bridge Street
London SE1 9GF

www.4thestate.co.uk

First published in Great Britain by Fourth Estate in 2015

1

MIX
Paper from
responsible sources
FSC™ C007454

FSC™ is a non-profit international organisation established to promote the
responsible management of the world's forests. Products carrying the FSC
label are independently certified to assure consumers that they come from
forests that are managed to meet the social, economic and ecological needs
of present and future generations, and other controlled sources.

Find out more about HarperCollins and the environment at
www.harpercollins.co.uk

For Will

And Babylon, the glory of kingdoms, the beauty of the Chaldees' excellency, shall be as when God overthrew Sodom and Gomorrah. It shall never be inhabited, neither shall it be dwelt in from generation to generation: neither shall the Arabian pitch tent there; neither shall the shepherds make their fold there. But wild beasts of the desert shall lie there; and their houses shall be full of doleful creatures; and owls shall dwell there, and satyrs shall dance there. And the wild beasts of the islands shall cry in their desolate houses, and dragons in their pleasant palaces: and her time is near to come, and her days shall not be prolonged.

Isaiah 13:19–22

CHAPTER 1

GOOD TO BE BACK

'AH, SEFTON, MY FECKLESS FRIEND,' said Morley. 'Just the man. Now. Rousseau? What do you think?'

He was, inevitably, writing one of his – inevitable – articles. The interminable articles. The inevitable and interminable articles that made up effectively his one, vast inevitable and interminable article. The *über*-article. The article to end all articles. The grand accomplishment. The statement. What he would have called the *magnum bonum*. The *Gesamtkuntswerk*. 'An essay a day keeps the bailiffs at bay,' he would sometimes say, when I suggested he might want to reduce his output, and 'The night cometh when no man can work, Sefton. Gospel of John, chapter nine, do you know it?' I knew it, of course. But only because he spoke of it incessantly. Interminably. Inevitably. It was a kind of mantra. One of many. Swanton Morley was a man of many mantras – of catchphrases, proverbs, aphorisms, slang, street talk and endless Latin tags. He was a collector, to borrow the title of one of his most popular books, of *Unconsidered Trifles* (1934). 'It takes as little to console us as it does to afflict us.'

'*Respice finem.*' And 'May you never meet a mouse in your pantry with tears in his eyes.' Morley's endless work, his inexhaustible sayings, were, it seemed to me, a kind of amulet, a form of linguistic self-protection. Language was his great superstition – and his saviour.

To stave off the universal twilight that evening Morley had rigged up the usual lamps and candles, and had his reams of paper piled up around him, like the snow-capped peaks of the Karakoram, or faggots on a pyre, like white marble stepping stones leading up to the big kitchen table plateau, where reference books lay open to the left and to the right of him, pads and pens and pencils at his elbow, his piercing eyes a-twinkling, his Empire moustache a-twitching, his brogue-booted feet a-tapping and his head a-nodding ever so slightly to the rhythms of his keystrokes as he worked at his typewriter, for all the world as if he were an explorer of some far distant realm of ideas, or some mad scientist out of a fantasy by H.G. Wells, strapped to an infernal computational machine. A glass and a jug of barley water were placed beside him, in their customary position – his only indulgence.

It was already well after midnight. I had returned to Norfolk and St George's after two days in London, attempting to put my affairs in order and succeeding only in disordering them further.

'Rousseau?' I said. It was my job in these exchanges, I had soon realised, to bat the ball gently back to him, the warm-up to his Fred Perry, as it were, throwing him balls or titbits, that he might leap up and devour them. 'My interlocutor', he would sometimes introduce me to new acquaintances, or, alas, worse, 'My *bo*', one of those terribly unfortunate phrases he'd picked up from his beloved hard-boiled detective stories, and which got us into a number of scrapes over the years. Damon Runyon, Ellery Queen: I could never quite understand his enthusiasm for purveyors of what he might, in the argot, have called *shtick*.

'Rousseau. Yes.' I was finding it hard to think. I had, admittedly, in London, been drinking and indulging, even though I had promised myself not to return to my former habits and haunts, but had found it impossible to resist. Just forty-eight hours away from Morley and his high thinking and I had descended back down to the depths of my depravities.

'Come, come, Sefton. Rousseau?' He clapped his hands.

'Well . . .' I'd managed to catch the last train out of Liverpool Street for Norfolk, in the full knowledge that if I stayed a day longer the die would be cast for ever, and I would be adrift and out of employment again, at the mercy of Messrs Gabbitas and Thring, and worse . . .

'Hello? Dial 0 for operator?' He rapped his knuckles against the table. 'Hello? Operator? It's ringing for you, caller! Remind me why I employed you again, Sefton?'

I had at that stage been Swanton Morley's amanuensis, his assistant, and his 'bo' for approximately two weeks. And I had to admit that – apart from my time in Spain – it had been the strangest, most utterly disorientating and exhilarating two weeks of my life. It had also – not insignificantly – helped to solve certain personal and practical problems I had been facing in London. Which is why, after a hectic few days, I had returned again to the wilds of Norfolk ready to clock in promptly for work on Monday morning.

'Jean-Jacques Rousseau,' I offered, fossicking around in

my rather disordered mental store cupboard. 'Philosopher. Educationalist—'

'No! No! No! Come on, man. Wrong Rousseau!' said Morley. 'Henri. Or *Henri*, pronounced in the continental fashion.'

'Ah.' As if I should have known which continental Rousseau he had in mind.

'Here, here. Come, come, come.'

Morley beckoned me towards him. I edged carefully around the books and papers and looked over his shoulder at one of the large volumes spread out on the desk.

'Well. What do you think of that?'

The moon shone down brightly from the high window above the table, illuminating the book, which showed an illustration of an extraordinarily vivid, disturbed sort of painting, like the work of a brilliantly gifted child, depicting what was presumably supposed to be a lion sinking its teeth into what was presumably an . . .

'Anteater?' I said.

'Antelope,' said Morley. 'Though granted it's not entirely clear. The gaucheries of the self-taught, eh, Sefton?'

'Yes.'

'Not that you'd know anything about that, eh?'

'Well, no' – my privileged upbringing and education were a constant source of amusement to Morley, who had raised himself by his proverbial bootstraps, and who found it hard to take anyone seriously who did not possess bootstraps that needed raising – 'although—'

'Quite extraordinary,' he said.

'Quite extraordinary,' I agreed. 'Remarkable.' I was rather groggy from the after-effects of my journey, and all the tobacco, and drink and too little sleep – and even under the best of circumstances it was simply easier to agree with Morley.

He turned the page to another illustration. A lion eating a leopard. And another page: a tiger attacking a water buffalo. And another: a jaguar bringing down a white horse.

'Wonderful stuff, isn't it, Sefton?'

'It's certainly . . . interesting, Mr Morley,' I agreed.

'Interesting?' he said. *'Interesting?'* 'Interesting', I learned over time, was a trigger word. There were others. 'Literally', for example, used incorrectly, would send him – literally – mad. 'Effect', as a cause, infuriated him. His 'instant' was never quick. And he could never see the irony in 'irony'. His moustache bristled. 'Is that really an aesthetic category, Sefton, do you think? *Interesting?* Hmm? Acceptable to the philosophers and critics of taste in your alma mater, in the old wisteria-swagged ivory towers of Cambridge, do you think? Mr Wittgenstein? Mr Leavis? *"Interesting"?* A common term of approbation among your peers, is it?'

'Well . . .'

'God save us from *"interesting"*, Sefton. God Himself save us. Jesus Christ? Hmm? What do you think?'

'What do I think about Jesus Christ, Mr Morley?'

'"Interesting" sort of fellow, would you say? And what about – I don't know, take your pick – Tutankhamun? Captain Scott? Napoleon? Christopher Columbus? Any of them *"interesting"* in your books? J.M.W. Turner perhaps? J.S. Bach? *"Interesting"* at all, at all, at all?'

'Erm . . .'

'Never left France, Rousseau.' Morley suddenly switched tack, as he was wont to do. 'All this exotica derived entirely from images in books and magazines. And up here, of course.' He tapped his head with his fingers, one of his favourite gestures in his wide repertoire of gestures: he would have made a fine actor in rather broad Shakespearean roles, I always thought, or perhaps an understudy to Charles Laughton, though in looks of course, as has often been remarked, he resembled rather more a mustachioed Fritz Leiber, in his heyday in *The Queen of Sheba*. 'And the Jardin des Plantes,' he continued. 'Dioramas in museums and what have you – look at the lion there, looks like a stuffed toy, doesn't it? Product entirely of the imagination, Sefton. An orchestration of images, ideas and desires. And yet an instinctive understanding of the mysteries of the tropical, wouldn't you say? Look at that undergrowth.'

'Yes.'

'I think our friend Herr Freud would have something to say about Rousseau, wouldn't he, eh? Monsieur *Henri*, eh? Eh?'

'I'm sure he would, Mr Morley.' Though I wasn't sure entirely what it was Freud would have to say. Nor did I entirely care.

'Hmm.' He stroked his moustache. 'The tangles, you see, Sefton. Tangles. Tangles. You see the tangles?' I saw the tangles. 'And the deep lush vegetation. Vines. Lianas. Terrible confrontations in deep dusky dells with mysterious hairy beasts. Look at these gashes and wounds here.'

'Yes.'

'One doesn't have to be Viennese, I think, to have a guess, does one?'

'No, Mr Morley.' Or rather, *What, Mr Morley?* (Which is of course the title of his famous series of books of notes and

[6]

queries, published annually, containing answers to questions posed in the form of the book's title, thus, 'What, Mr Morley, is the meaning of the term *mah nishtana*, which I have heard some of my Jewish neighbours exclaim, and which I believe may be either Hebrew or the Jewish language of Yiddish?', or 'What, Mr Morley, is the best way to remove coal dust from my antimacassar?')

'Not quite top rank though, is it?' continued Morley. 'In all honesty? I think we'll grant him an *accessit*, shall we?'

'A—'

'Second prize medal. Forgotten all your Latin?'

'Ahem. Well. That sounds about . . .'

'The great untaught, you see, Sefton. All that power and originality combined with sometimes shocking naivety. The child's perspective, one might say. The sublime cheek by jowl with the ridiculous. One of life's great mysteries, wouldn't you say?'

I couldn't have agreed more.

'Yes,' I said.

'Good.'

'And who's the article for, Mr Morley?'

'*Sunday Graphic*. Just a little *jeu d'esprit*, as Mr Rousseau himself might say.'

He poured himself a fresh glass of barley water, and stared at me inquisitively.

'So, my young fellow, how was London?'

'It was fine, thank you, sir.' I never spoke to Morley about my other life. It did not seem appropriate.

'Good. Good. You'll be delighted to know that in your absence I've finished *Norfolk*.'

'Finished it?'

[7]

'That's correct. *Aquila non capit muscas* and what have you.'

We had only returned from our first adventure around the English counties on Sunday. This was a week later. Which meant that he had written a book . . . in a week?

It took me a moment to gather my powers of speech.

'But I thought we were going to . . .'

'We have a strict schedule to stick to, Sefton, remember. If we're going to cover everything by 1940. Uphill all the way, I'm afraid. No time for slacking.'

'No, of course.'

'Or shilly-shallying.'

'No.'

'Or funking.'

'No, absolutely. No slacking. No shilly-shallying. No funking.'

'Precisely! So I took the liberty of writing up most of my notes myself – to save you time. You'll be copy-editing and proofing this week. We want to have it more or less ready for the presses within two weeks. Photographs and what have you. Excellent photographs, by the way, Sefton – though a little bit more artistic, next time, eh?'

'More artistic, Mr Morley?'

'Well, you know. Something a bit more . . . Man Ray perhaps?'

'Really? Man Ray?'

'Yes, you've come across him?'

'I think so, yes.'

'Or . . . I don't know, maybe not Man Ray, Sefton. But something. We need to capture the public's imagination, man. Give them something new. Something fresh. Something ... unexpected.'

'I'll do my best, Mr Morley.'

'Good! Bit of experimentation, man. But not too much.'

'Very good, Mr Morley.'

'And then as I say, we should have everything ready for publication by the end of October. *The County Guides* – book number one.'

'That's ... good.'

'And in the meantime we shall move on swiftly to book number two.'

'Right. I'll be staying here then, to do the copy-editing and proofing on book one?'

'Here?'

'St George's? Norfolk?' I could imagine myself curled up by the fire in the library, leisurely correcting Morley's proofs, cigarettes and coffee to hand.

'Not at all, not at all, not at all, Sefton. Not. At. All. No, no, no. We're all packed and ready to go again, my friend, first thing in the morning. You're going to have to get accustomed to the pace of life here, old chap. You'll be editing en route to our next county.'

'I see.' I was tired already. 'Will Miriam be joining us?'

'She will, indeed. For better and for worse. Until you've got the hang of things.'

'I think I've probably—'

'Also, she needs to ... get away for a while. I have spoken to you about Miriam before, Sefton, you will recall.' He narrowed his eyes rather as he spoke.

'Yes.'

'And you have clearly understood my concerns?'

A bit of experimentation

'Yes, yes, of course, Mr Morley.'

'Wild.' He shook his head. 'Untameable.'

'Well, I wouldn't say—'

'And it'll take a better man than you to tame her, Sefton. With all due respect. There's talk of another engagement . . .'

'I see.'

He gazed up at the window above the desk. It was a clear night sky.

'There's a storm coming.'

It wasn't immediately clear to me whether he was speaking literally or metaphorically; he spoke often of gathering storms. It wasn't always clear whether he meant rain, or Miriam's doomed engagements, or the imminent collapse of human civilisation. Or all three.

'Do you ever think about the future, Sefton?'

'Occasionally, Mr Morley. Yes, I do.'

'And when you think about the future, what do you think?'

'Erm . . .' An answer, obviously, was not required.

'When I think about the future, Sefton, I think that what we are doing now will be seen largely as an irrelevance, alas. The book will become a decorative art object, and as for newspapers . . .' He shook his head. 'There will be endless wars. Famines. And the England that we know and love will have entirely disappeared. We will achieve a classless society, not because we have all been raised to new heights, but rather because we have all been dragged down to the same depths.' When speaking of heights and depths, Morley illustrated the point with his usual gestures.

'I see.' This was a version of a speech I had already heard him utter on numerous occasions.

[11]

'People's bodies will seize up, Sefton, due to their un-thinking reliance on machines. Men and women will balloon in size, like vast blimps, and go bouncing around our towns and cities, crushing one another in their hurry to acquire more and more of less and less that is truly good. Don't you think it's possible, Sefton?'

'It's certainly not im—'

'But one day, I believe, man will overcome himself. He will rise from his slumber. He will slip the bounds and trammels of this earth. He will transcend his small concerns and reach for the stars! He will travel . . . to the moon! Do you think it's possible, Sefton?'

'Again, it's entirely—'

'Not in my lifetime, perhaps. But in yours. It will be wonderful: an opportunity to start all over again, eh? Not granted to every man, Sefton, is it?'

'No, Mr Morley.'

'But in this brave new world I believe there will be so much going on that no one will care to remember what we have lost.'

'Indeed.'

'Which is our task, of course, Sefton! To act as recording angels, if you like. No more. No less. Quite a calling though, eh?' His rambling speech seemed to have cheered him – as his rambling speeches so often did. I wondered some-times if he spoke merely for the sole purpose of his own encouragement.

'Yes. Indeed.'

He stared at me again. 'You seem rather liverish this eve-ning, Sefton, if you don't mind my saying.'

'Yes, well, I . . .'

'Time for your beauty sleep, perhaps.'

'Well, I am rather tired, Mr Morley.'

'*Raram facit misturam cum sapientia forum*, Sefton.'

'Quite. So . . . unless there's anything I can do for you here . . .'

'No, no, no. The cottage won't be ready for a while, I'm afraid. I've spoken to Wilson about it. It's going to need quite some fixing up. In the meantime we'll put you upstairs in one of the attic rooms, if that's still OK? Same room as before. All set up for you.'

'That's wonderful, thank you.'

'Eaten?'

'I had a sandwich at Liverpool Street.'

'*Cheruntis pabulum*! You can find yourself something in the kitchen if you'd like. Cook made a wonderful mutton and parsnip soup a few days ago. It's maturing rather nicely.'

'No, thank you.'

'What's the Korean dish?'

'I'm not sure, Mr Morley.'

'*Kimchi*! That's it. Rather reminiscent. I was there just after the Japanese occupation. Pretty grisly. Merciless . . . Anyway. Probably best to avoid the soup in your condition. I'll bid you goodnight. Must just finish this.' And with that he turned back to his books and his typewriter, and the endless words began to flow again.

∽ ∾

Upstairs, as I walked down the long corridor towards my room up in the attic, the echo of Morley's typewriter in the distance, a door happened to open and Miriam walked out. She was smiling inwardly, it seemed to me: there was a look of satisfaction on her face, of satiation, one might almost say, as if she had . . . Well . . . I had enjoyed a rather long weekend in London and was tired; my imagination was doubtless running away with me. Her hair, I noted, was a blonder shade of blonde than I remembered, her cheeks were flushed, and she was wearing a nightgown made of a silvery silk, creating an effect that in the half-lit corridor might be described as simultaneously ethereal and electrifying, shuddering almost, as if one had bumped into Carole Lombard herself, made-up, half dressed, lit, on set, and ready to take her call . . .

'Oh, Sefton. You're here!' she gasped, clutching her nightgown more closely to her. 'Sorry, I was just . . .'

'Yes. Good evening, Miss Morley.'

'Back for more then? We haven't put you off?'

'No. No. Not at all.'

'You were in London?'

'Yes, I was.'

'I hope you had fun?'

'I . . . did. Yes. Certainly.'

'Good. I think we're going to have fun, aren't we, Sefton?' She was standing alarmingly close to me at this point, so close that I began to feel rather vulnerable, like the poor antelope in Rousseau's painting.

'I'm sure we will, Miss Morley.'

'You . . . and me,' she said.

'And your father, of course.'

'Hmm.'

She walked off then, turning only to wave goodnight and

to cast the mystery of her smile before me, like a cryptic invitation, or a code I was supposed to crack.

I entered my room and lay down on my bed, exhausted.

God, it was good to be back.

CHAPTER 2

PRANIC BREATHING

As Morley had predicted, there was a storm. I stood watching it from the window of my room as the lightning at first flickered feebly in the distance and then, as it came closer, began flashing through the darkness, illuminating both sky and earth, thunder reverberating everywhere, the whole building humming in response, it seemed to me, window frames squealing, until finally, after all the tumult, the soft rain came splashing down, dripping from the eaves above my little dormer window as though the house itself were weeping.

Eventually I fell asleep, with the assistance of only a couple of pills, and topped up with no more than half the bottle of brandy I'd brought with me in case of emergency, and which I'd intended to last me for some time. And then, as usual, I woke early, tense from another terrible dream – Spain, gunfire – in Laocoon-like distress, twisted, hot and uncomfortable, the sheets tangled tight around my body. Freeing myself from the bed, I rose, splashed myself with cooling water from the washstand, threw open the heavy damask curtains and stood by the open window, allowing the morning air to calm my racing thoughts. As I gazed out across the vast north Norfolk landscape, my previous life – all my indulgences and regrets, my lies and my mistakes – suddenly seemed far away. Everything seemed invigoratingly fresh and new. All that mattered now, I tried to convince myself, were the *County Guides*.

All I had with me were the clothes that Morley had kindly provided me with, a wash kit, some shaving gear and a few books. My humble *tout ensemble*. Having given up my digs in London I no longer had a permanent home: it seemed now as if every room I stayed in was almost immediately cleansed of my presence. Before leaving London I had purchased a few books to accompany me: George Orwell's *The Road to Wigan Pier*, Eric Partridge's *A Dictionary of Slang and Unconventional English* and a second-hand edition of Pound's *A Draft of XXX Cantos*, published by the Hours Press in Paris, the hessian cover already worn thin. I was on another self-improvement jag. Not in the mood for either Orwell or etymology, I began flicking through the Pound, trying to find something at least half-readable, until I came to Canto XXX, and the poem beginning 'Compleynt, compleynt I hearde upon a day':

> *All things are made foul in this season,*
> *This is the reason, none may seek purity*
> *Having for foulnesse pity*
> *And things growne awry;*
> *No more do my shaftes fly*
> *To slay. Nothing is now clean slayne*
> *But rotteth away.*

Both inexplicably cheered and thoroughly depressed, I shaved and dressed and went downstairs. I thought I would go outside to smoke. It was, by this time, about 5.30 a.m.

To my great surprise, as I walked quietly outside and around St George's, along the path fringed with flowers and grasses that leads eventually under the narrow archway tangled with roses, and past the yew hedges down towards the model farm and the orchards, I came across Morley standing on the lawn outside his study. He was dressed only in a pair of pure white underpants and a white vest, without shoes or socks. His eyes were closed and his arms outstretched, as if in an enormous embrace, and the grass was thick with rain, and his breath rose from him like ... I can only properly describe it as like steam rising from a dish of potatoes, though Pound would perhaps have described it as like steam from a bowl of rice, or Yeats perhaps as a grey mist, Auden as like a cigarette smouldering in a border, and Eliot – I don't know – as a kind of god river sweat? I wonder sometimes if I'll ever write a poem again, and indeed if I ever truly wrote one. If nothing else, my time with Morley convinced me of my own limited capacities as a writer.

The gardens and grounds of St George's stretched out far behind Morley, in bright greens and in grey-green hollows of mist. He appeared in that moment, I thought, almost a kind of Christ figure, hanging suspended over the early morning English landscape. It was a strange and particular scene, and yet also somehow entirely everyday – and of course rather comic and banal. As Morley himself often liked to remark, the juxtapositions and non sequiturs of everyday life are often more astonishing than even the most extraordinary work of art. 'There is no such thing as the avant-garde' –

this was one of his favourite sayings, repeated in a number of his books, including *Morley's Style Manual for Writers and Editors* (1936) and *Art for Art's Sake* (1939) – 'there is only the *garde-en-retarde*. All artists are catch-up artists and merchants in nostalgia.'

In his semi-clad reverie he didn't seem to notice me, so I stood behind a large shrub, finishing my cigarette, watching him silently from a distance. A big grey-backed fox – that old type of fox that one rarely sees any more – came prancing across the lawn, came towards him, glanced up, flirtatiously almost, and then trotted on, doubtless towards its breakfast in the hen-house and the orchards. Birds called – let's say, for the sake of argument, that they were blue tits, willow warblers and chiff-chaffs, though at the time, in all honesty, I could not have recognised any of their calls, having only in recent years taken up Morley's frequent admonition to make myself familiar with birdsong and the sounds of nature – and a couple came and settled so close almost as to rest upon him.

And then the sun suddenly cast a blaze of light across the scene, further illuminating the brilliant damp green, and Morley's dazzling white underclothes, and his glaring white moustache, and his pale white skin, and this was one of those moments, I think, when I began to understand the true paradoxes of Morley, and of my strange relation-ship with him. During our time together I think I tended to think of him as a kind of mechanism, rather like an electric appliance – an animation of a man, unnatural, Karloffian almost, like Dr Frankenstein's monster, twitching with life, a creature of unnatural habits and abnormal brain. And yet there was simultaneously this other very marked aspect of his personality, which one might describe as botanical and germinal, organic perhaps, his thoughts and ideas growing slowly and gently within him and from him as a tree might throw forth branches, or a flower blossom. This combination of the natural and the mechanical, the extraordinary and the everyday, the practical and the poetic, the physical and the metaphysical, always made him seem larger than life, macrocosmic almost – and, it has to be said, utterly bizarre.

After some moments of inactivity, he started rocking his head backward and forward, breathing in on the upswing, and out on the downswing. He did this for about a minute, and then began to prepare for a series of exercises that seemed to require the removal of his underwear. I coughed, involuntarily, and he opened his eyes and spied me on the path.

'Ah, Sefton. Don't be shy. Come on over.' He glanced down. 'Almost an inch, I'd say. What do you think?'

I walked rather shyly across the damp lawn towards him.

'Right,' I said. I didn't know what to reply.

'Of rain, man. Last night.'

'Ah.'

'Refreshing, isn't it? A good old autumn storm. We had hailstones last year in September that shattered the glasshouses. Tore the plants from their pots. Beware nature, eh, Sefton? Just communing myself, here. Connecting to the old vital forces. Care to join me?'

'No, I'm fine, thank you.' I took out another cigarette and lit it.

'Still smoking?'

'I'm afraid so.'

'Won't do you any good, you know. Chains of bondage. *Nil tam difficile est quod non solertia vincat.*' He began swinging his arms in contrary motion. 'We need you in peak condition, man, if you're going to stay the course with the *County Guides*. It's no holiday.'

'No,' I agreed.

'An endurance test really. Test of strength. Of mettle. Of one's inner resources, eh?'

'Indeed.'

His arm-swinging had by now become alarmingly vigorous.

'You want to try this, Sefton. You're familiar with pranic breathing, I take it?'

'Pranic breathing?'

'Taught to me by a man in Paris, many years ago – *respiration pranique*. Haddo. Funny sort of fellow. Your sort.'

'My sort?'

'You know, bohemian. Bit of a fraud, actually. Claimed he could live without food or water and that he existed merely on the energy of the sun.'

'Is that possible?'

'Obviously not. Met him in a restaurant one night, tucking into a *fricandeau à l'oseille* and a bottle of German hock. Anyway. Most people don't breathe at all properly, Sefton, as you know. Essential, breathing.'

'Yes. I suppose it is.'

'I found the technique very useful, after my wife ...' Morley rarely spoke of his wife, and when he did he was often overcome with such emotion, such an intense turmoil, such a storm, that he was simply unable to speak, as if he were momentarily gripped by a pain beyond words. He would literally stall and stop, like one of his cars, and then he would blink, and clear his throat, and continue on again, as now. 'The breath, you see, gets interrupted all the time.' I thought I saw a tear in his eye. 'Shallow breathing – curse of our age. I might write a little pamphlet, actually. In fact, make a note could you, Sefton? I don't seem to have my notebook or cards with me.' He patted at his underpants, as if fully expecting to find a notebook tucked away there.

I felt in my own pockets for a notebook, but found none. Not that it mattered. The storm had passed. Morley moved on.

'Girdling,' he said. 'Medieval monastic practice. Prevents a man being caught short. I've spoken to you about it before?'

'You have, Mr Morley, yes.'

'Good. Anyway. Fear, anxiety, anger – all stored in the breath, you know. If people were given basic lessons in good consistent, circular breathing I think everyone would be much happier. Don't you think so? Moves energy from the body, proper breathing. Energy in motion. Here.' He reached out towards me and placed his hands on my belly. 'Breathe in.' I breathed in. 'And breathe out.' I breathed out. 'Yes, as I thought. You should be breathing from the diaphragm, Sefton. When you take a breath, you're inhaling from the chest. You need to take a proper breath.' He kept his hands on my belly. 'Go on. Try again. From the diaphragm. Here. Not here.' He tapped my chest.

The more I thought about diaphragm breathing, the less I seemed able to do it.

'You're constricting on your exhale, man. You're not letting go. How did you sleep?'

'Not well, I'm afraid.'

'Hardly surprising. Poor breathing robs us of energy and doesn't allow us to rest properly.'

'I think it was more because of the thunder, ' I was about to say, and also perhaps because of the half-bottle of brandy, and the pills and the dreams, but he had taken his thumb and index finger and pressed my left nostril with his thumb, making speech difficult.

'There we are. Breathe in. Hold for three.'

And then he pinched the bridge of my nose, before pressing my right nostril with his index finger.

'And now exhale through the left for a count of six. One. Two. Three. Four. Five. Six. Good. And again.' More nostril-pinching.

I had only recently been in a Soho club where—

'Hold for three. Good. And exhale for six. Etcetera. Don't worry. We'll get there, Sefton. We'll get there.'

He began walking back towards the house. I followed: what else could I do?

'I am not – as you know – entirely ecumenical in my outlook, Sefton, but I do think there are some things we could profitably learn from our Hindu brothers and sisters. And Confucians. Buddhists. Taoists. Do you know the Waley book on the Tao Te Ching?'

'Erm . . .'

'Worth looking up. Jainism also. Ever come across any Jains?'

'I think I may have come across one or two Janes in my time, yes, Mr Morley.' I grinned.

'Are you being facetious, Sefton?'

'No.'

'Good, too early in the morning to be facetious, Sefton.

And too late in the day, I fear. The Jains, man. *Jains*. There's a beautiful white granite statue of Bahubali, on a hill near Sravanabelagola I think it is – visited it once. Long time ago. Astonishing piece of work. Sixty foot tall, and they have this quite extraordinary ceremony where they anoint it with milk and saffron and what have you. Marvellous. Quite extraordinary. Anyway, as I was saying, *prana*, Sefton – the life force. Powerful thing. Very popular notion in all Asiatic religions: *qi* among the Chinese, of course. Odic forces I think are probably the closest we come in the West. Personally, I am trying to develop my *apana*, the long down breath, which reaches down all the way to the root *chakra*.'

Frankly, I found it a little early to be discussing Jainism, *qi* and *chakras*, but fortunately, in characteristic style, Morley soon switched subject matter again as we entered his study through the French windows, and several of his many dogs came bounding towards us. One of his particular favourites – an Irish terrier named Fionn mac Cumhaill ('pronounced MacCool, Sefton, please, in the Celtic fashion') – never seemed to warm to me and stood protectively now at Morley's side, with the clear intention first of growling at me, and then very possibly barking, chasing, biting and savaging.

'Irish dogs,' said Morley. 'Like Irish men. Or women, for that matter. Not to be trifled with. *Cave canem*, Sefton – as they said in old Pompeii.' He stroked the dog absent-mindedly. 'You really do need to learn how to handle animals, Sefton. They can sense fear, you see. Like children. One should simply fondle them – thus – when they're near.' He fondled the dog, thus. 'But without appearing to pay them much attention.' He then duly paid the dog no attention. 'Very much like the Irish ... So. Anyway,' he said, striding

Fionn mac Cumhaill (pronounced in the Celtic fashion)

around in his underwear, as if it were the most natural way to conduct a meeting. 'There's Norfolk.' He pointed to a pile of typed papers, stacked on the floor next to boxes of index cards: the work of the past week. What was impressive was not only his uncanny ability to produce copy but also his capacity for processing information of all kinds; he had a method of both overseeing and arranging material that was entirely his own, or certainly that I had never encountered before and that required the constant categorising, filing and sub-categorising and refiling of his papers and notecards. He often worked through the night, shuffling papers.

He pointed to another teetering pile of papers on a desk.

'And there's some correspondence we should probably sort before setting off, Sefton. There's been quite a lot of talk about what happened in Norfolk, as you know. I'd like to avoid any such troubles on our next trip.'

'Of course.'

'Anyway, I cleared a couple of dozen letters before going to bed last night, but I'd like to get them all done before we leave.'

'I see. It seems like rather a lot,' I ventured. I imagined that such a pile of correspondence might take several days to work through.

'And what is our motto here, Sefton?'

'No slacking.'

'Correct.'

'No shilly-shallying.'

'Precisely.'

'And no funking.'

At that moment Miriam appeared at the study door. She was dressed and made up, as usual, in a fashion that

The County Guides: Norfolk, in preparation

suggested that she was about to arrive fashionably late at a cocktail party, probably somewhere in Kensington, thronged with wealthy and elegant suitors.

'Hard at it already then, boys?'

'Ah, Miriam,' said Morley. 'You're uncharacteristically bright and early.'

'Good morning, Father. Yes. The storm kept me awake in the night. I was terribly disturbed. And what about you, Sefton? Another long and lonely night?'

'I slept as well as could be expected, Miss Morley.'

'Glad to hear it.'

'We'll be leaving at seven, children,' said Morley. 'Quick breakfast, and on the road. I want to be in Devon by night-fall.'

'Devon?' I said.

'And when is your speech, Father?'

'Tomorrow. Founder's Day.'

'You're giving a speech?' I said. 'In Devon.'

'Yes, I thought we'd kill two birds with one stone. I've been asked to give the Founder's Day address down at All Souls, Sefton. They've just moved into new school buildings down there somewhere. Where is it, Miriam?'

'Rousdon, Father.'

'Rousdon, yes, that's it, and—'

'Or *Rouse them*, Sefton,' said Miriam coquettishly.

'So the plan is to base ourselves there and tackle Devon. Book number two. How does that sound, Sefton?'

'Mad,' said Miriam. 'Utterly, utterly mad. As usual.'

'Super,' I said.

'Oh, please,' said Miriam. '*Soo-per*. If you'd wanted some-one to soft-soap you, Father, you could have employed a masseur.' She raised a quizzical eyebrow towards me.

'Thank you, Miriam,' said Morley. 'Let's fight nicely, shall we?'

'Sorry, gents. Must pack,' said Miriam, leaving as abruptly as she'd arrived, glimmering as she went.

'Untameable,' said Morley, shaking his head. 'Wild, Sefton. Utterly wild. Like Devon.'

The Lagonda

CHAPTER 3

GATEWAY TO THE RIVIERA

AFTER A BRIEF but exhausting breakfast – Morley expatiating on the history of sausages, the music of Wagner, the music of birdsong, the symbolic meaning of the human hand, and the decline of smithying ('It's the bicycles I blame, Sefton, not the cars, and of course people getting rid of the pony and trap') – Miriam and I loaded the Lagonda and prepared to set off. The weather was sullen, and so was Miriam. After everything had been loaded – massive stationery supplies, mostly – I assisted her in lashing a couple of long planks to the side of the car.

'Careful with the paintwork, Sefton, or you'll have to touch it up. We wouldn't want that, would we?'

'No, Miss Morley,' I agreed.

'Ah,' said Morley, appearing fortuitously with his trusty Irish terrier. He tapped the long wooden boards with a great deal of proprietorial pleasure. 'They arrived then?'

'Apparently,' said Miriam.

'Beautiful, aren't they, Sefton?'

'Yes,' I agreed. My attention was elsewhere: I was

attempting to fondle the dog, and simultaneously to ignore it, as Morley had advised. But the dog was not impressed – the damned thing was tugging determinedly at the turn-ups on my trousers.

'Finn!' said Miriam sternly, and the dog immediately stopped and trotted off. Miriam gave me a pitying smile.

'Absolutely beautiful,' Morley was saying to himself, about the boards, which were indeed beautiful – sleek, rounded, polished – though I had absolutely no idea what on earth they were.

'Solid ash,' said Morley. 'Had them made by Grays of Cambridge – the cricket chaps. Not cheap. But worth every penny. They finish them with the shinbone of a reindeer. Did you know?'

'No.'

'Gives a lovely finish.'

'And they are . . . ?'

'Surfboards, of course,' said Morley.

I must have looked, I suppose, rather nonplussed. It was still early in the morning.

'Really, Sefton, have you never seen a surfboard?' said Miriam, delighted.

'No. Of course I've seen . . . surfboards and . . . surfboard-ing, but—'

'Well, you're in for a treat,' she said.

'Yes,' agreed Morley. 'It's very—'

'Liberating,' said Miriam.

'Yes,' agreed Morley. 'Liberating is exactly the word. Like flying. Being free.'

'It'll be a new experience for you, Sefton,' said Miriam.

'Hawaiian in origin, obviously,' said Morley, as he climbed

into the back of the car, and Miriam fitted his portable desk with his typewriter stays. 'I've done a little research, I think our best bets are north Devon. Saunton. Croyde. Round about there.'

'We could camp on the beach!' said Miriam, clapping her hands, and then carefully slotting Morley's favourite travelling Hermes typewriter into place.

'It sounds like it's going to be quite an adventure,' I said, climbing into the back next to Morley, who unceremoniously dumped the manuscript of the Norfolk book and a pile of index cards into my lap.

'Let's hope so!' said Miriam, climbing into the front, and starting up the engine, which gave its customary pleasing growl. 'Better than bloody Norfolk anyway.'

'Language, Miriam,' said Morley.

'I need adventure, Father.'

'I know, my dear – don't we all. And Devon is of course the great county of adventurers and explorers. Scott of the Antarctic – from?'

'Plymouth?' said Miriam.

'Correct. And Sir Francis Drake, the old sea dog, born near? Sefton?'

'Erm. Plymouth?' I said.

'Tavistock. So we'll have to pay respects. And we'll also have to visit Sir Walter Raleigh's bench ends in All Saints, East Budleigh.'

'Great,' I said, as Miriam raced the car down St George's long drive.

'And a trip to Axminster, home of the eponymous carpet. Exeter, obviously. And Ottery St Mary.'

'Utterly St Mary!' said Miriam.

'Ever heard of it, Sefton?'

'No, I—'

'Shame on you. Church modelled on Exeter Cathedral, Samuel Taylor Coleridge was born there. Ring any bells?'

'Erm.'

'Yawn,' said Miriam.

'And speaking of bells, it has a clock, I think, that's said to date from the fourteenth century, and which is one of the only pre-Copernican clocks in the country—'

'And there's surfing,' said Miriam. 'Which way, Father?'

'Left.'

∽ ∾

And so the conversation and the journey continued across country and down to Devon, hour after hour after endless hour, Morley, like Pliny the Elder, continually making notes along the way – 'Lavender! Roses! Gypsophila! Dry-stone wall!' – while I corrected his work on the manuscript of the Norfolk book, and Miriam smoked innumerable cigarettes and offered the occasional taunt and barbed aside: she was, as usual, determined to provoke. Somewhere in Essex, for example, I think it was, we passed a woman riding a horse and this excited a typical little Miriam provocation. She often spoke like someone trying to get around the Hays Code.

'Medicine may well have something to say on the subject of whether women should ride astride once they have reached maturity,' Morley had remarked. 'Side saddle is surely the appropriate method, wouldn't you agree, Sefton?'

'I'm not sure,' I said.

[34]

'Oh, come, come,' said Miriam, cocking her head rather. 'Surely you must have an opinion on the question of women's riding styles?'

'It is a matter about which I have no opinion whatsoever,' I said.

'Such a shame,' she said, revving the engine unnecessarily.

'Thank you,' said Morley. 'No need.'

∽ ∾

For navigational purposes Morley had cut up and mounted onto thin oak boards a large *Philip's Road Atlas of Britain*, dividing England county by county into squares of approximately nine by six inches. It was my job to arrange these giant county playing cards, as it were, into some kind of meaningful hand, and then to deal out the route, card by card, to Miriam, with Morley adding his own inevitable comments and elaborate instructions: 'Avoid Cambridge at all costs, Miriam – whole place stagnant with marshes and dons!'; 'Ah, yes! Beautiful lute-like Berkshire! Belly to the west, neck to the east!' Etcetera, etcetera. Morley would also make requests for ludicrous detours and stopping points – 'Do we have time for a dawdle through Hampshire?' 'Up to Bristol? Cardiff?' – which Miriam, thankfully, resisted.

'This is the route, Father, that we are sticking to, if we wish to arrive any time today. Repeat after me: Norfolk, Cambridgeshire, Bedfordshire, Buckinghamshire, Berkshire, Wiltshire and Dorset.'

'And Devon!' cried Morley.

A giant county playing card

'Obviously,' said Miriam. 'No slacking. No shilly-shallying. No funking.'

'No Bristol?' said Morley.

'Correct,' said Miriam. 'And no Bath, no Basingstoke, no Bournemouth. So please don't ask. I have the wheel, Father. Mine is the power.'

'Onwards, Boudicca!' cried Morley. 'To defend the nation!'

We stopped for a filthy tea somewhere near Salisbury, at the inexplicably named Nell Gwynn Tea-Rooms, a place decorated both inside and out with an unfortunate combination of fake wooden beams and very shiny yellow bricks.

'A Tudorbethan lavatory,' said Miriam, as we pulled up. 'How quaint.'

'Worse than Mugby Junction,' said Morley, which seemed to be an allusion to something or other: it certainly made Miriam laugh. They often enjoyed little jokes like these, based on a lifetime's shared experience and reading: I imagine Milton and his daughter might have enjoyed similar happy reminiscences. Our Nell Gwynn tea consisted of cold potato soup and rather hard and arid little rolls which produced in us all such indigestion that we had to consume several packs of Morley's favourite mints in order to overcome the aftertaste. (These mints – Bassett's People's Mints – are not to be confused with actual Morley Mints, which were at one time produced by the manufacturers of Uncle Joe's Mint Balls, and which Morley consumed in incredible quantities. 'Insufficient weaning,' Miriam would traditionally reply, when Morley asked for another of his mint balls, and 'Oh, do spare us your Freud,' he would traditionally respond, popping another into his mouth.)

∽ ∾

And then finally, towards evening, after much indigestion and some confusion in my dealing of the county cards – I had accidentally confused Somerset with Dorset, sending us on a rather round-about route – we made it to Honiton. The weather had remained calm all day, but now the sky closed in again, menacing, threatening more rain. This did not, however, dampen Morley's mood.

'At last!' he cried. 'Honiton! Gateway to the Riviera!'

I looked around as we sped through the streets – street, really – of Honiton.

'Really?'

'Indeed, Sefton. Welcome to Devon! So, what are we looking forward to most in Devon, Sefton?'

'Erm . . .'

'Yes, Sefton,' called Miriam. 'What are we looking forward to most in Devon?'

'In Devon?'

'Yes,' said Morley. 'Or Dumnonia, as I believe the ancient kingdom was once called.'

'And don't say the cream teas!' called Miriam from the front seat.

'The . . .'

'Moors, of course,' said Morley. 'Yes. Correct. Dartmoor. Exmoor.'

'Of course,' I said.

'And it is renowned for what else, Devon? Topographically, geographically, I mean?'

'Well, there are the moors, obviously, and ...' I was struggling rather.

'The fact that it is the only one of our counties to be in proud possession of not one but two coastlines!'

'Ah.'

'Correct! And any other particular places and sights of interest? I am myself particularly looking forward to visiting Torquay United, Exeter City and the mighty Argyle. But you're not a fan of association football, are you, Sefton?'

'Well, no, I'm more of a—'

'Lah-di-dah?' said Morley. 'But we'll say no more about it. What about you, Miriam?'

'I can't wait to just strip off and get into the water,' she called. 'I've brought my costume. Have you brought yours, Sefton?'

I forbore to answer.

'It's emerald green,' she said.

'And some rockpooling perhaps,' said Morley. 'Crabbing. I do love a spot of crabbing.'

'And surfing,' said Miriam.

'Indeed,' said Morley. 'Now, Devon: patron saint? Sefton?'

'St Petroc?' said Miriam.

'Good guess. But wrong. Cornwall, Petroc. Though I believe he did pass through on his way down. St Winfrid I think is Devon's, isn't that right?'

'Possibly, Father.'

'Also the patron saint of?'

'Germany?' said Miriam.

'Correct.'

[39]

'And?'

'Don't know, don't care.'

'Brewers,' said Morley.

'Sefton will feel right at home then.'

I blushed rather.

'And we must make a visit to the Dartmouth pixies, Miriam, while we're here. Or *piskies*, as I believe the locals call them. *Pharisees*, as they are known in Sussex. The little people. They like to ride ponies and lead unwary travellers to their doom in the bogs on the moors, isn't that right, Miriam?'

'Yes, Father.'

'Pixies?' I said.

'Indeed.'

'You're not serious?'

'Deadly,' said Miriam. 'Deadly serious.'

'Pixies?'

'Oh yes,' she said. 'Absolutely. Father is as serious about his pixies as Conan Doyle was about his fairies. Didn't you know? Deadly, deadly serious.'

'I see,' I said. 'Well, I suppose we must allow for the possibility of—'

'Of course he doesn't believe in pixies, Sefton!' cried Miriam.

'Joke!' cried Morley. 'Jolly good, Miriam.'

They roared with laughter: they had a curious sense of humour, the pair of them.

'Pixies!' cried Morley, tears coursing down his face. 'Pixies!'

'Pixies!' cried Miriam, sobbing with laughter also.

'Do you think I have entirely taken leave of my senses?'

This was not a question that required an answer. He wiped the tears from his eyes.

'People will believe anything, won't they?' said Miriam.

'Indeed they will, my dear,' said Morley. 'Indeed they will.'

'Ghoulies and ghosties!'

'Gremlins and goodness knows what,' said Morley. 'Do you know Yeats's poem "The Land of Heart's Desire", Sefton?'

'I'm—'

He began to intone, in Yeatsian fashion:

> *The Land of Faery*
> *Where nobody gets old and godly and grave,*
> *Where nobody gets old and crafty and wise,*
> *Where nobody gets old and bitter of tongue.*

'Pure fantasy,' said Morley. 'Absolute nonsense.'

'Pixies!' cried Miriam.

'Pixies!' echoed Morley. 'Marvellous! Marvellous!'

And so, in characteristic fashion, we arrived at our destination.

CHAPTER 4

THE VERY BOUNDARIES
OF ENGLAND

ROUSDON, according to White's *History, Gazetteer and Directory of Devonshire* (1850) – a copy of which Morley had usefully brought with us, along with several other dusty old directories, including Pigot's, Kelly's and Slater's, and a small suitcase-worth of up-to-date guidebooks to the geography, topography, history, culture, coastal scenery and cider-making heritage of a county that most of them insisted on referring to, inevitably, at some point in their Exmoor sheep-herd-like ramblings as 'Glorious' – 'is an extra parochial estate belonging to R.C. Bartlett Esq., and lying within the bounds of Axminster parish, adjoining the great landslip of Dowlands and Bindon'.

This hardly does the place justice. Rousdon is not merely extra parochial. It is ultra-extra parochial. It is far, far, far beyond the parochial. It might best be described as a place at the edge of the world.

The land, with its few original buildings, according to all accounts, was purchased some time around 1870 by a Sir

Henry Peek, who undertook various schemes of improvement, including rebuilding the existing church, providing a small school, the vast mansion, a coach house, a bake house, farm buildings, cottages, a walled garden, tennis courts, and every other possible kind of dwelling, convenience and requisite for what became effectively a small private village. The Peek family – latterly Peek Brothers and Winch – had made their fortune as importers of tea, coffee and spices, and Rousdon does indeed have rather the feeling of a plantation complex, 'with all the appearance of having been planned by the Tudors, built by the Jacobeans, and completed by the Victorians', according to Morley in *The County Guides*, 'and with perhaps just a touch of the Lombardic, in what one might generously describe as an act of freestyle Anglo-Euro-Renaissance *sprezzatura*'. For all its undoubted pizzazz and *sprezzatura*, the estate's development was in fact overseen and undertaken by a redoubtable Englishman, Ernest George, who was one of Morley's great heroes, and responsible also for Cawston Manor in Norfolk, one of Morley's favourite English houses, and Golders Green crematorium – undoubtedly his favourite crematorium.

The estate is approached by a long driveway, though since it was dark by the time we arrived, having stopped off at Lyme Regis in order for Morley, in his words, to 'acquaint myself with some ammonites', I wasn't aware initially of the extraordinary dimensions of the place and it wasn't until we – just – managed to stop the car at the bottom of a steep, deep dark lane, our having taken another wrong turning in a maze of roads, that I realised that the entire estate seemed to have been built along a clifftop that dropped precipitously down to the sea.

Rousdon isn't just isolated: it is simply on its own. It is one of the very boundaries of England. And we were about to go sailing headlong over the edge of it . . .

Morley, as usual, was expounding on some subject or another, Miriam was energetically riposting, and I was doing my best to keep the peace. None of us was paying much attention to what was ahead. Fortunately we were travelling slowly, and it seems we all at once caught a glimpse of the cliff's edge and the moon on the sea beyond it. Miriam gave a yelp, Morley uttered, accurately, if not entirely helpfully, '*Thalatta! Thalatta!*' and I realised that if nothing was done then the fate of the overloaded Lagonda, stationery, surfboards, passengers and all, was going to be not dissimilar to that of the steam train in Buster Keaton's *The General* (a film that Morley writes about at great length in his book *Morley Goes to the Cinema*, published in America as *Morley's Movies*, a misleading title which rather implies that Morley himself were a film star, which he most certainly was not; his personality, if anything, was too big, too boisterous and too boundless for the silver screen; he was, I often thought, a strictly novelistic character, a panoramic soul from a panoramic story, of the kind found in the pages of Balzac, or Victor Hugo).

I yelled 'Stop!', leapt up out of my seat, leaned across and yanked on the handbrake. Miriam stamped on the footbrake, and Morley . . .

Morley had leapt out of the car – I thought initially to save himself from what might have been certain death. As it turned out, to my astonishment, he'd leapt out only to get *closer* to the cliff edge, where he immediately launched into another recitation. This time it was Kipling, 'Mandalay':

Ship me somewheres east of Suez, where the best is
*   like the worst,*
Where there aren't no Ten Commandments an' a
*   man can raise a thirst;*
For the temple-bells are callin', an' it's there that I
*   would be –*
By the old Moulemein Pagoda, looking lazy at the
*   sea.*

'Well,' said Miriam, rather breathless, 'we certainly seem to have found the limits of the estate, Sefton.'

'Quite,' I agreed.

'I could have sworn the sign for the school pointed down this way.'

'Apparently not,' I said.

'Did you see the sign, Father?'

'Sign?'

'For the school?'

'No idea,' said Morley. 'But I think we might be able to climb down here, actually. Onto a little beach.' He was standing perilously close to some loose scree.

'Father!' called Miriam. 'For goodness sake, not tonight!'

'A night-time descent might be rather fun,' said Morley, staring down, illuminated by the headlamps of the car and framed by the bright-lit moon, making him appear rather like his own ghost, or a velvety shadow puppet.

'We're going back to find the school, Father.'

'But—'

He had edged close enough now for us both to be concerned about his safety.

'Should I?' I asked Miriam.

'Would you mind awfully?' she replied.

And so I jumped out of the car and edged close enough to Morley to make a grab at his clothes if he were to lose his footing.

'What do you think, Sefton?'

'It is certainly a steep cliff-face, Mr Morley. And we're all rather lucky not to be heading over the edge.'

'Five-hundred-foot drop, would you say?'

'Something like it,' I said.

'V. diff., do you think?'

'V. diff.?'

'Climbing-wise.'

'Yes,' I said, not entirely sure what he meant.

'Straight down to a nice little hidden beach.'

'Indeed. Quite a drop.'

'Into the ocean.'

'Indeed.'

'The abyss – *tehom*, in the Hebrew, isn't it? "Draw me out of the mire, that I may not stick fast: deliver me from them that hate me, and out of the deep waters. Let not the tempest of water drown me, nor the deep swallow me up: and let not the pit shut her mouth upon me." What is that? Psalms . . . 68? 69?'

'I don't remember exactly.'

'Ever done any mountaineering of any kind, Sefton?'

'I can't say I have, Mr Morley, no.'

'Well, we'll have to put that right. I was lucky enough to have climbed with Mallory and Sandy Irvine. Long time ago. Do you know Lisle Strutt?'

'No, I'm afraid not.'

'Glad to hear it. President of the Alpine Club. I resigned in protest. Not a fan.'

'Father, come on!' said Miriam. 'Enough shilly-shallying. It's late.'

'Next trip, we'll bring along some rock boots and rope and see where it takes us, shall we?'

'That sounds like an excellent idea,' I said. 'I look forward to it.'

'Not tonight though, chaps, eh?' cried Miriam, who had lit a cigarette and who seemed to have instantly recovered from our near-death experience and was enjoying the cool breeze from the sea. She, like her father, rather enjoyed risk-taking, near-misses and every other kind of calamity. Neither of them, of course, had ever been to war.

'Thing to remember, Sefton,' said Morley, as we made our way back to the car, 'is that the top of the ascent is the most dangerous part of any climb. The summit, you see. Gets the old heart racing.'

'Is your heart racing, Sefton?' said Miriam, as we clambered back into the car.

I was in fact feeling my stomach grumbling – we hadn't had anything to eat since our filthy Nell Gwynn buns.

'You know, we could camp out here for the night,' said Morley. 'Do you remember we used to do that when you were young, Miriam? In the old Standard? It had the detachable front seats, and your mother would—'

'Not tonight, Father,' cried Miriam.

'"Only the road and the dawn,"' said Morley, '"the sun, the wind and the rain, / And the watch fire under stars, and sleep and the road again."'

'Not tonight, thank you, Father!'

'Very well,' said Morley.

'Onwards!' said Miriam.

'Or backwards,' said Morley, 'to be accurate.'

'Thank you, Father.'

Eventually managing to reverse back up the lane in the Lagonda – after much pushing and the grinding of gears – we picked up another route and soon found ourselves stopping in a courtyard outside an enormous building that by all appearances – mullioned windows, finialled gables, coats of arms and what-not – had to be the main Rousdon manor house. We had arrived at All Souls.

CHAPTER 5

A SODALITY OF PEDAGOGUES

AT THE SOUND OF OUR APPROACH the vast door of the manor house was swung open by a worried-looking young woman, apparently a nurse, who was done out in a most striking outfit, consisting of a blood-red dress with a white apron over it, and a little Sister Dora cap perched jauntily on her head, which gave her the appearance of someone having just rushed panicking from performing some particularly grisly surgery. From behind this rather ghoulish creature first came there a voice, and then a man, shuffling into view.

'Do I hear John Bull's roar?' cried the voice. 'The People's Professor?'

'You have been in Afghanistan, I perceive,' Morley said to the figure who now stood in the doorway. Their exchange of words caused much mutual amusement – it was some kind of private greeting, I understood. There was then a prolonged and vigorous shaking of hands – the two men seemed to operate on the same frequency and gave off exactly the same vibration of relentlessly hearty vigour – and Morley then introduced us.

'This is Dr Standish,' he said. 'Headmaster of All Souls.'

'Well, well, well,' said Dr Standish. 'What do we have here?'

What *we* had here was a man who might almost have been Morley's double, though perhaps a little more careworn, his face perhaps rather coarser-featured, his cheeks perhaps a little redder and rounder, his moustache rather more drooping, and his eyes small and hard and bitter, like a blackbird's.

'This is my assistant,' said Morley, 'Mr Stephen Sefton.'

'Your Boswell, eh, Swanton?' said Dr Standish, in a rather sniggering fashion, I thought.

'I don't know about that,' I said. We shook hands: he gave off a slight whiff of lavender, as though having only recently bathed.

'I have always been of the opinion,' said Morley, 'that the Great Cham was in fact a fictional character invented by the scheming Scotsman as a way of making a reputation for himself.'

'Ha ha! Very good!' said Dr Standish, smiling and showing a set of gleaming teeth. 'Though I'm sure such treasonous thoughts are far from the mind of your young assistant.'

'Indeed,' I agreed. Nothing could have been further from my mind.

'And this is my daughter,' said Morley.

'Charmed,' said Miriam, offering her hand, and simpering rather.

'Well, well,' said Dr Standish. 'You have grown up since last we met.'

'Indeed, we are now full-grown,' said Miriam, hoisting

Puer Aeternus, The Eternal Boy

herself up to her not inconsiderable height, and gazing at him, mesmerisingly, in her fashion, over her cheekbones.

'You haven't aged, though, Headmaster,' said Morley.

'Well, teaching keeps one young, I suppose.'

'*Puer Aeternus*,' said Morley. 'The Eternal Boy.'

'Indeed,' said Dr Standish. 'No need to stand on ceremony though, old friend. Come in, come in, come in!'

⌇ ⌇

Given Morley's well-known quirks and attributes – his extraordinary working habits, his odd detachment from others, his fixation on objects, his obsession with classification, and his complete and utter inability to understand or to be able to empathise with others – one might have suspected that he would have found close relationships almost impossible to maintain. In fact, as I was to discover during the course of our time together, he was a man who attracted and enjoyed the company of all sorts of individuals, of both sexes, of all ages, all classes and all kinds. Of course above all he attracted fans, with whom and about whom he was always polite and courteous. Much of my time was spent protecting him from these fans, and from all sorts of other less well-meaning hangers-on and acolytes. (He was most often beset and troubled by those whom one might call Morley-mimickers: one thinks most readily perhaps of Frederick Bryson and John Fry, Morley-mimickers of brief renown. Such individuals often started out as fans, became acolytes, and then attempted to actually *become* Morley – 'stealing our bread from the table', as Morley often complained – trying to forge careers as hacks and popular writers, though none of them could match Morley's own ferocious output. About such types Morley could be surprisingly and shockingly discourteous. Bryson, for example, I recall him once describing as a 'sunburned nut': he famously kept a house on the French Riviera. And Fry he often referred to simply as 'the Pygmy': he was a man famously short in stature.) But Morley also had real *actual* friends, and Dr Standish was one of them: he had contributed to a number of volumes edited by Morley for the edification of the young, including *Manners Maketh the Man: A Guide for Parents and Teachers* (1932), and *A Boy's First Fingering: Easy Piano Pieces for Small Hands* (1934).

∽ ∾

While the two men caught up with all their news and gossip, Miriam and I were shown through by the nurse to what seemed to be the old drawing room of the manor house, which had been converted into the school's staff common room. The transformation had been entirely successful – and was, of course, quite appalling. Noticeboards had been erected on the oak-panelled walls, a long coat-rack was hung with gowns and mortarboards, and where there once might have been pleasing arrangements of bibelots, vases and ornaments there was now a mess of packets of chalk, cigarettes, brass ashtrays and bottles of ink. An elephant's foot umbrella-stand in one corner held a quiver of canes, ranging from a thin-strip willow to a heavy hardwood beater. Windows high up allowed for no views, and little natural light. I knew exactly what the place had become, having wasted so much of my time over the course of the past five years in similar rooms throughout the country. It was a place for the gathering of the unredeemed before their trials: we had come upon a sodality of pedagogues.

We entered into a thick fug and hubbub of tobacco being smoked, of jokes being cracked, of sherry glasses tinkling, of the crackle of corduroy and tweed, and of the infernal sound of a gramophone playing music of a Palm Court trio kind – 'the music of the damned', Morley would have called it – but upon our entrance all noise abruptly ceased. From deep within the fug a dozen or so pairs of eyes fixed upon us. Only the Palm Court trio played on: the dreaded sound of Ketèlbey's 'In a Persian Market', a tune regarded by Morley with particular horror ('self-aggrandising nonsense' is his memorable description in *Morley's Lives of the English Composers* (1935)). The room also had the most extraordinary smell: rich, thick and rank. I couldn't quite put my finger on it, but in this stench, and to the sound of Ketèlbey's self-aggrandising nonsense, the gathered crowd smoked and stared at us, breathing as one.

'Oh don't mind us!' said Miriam, entirely undaunted, and indeed clearly relishing the attention. 'At ease, at ease. We're only the school inspectors.' And then turning to me, in the *sotto voce* remarking manner that she had unfortunately inherited from her father, she said, 'Not sure that we'll pass them, eh, Sefton? Seem like rather a rum bunch, wouldn't you say?' Clearly meant as a joke, the silence that greeted these remarks might best be described as stony, and the atmosphere as icy – until, as the sound of Ketèlbey faded away, a man boldly separated himself from what was indeed a rum bunch and came towards us, like a tribal leader stepping forward to greet the arrival of Christian missionaries.

A sodality of pedagogues

'I'm Alexander,' he said, 'but everyone calls me Alex. Delighted to meet you.'

Alex shook my hand in an appropriately brisk and friendly manner but he took Miriam's hand with a rather theatrical flourish, I thought, and then he kissed it, lingering rather, bowing slightly – all entirely unnecessary. He then gave a quick glance to his colleagues, which seemed to be the signal for them to resume their conversations. Sherry glasses were once again raised, and someone set the Palm Court trio back upon their damned eternal gramophone scrapings. The natives were calmed and reassured.

Alex was tall, long-legged, dressed in a dark double-breasted suit, and had what one might call confiding eyes. Miriam – who knew the look – offered her confiding eyes back. I feared the worst. There was no doubt that Alex had a commanding presence: he rather resembled Rudolph Valentino, though with something disturbingly super-sepulchral about him that suggested not the Valentino of, say, *The Sheikh*, but rather a Valentino who had recently died and then been miraculously raised from the dead. He also had the kind of deep, capable voice that suggested to the listener that one had no choice but to trust and obey him, and an accompanying air of bold determination, of knight-errantry, one might say, as if having just returned from the court of King Arthur, in possession not only of the Holy Grail but of the blood of Christ itself. I conceived for him an immediate and most intense distaste. Miriam, on the other hand, was clearly instantly smitten and the two of them fell at once into deep conversation.

Feeling rather surplus to requirements, and dreading an evening of talking about the state of modern education with a group of teachers – having long since forsworn all such utterly pointless conversations – I excused myself to go and arrange for the unloading of the Lagonda.

Out in the school's forecourt I lit a cigarette and gazed up at the building. The place had a medieval aspect about it, like some kind of monastery, rather ponderous in style, and yet also at the same time strangely promiscuous, self-fertile almost, appearing to consist of numerous buildings grow-ing into and out of one another, clambering over and upon itself with gable upon gable upon turret upon high tiled roof, writhing and reaching up towards the dark heavens above.

As I glanced up and around I fancied that I was being watched – and indeed for a moment I thought I saw the small white faces of young boys pressed up against mullioned window panes in the furthest and highest corners of the buildings. But when I turned again, having stubbed out my cigarette, they had gone.

The sensation of being watched, however, strongly per-sisted: it was almost as if someone had clapped me on the shoulder, or slapped me on the back; I felt eyes upon me. The air felt cold, as if someone had rushed close by. I turned quickly again, this time looking down around the forecourt and out towards the fields – and there in the moonlight I saw a man. He stood by the hedge beyond the lane, under the shelter of a tree.

'Hello?' I said instinctively.

'Hello,' he replied softly, his voice carrying clearly across the still night air.

'Are you watching me?' I asked. I didn't know what else to say.

He stepped forward then, out from the shade of the tree,

and I saw that he was dressed in old, stained muddy clothes
– pig-skin leggings and an old battledress coat – with an unlit
lantern in his hand. He was perhaps in his early twenties,
with a light beard fringing his cheeks, a grey cap upon his
head.

'You're out walking?' I asked.

'No,' he said.

'Well, who are you and what are you doing?' The man
struck me as a reprobate.

'Who am I? I might be asking you the same, sir. Who are
you? And what you be dwain? You a parent?'

'No.'

'Teacher?'

'No.'

'Who are you then, sir, and what you be dwain? You're
not from round here.'

'No. That's correct. My name's Stephen Sefton and I'm
here with Mr Swanton Morley, who is giving the Founder's
Day speech tomorrow.'

'Is that right?'

'Yes. And you are?'

'I,' he said slowly, 'am Abednego.'

'Ha!' I couldn't help but laugh. 'Really? And you don't
happen to have two brothers named Shadrach and Meshach
I suppose?' He did not answer. He now stood no more than
a few feet away from me, staring at me hard. I could smell
cider on his breath. 'Well, and what's your business here this
evening, Abednego, if I might ask?'

'I'm watching the comings and goings,' he said.

'I see. You're the night watchman, then, or a porter?'

'You might say that.'

'So Dr Standish would be aware of your activities?'

'Standish knows all about me. And we know all about him.'

'Good,' I said, not entirely reassured, but wishing to be in conversation with this odd young fellow no longer. 'Well, I'm just unloading the car here . . .'

He had already turned and walked away.

～ ～

The contents of the Lagonda eventually unloaded into the school entrance hall, I separated my own travelling items from Miriam's and Morley's and picked up the Leica, fancying that I might perhaps take some photographs of the buildings. But as I was about to do so a loud gong sounded, summoning the teachers to dinner. As they flooded through the hall I found myself caught up among them as they trooped towards the dining room. Alex, walking alongside Miriam, spotted me with the camera and paused on his way past.

'Camera fiend are we, Mr Sefton?'

'I just take a few photographs,' I explained. 'For Mr Morley's books.'

'I'm a keen photographer myself. We have a modest little darkroom down in the basement if you'd like to see it some time.'

'Tomorrow perhaps.'

'I think you'll be impressed,' he said confidingly. 'I think we may have many interests in common, Mr Sefton.' And then he swept Miriam before him into dinner.

CHAPTER 6

RECOMMENDATIONS OF WHERE TO VISIT

WE ENTERED A VAST HALL and shuffled up onto a dais, around a long oak refectory table that bore the scars of age and half a dozen wax-encrusted candelabras. The hall was suffering from a split personality: it was a room divided among itself. Below and beneath the grand oak refectory table on its dais, set at right angles, were rows of rough pine trestles and cheap steel chairs, clearly of an inferior kind. The walls sported crude brown-painted wainscoting below, but vast swathes of old William Morris paper above. There were enough fireplaces to be able to warm the place on the coldest of evenings, and a scattering of three-bar electric fires which might do no better than warm the feet. Exquisite crockery and cutlery were laid on our table, along with battered enamelware jugs and chipped, thick glass tumblers. The unmistakable sweet smell of wax and polish: and the underlying stench of sweat and cabbages. All the usual contradictions, in other words, of the English public school.

Mr Woland Bernhard and his
excellent and idiomatic English

I found myself next to the maths master, a Mr Woland Bernhard, who was possessed of boyish good looks and tremendous enthusiasm. He was also German: 'But not of the bad kind!' he was quick to point out. He spoke, of course, excellent and idiomatic English. 'Yes, yes,' he insisted, when I gestured to take the space next to him, 'take a pew, take a pew.' Before we had a chance to take our proverbial pews, the headmaster spoke.

'Ladies and gentlemen, we are privileged to have with us this evening my dear friend Mr Swanton Morley, known to many of you no doubt as the People's Professor. One might say that Mr Morley is in the same business as us here at All Souls: the education of the ignorant and the—'

'Ineducable,' quipped one of the teachers, to the delight of many of the others.

'Thank you, Mr Jones,' said the headmaster. 'As you know, I invited Mr Morley here to give tomorrow's Founder's Day address' – there was some mumbling and grunting around the table at this, I couldn't tell whether in approval or disgust – 'our very first Founder's Day at our magnificent new location here at Rousdon. I wonder if Mr Morley might like to say the grace for us?'

There was no need to ask: never one to miss an occasion for preaching or performance, Morley ceremonially bowed his head, took a deep breath, and delivered a faultless grace. In Latin, naturally:

Exhiliarator omnium Christe

Sine quo nihil suave,
nihil jucundum est:

Benedic, quaesumus, cibo et potui
servorum tuorum,

Quae jam ad alimoniam corporis
apparavisti;

et concede ut istis muneribus tuis ad
laudem tuam utamur

gratisque animis fruamur;

utque quemadmodum corpus nostrum
cibis corporalibus fovetur,

ita mens nostra spirituali verbi tui
nutrimento pascatur

Per te Dominum nostrum.

'Very good,' said my mathematician friend, settling into his chair. 'A classicist, your friend?'

'Of a kind,' I agreed. Morley's stock of Latin tags, sayings and graces was seemingly inexhaustible, though his precise grasp of the grammar of any language other than English was, according to some critics, rather uncertain. He did not believe, for example, in what he called 'traditional grammar', propounding instead what he called a 'theoretical grammar', which he thought applied to all languages equally. This meant that he spoke Spanish as if it were English, and French as if it were German. He was also extremely disparaging of anything resembling what he called 'punctuational patriotism', insisting at all times on using only the very simplest of punctuation marks: he despised my frequent recourse to colons and dashes, which he felt were

entirely unnecessary and a barrier to world peace and understanding. His ideas on the subject – which can be found in
Morley's Modern Multilinguist (1928) – had been formed
through his correspondence with Mr Ludwik Zamenhof, the
creator of Esperanto, and a man who Morley regarded as a
kind of secular saint.

'Now, do tell me, what do you think of our new school,
Mr Sefton?' asked my new German friend, whose manners
and whose grammar were both impeccable.

'It is quite lovely,' I said, not untruthfully, 'what I've seen
of it.'

'Yes,' he agreed, cracking open a starched but rather
stained napkin and tucking it into his shirt collar. 'You are
correct. It is lovely. And tomorrow you will enjoy also the
farm and the dairy and the pumping house. You may know
we also have a bowling alley, for the boys, and a rifle range.
Tennis courts. And our own little observatory.'

'Really?' I said, not paying much attention to him. I was
too busy watching Miriam across the table: she was busy
flirting with Alexander.

'We have everything we need here. It is our own little
community.'

'Very good,' I said.

'And Dr Standish is our leader,' he added.

'Yes.'

'An excellent headmaster,' he said. 'Despite what some
people say.'

'I see.' Parts of this conversation I must admit I missed
entirely.

'A headmaster must exert total control over a school.
Otherwise . . .'

His 'otherwise' trailed off rather, at the very moment at which plates of soup were set before us, and I looked away from the playful Miriam and Alexander and returned my attention to my mathematical friend.

'Sorry? You were saying?'

'Otherwise . . .'

'Uh-huh. "Otherwise"?'

'Otherwise? Well. A good leader must be feared and respected,' said my friend, factually. Perhaps because of his accent, or perhaps because I hadn't been listening closely to what he was saying, I wasn't entirely sure if he was referring to the school or to a nation. 'But. A glass of our modest *vin de table*, Mr Sefton?'

'Thank you,' I said.

He poured and we shared a toast.

'To knowledge!' he said.

'Indeed.'

'Now, eat!' he said.

I had a bellyful of People's Mints and a day of Morley behind me. I did not argue.

∽ ∾

Dishes were served and conversations undertaken. At the head of the table, deep in reminiscence, Morley and the headmaster carried on like long-lost brothers. The meal itself was a curious affair. Dr Standish was apparently a recent convert to the cause of vegetarianism, and was determined that all meals in the new school were to be prepared with ingredients from their own farm. Setting the example, he dined, therefore, on a small dish of carrots and a bowl of

[65]

new potatoes that looked particularly dull and surly – grey-brown, speckled, about the size of bantam eggs, and rather few in number. For the rest of us, however, there were plates of steak, grilled lamb and whole chickens, fresh bread and pats of butter the size of cricket balls: a veritable feast.

～ ～

On my right sat the school nurse, the woman who had greeted us on our arrival, a Miss Horniman. She was a young, round neurotic thing who wore Harold Lloyd glasses and picked at her food absent-mindedly like a schoolgirl and who kept telling me how terribly lucky she was to have a job at the school, and how brilliant and creative were all the staff, particularly Alexander, of course, with whom she occasionally exchanged glances across the table – just as I exchanged glances with Miriam – and with whom she was clearly in love. Her paean to All Souls, to its staff and pupils, and to the extraordinary Alexander in particular soon became rather tiring.

'He takes photographs you know,' she said. 'He's terribly modern and up-to-date. He's taken photographs of all of us here in the school.' I momentarily entertained an image of her lounging on a divan, her innocence protected with a carefully draped Chinese shawl, or perhaps a strategically placed puppy, her eyes glowing like ruby sparks behind the Harold Lloyd glasses, and Alex hovering over her greedily with his lens . . .

'Really?' I said. 'I also take photographs—'

'And he paints,' she said. 'He's influenced by the sur-realists, you know.'

'Yes. He certainly looks like a man who might be influenced by the surrealists.'

'And he makes sculptures – clay models. Bronzes.'

'Is there no end to his talents?' I asked. This was not, I must confess, intended as an entirely serious question, but Miss Horniman took it entirely as such.

'Really, I don't think there is,' she said, 'he is so extraordinary.' She then duly launched into a list of his various other accomplishments, including his athletic prowess, his culinary skills – he was reputed both to be able to boil spaghetti – 'Italian spaghetti!' she exclaimed – and to make a fine mayonnaise – and his amazing ability on the recorder. 'And he plays the organ!' she concluded. 'He writes his own tunes!'

'He is like J.S. Bach himself,' I said.

'Yes,' she agreed.

'Crossed with Pablo Picasso and Auguste Escoffier.'

'Exactly like J.S. Bach crossed with Picasso,' she said. 'And Escoffier! Exactly!'

All the time, opposite us, Alex and Miriam continued deep in conversation, Miriam occasionally looking across the table in my direction, with what could only be described as a mischievous glance.

Tearing through a slice of perfectly pink lamb, I turned back to my German friend, Woland, who proceeded to discourse enthusiastically upon his love of the English countryside, explaining that he had hiked the length and breadth of Devon with nothing but his trusty knapsack on his back and the goodwill of the local people to guide him. Unaware of the torrent of tiresome trouble I was about to unleash, I then foolishly revealed that we were here not just for Founder's

Day but were intending to explore Devon for the second volume of *The County Guides* series, and I asked, innocently, if perhaps he could recommend anywhere that we should visit? This was a terrible, terrible mistake.

In later years I learned not to mention our purpose to others, in case what happened then happened again – though of course it often happened anyway. Everywhere we visited during our time together working on the books we found people excessively proud of their counties, as though of some prize cow, or a local cheese, and intent upon offering recommendations of where to visit in order best to enjoy the local delights. It was like listening to parents extolling the virtues of their children – which is to say, deeply tiresome.

'Ah!' said Woland, flexing his fingers in preparation for what was clearly going to be a serious bout of totting up. 'Recommendations of where to visit?'

'Yes, that would be very helpful, if you have any.'

'Beer,' he said definitively.

I thought I'd misheard him.

'Beer?' I said. 'No thank you, I'm fine.' We were by this stage in the meal drinking a red wine so sweet that it might almost have been used for communion.

'*Nein! Nein! Nein! Beer.* Beer?'

'Beer?'

'A fishing village, not far from here, just a few miles. Surely you know Beer, Mr Sefton? I thought it was famous in England? The stone from Beer, it has been used in the Tower of London?'

'Of course. The stone from Beer, yes, used in the—'

'And it has a lovely sheltered bay.'

'Good.'

'And white cliffs – and a stream that runs down the main street, leading to the beach.'

'Sounds absolutely lovely.'

'And of course the caves.'

'The caves?'

'Yes, the quarry caves. Would you prefer for me to write this down?'

'No, it's fine. I can remember, thank you.'

'Good. So. When they have quarried the limestone it has left these . . . what would you say? Caves?'

'Caverns?'

'Yes, caverns. Used for smugglers. Wonderful. The stone of Beer was first quarried for the Romans, I think.'

'Really?' I rather wished I was drinking beer, rather than hearing about it.

'Very big underground rooms, chambers. The rooms are the reverse image, you see, of the great halls and cathedrals quarried from them.'

'Yes, that does sound very interesting,' I said, feigning enthusiasm.

'Where else?' wondered my friend. 'Where else would you like to visit?'

'I'm not sure,' I said. 'I think we probably have an itinerary that will see us through . . .'

He called across the table to a thin man, Mr Jones, a Welshman, who had earlier made the quip about the ineducable, and who was now engaged in the business of dismembering half a chicken. Woland explained to him the purpose of our visit.

'Beer, Jon. They are visiting Beer. But where else should they visit?'

'The Royal Oak at Sidbury?' said the hilarious Jon Jones, the Welshman, pausing momentarily in his chicken-parting. 'And the Turks Head at Newton Poppleford?'

'Not just pubs, Jon!'

'Only joking,' said Jon, obviously, his mouth now full. 'What about the caves? They should probably visit the caves.'

'Yes, I have already suggested the caves,' agreed my German friend. Jon Jones the Welshman had by this time nudged the woman on his left, and explained our purpose to her, and she had dutifully nudged the person on her left, who had explained our purpose to them, and etcetera, until soon I had recommendations from almost everyone seated at the table. In south Devon alone we were encouraged to visit Branscombe ('Thatched forge, terribly pretty, longest village in the country'), Budleigh Salterton ('You simply must go to Budleigh!'), Colyton and Colyford. Exmouth. Seaton. Shute Barton Manor. Ilfracombe. The moors. Great houses. Battlements. Tudor gatehouses. The usual.

Fortunately, by the time we had reached dessert – of which there was an abundance, including huge fruit flans of cherry, raspberry and apple, with bowls of thick cream – I had managed to move the conversation forward. Unfortunately, the conversation we moved forward towards was education, a topic of course of great importance but frankly of strictly limited conversational interest, but upon which and about which my dear German friend, mid-flan, was very keen to offer his many insights.

'You see, with teaching it is as it is with cooking, Mr Sefton.' He clapped his hands together as he spoke, and then paused to ladle more cream into his bowl. 'First' – he clapped again – 'you take your boy, yes?!' He chuckled. 'Some young barbarian with all the qualities of the natural savage – raw, if you like, yes? A hard apple, perhaps? Or a nut. A sour cherry. And then you chop him up, and you break him down, and you add your spices and your sugar and cream, and you combine him with all these other ingredients and – *voilà!*' He held a spoonful of fruit flan aloft. 'He becomes this delicious, delightful new thing. A young man!'

'Quite,' I said.

'Good enough to eat!' pronounced Woland, eating his spoonful of creamy flan.

Miriam called across the table; she had been taking a quiet interest in our conversation.

'You do know Mr Sefton was a schoolmaster himself for a long time. Isn't that right, Sefton?'

'No?' said the German, his mouth half full. 'But you should have said! You know exactly what I am talking about.'

'Well, perhaps not quite—' I began.

'And then he went to fight in Spain,' said Miriam. Unfortunately, this announcement coincided with a sudden lull in the table's conversation.

'Spain?' said Alex.

'See any action?' asked Jon Jones the Welshman.

'A little,' I said, which was the answer I gave to anyone who asked such a stupid and offensive question.

'Perhaps you'd be prepared to instruct the boys in a little rifle shooting?' said Jon Jones. 'We have an excellent little cadet corps here.'

'No, thank you,' I said.

'Signalling, perhaps?'

'No, thank you.'

[71]

'Ah, that's such a shame. We took some of them to a camp at Aldershot last year. Do you remember, Bernhard?'

'I do, Jon, yes.'

'Yes, a great success,' said Alex. 'Great success.'

Our conversation, unfortunately, was now the conversation of the table.

'Perhaps we could persuade you to assist the boys with some PT?' said Dr Standish, from the top of the table. 'Alex is on a mission to get our boys fit, aren't you, Alex?'

'I am indeed, Headmaster.'

'We were all rather shamed, I think, by our dismal showing at the Olympic Games. Can't let the Germans take over, can we – with apologies, Mr Bernhard.'

'Not at all,' said Mr Bernhard jovially. 'Not at all!'

'We have a gymnasium in one of the outbuildings, if you're interested.'

'And God's gymnasium all around you,' said Morley.

'Indeed,' said Dr Standish.

'Actually, I was thinking of taking the boys surfing while I was here, if they might be interested?' said Morley.

'Surfing?' said Dr Standish.

'Riding the waves on a wooden board?' said Alex. 'Is that correct, Mr Morley?'

'It is indeed,' said Morley.

'Well, that certainly sounds like a jolly enterprise,' said the headmaster. 'Why not? Perhaps the day after Founder's Day, if you're able to stay on?'

'Sounds splendid. I'll get something arranged,' said Morley.

Conversations then devolved once again and Mr Bernhard turned to me.

'Now, we must discuss your educational theories and pedagogical practices, Mr Sefton.'

～ ～

I was delighted when we retired to the staff common room for coffee and cigars.

～ ～

Pre-prandial sherry, wine, port and flagons of local cider had been drunk with the meal, which had had the inevitable effect, and I prepared to leave the common room when a number of the teachers began serenading one another with renditions of songs by Layton and Johnstone – 'It Ain't Gonna Rain No More' and other hideosities – and the drama teacher was warming up for her apparently hilarious imitation of Queen Victoria. Also, someone had produced from somewhere a ukulele – dread instrument – and Morley had begun tuning it up, with 'My-Dog-Has-Fleas', which everyone seemed to find hilarious. This did not bode well. The common room also sported a rickety old yellow-toothed piano in one corner: I foresaw honky-tonk and possibly Gay Gordons on the horizon.

I went to make my excuses to Dr Standish.

'Ah, yes,' he said, taking me by the elbow and leading me away from the crowd. He lowered his voice. 'I'm afraid some of the rooms are not yet completed. I wonder if it would be an awful inconvenience if we were to ask you to lodge down at the farmhouse? It's just a very short walk, past some of the teachers' houses. I've asked them to leave some lamps on so you can find your way to it in the dark.'

'That's fine,' I said, wishing I could simply curl up and go to sleep right there.

'Mr Morley and his charming daughter will of course be staying here in Peek House with us.'

'Of course.'

'I can have your case sent down for you, if you'd like?'

'No, that won't be necessary, I can take it myself.'

'Very good. The couple down at the farmhouse are expecting you: you'll find them very welcoming.'

I went to say goodnight to Morley.

'Ah, Sefton. Retiring for the night?'

'Yes, Mr Morley.'

'All work and no play?'

'Indeed.'

'Glad to be back among your own, though?'

'My own?'

'Teachers,' he said. 'You were a teacher, weren't you?'

'I was, Mr Morley.'

'You know, Sefton, I had quite forgotten,' he continued, 'how much fun are teachers!'

'Aren't they just,' I said.

He leaned in close and spoke in a whisper. 'And how repellent are their table manners. Goodnight, Sefton.'

'Goodnight, Mr Morley.'

It was a beautiful clear moonlit night, the violet-black sky full of stars. I remembered nights like it in Spain – shells bursting in the darkness. I walked in the bright darkness down to the farmhouse, past fields and labourers' cottages, half expecting to see Abednego again, out walking the grounds. But everywhere was quiet and deserted.

The night air was cool. Autumn was beginning to make itself felt. Nature was on the turn.

CHAPTER 7

TO RECORD EVERY DETAIL

I was met at the farmhouse by an elderly couple who had reached that inevitable stage in married life where they had begun to resemble one another: both silver-haired, both dark-skinned, both poorly dressed in clothes little better than rags, and both with deep brown melting eyes. It was like being greeted by a pair of very old and mournful mongrels.

The lady of the house introduced herself as Mrs Gooding and kindly offered me a cup of tea and a tongue sandwich, which she had already prepared, and which sat lolling expectantly on the kitchen table, attended by lazy flies. I declined the tongue sandwich.

'But you'll have a cup of tea, of course?'

'I will, thank you, madam, yes.'

The man of the house, Mr Gooding, sat in a low chair by the kitchen range. He grimaced upon my entry, baring his teeth at me, which were rather few, and those few a troubling black and yellow. He looked like a man with a mouthful of wasps.

'Good evening, sir,' I said. 'I'm Stephen Sefton. You're kindly putting me up, I understand?'

Mr Gooding stared at me in his rotten, waspish, gap-toothed fashion, while Mrs Gooding poured the tea from the big black tinker's kettle set on the range.

'Oh yes, that's right,' said Mrs Gooding, ladling milk and sugar into my tea. 'The headmaster told us you were coming.'

'Good.'

Mr Gooding growled a little at the mention of the head-master.

'Don't mind him,' said Mrs Gooding. 'Have you come far?'

'Norfolk,' I said.

'Norfolk!' she said, as if it were the moon. 'My my. That is a long way.'

'Yes,' I agreed, sipping at the scalding sweet tea. 'It is. Do you know I think I might turn in if that's—'

'Where is Norfolk?' said Mrs Gooding. 'I just can't picture it.'

'It's over in East Anglia,' I said.

'East Anglia,' she said. 'Is that somewhere in London?'

'Yes. Well, it's . . . near, I suppose. Nearish.'

'Is it a town?'

'It's a county.'

'Ah, of course. Nor-folk,' she said, emphasising the *folk*.

'Anyway. It's been a long day, so—'

'Would you like some pie and custard?'

'Well, that's very generous of you, but—'

'We're coming to the end of our supply of blackberry and apple, I'm afraid. But they'll be a new crop soon. And we've a nice beest custard to go with it.'

'Erm . . .' I wasn't entirely sure what a beest custard was – assuming it might be a 'beast' custard, containing—

'He loves a nice beest custard.' She nodded towards her husband.

'A beest custard?'

'You don't have those in Nor-folk?'

'It's possible we do. I'm actually from London myself, but Mr Morley is—'

'From the beest milk?'

'The beest milk?'

'Third milking, lovely for making custards. Nice rich custard. Sort of . . .'

'Meaty,' piped up Mr Gooding. 'A good beest custard.'

'I don't think I will, if that's OK,' I said. 'I've just had a rather substantial meal down at the—'

'Good,' said Mr Gooding. 'All the more for us.'

'Now, don't mind him,' said Mrs Gooding. 'He's only joking.' And then she added, lowering her voice, 'It's just he's lost more chickens.'

'Losht more chickens,' repeated Mr Gooding.

'Oh dear,' I said. 'Well, I'm terribly sorry to hear that.'

'Foxes,' said Mrs Gooding.

'Foxes!' repeated Mr Gooding, spitting on the range.

'Don't that do that, Solomon,' said Mrs Gooding. 'We've company.'

'Anyway,' I said. 'Foxes. Terrible menace, but—'

'I've never met a fox that opens the door and shuts it behind him,' said Mr Gooding, in a sudden outburst.

'Solomon!' said Mrs Gooding.

'It's them boys,' he said. 'Bloody boys.'

'Surely not,' I said.

'Don't take any notice of him now,' said Mrs Gooding. 'It's just the shock.'

'Jhust the schock!' repeated Mr Gooding, who spat again on the range. 'We never had any trouble before the school came.'

'Anyway,' said Mrs Gooding, 'you're wanting your bed.' At which she hurriedly ushered me up a narrow staircase to a little room above the kitchen: drab, damp, undecorated and grubby, with distemper peeling from its walls, a dark dank wooden ceiling, a bed, a half-broken chair, and a small steaming iron stove. This was to be my billet.

'There we are. This is you,' said Mrs Gooding.

'Thank you,' I said.

'You let me know if you need anything.' And she bustled away.

I heard raised voices from downstairs.

It was the sort of room where one might imagine Keats – or more likely Chatterton – writing lonely verses. I did not that night write any verses, lonely or otherwise. Despite the poverty of the room and its decoration it was, like Mrs Gooding, entirely sincere. The sheets on the bed were crisp and dry and the pillows downy, and it had indeed been a long day, and so I lay down gratefully and immediately fell asleep, with the sensation almost of drowning in the embrace of some vast welcoming creature.

∽ ∾

When I awoke the next morning I was shocked to find myself still dressed in my clothes. Resisting the temptation to practise my pranic breathing I instead smoked a cigarette lying on the bed, then straightened myself up and went downstairs, where I found no sign of the Goodings, though in the kitchen the big black tinker's kettle sat rattling on the range, and a plate of farm bread and butter with apple jelly was set out invitingly on the table. I poured myself a cup of tea, took a slice of the bread, and sat down on an old wooden chair by the range to smoke, to compose myself and make my plans for the day.

Morley's speech was scheduled for three o'clock that afternoon, my farming hosts seemed to be at work already, Miriam would not be up for hours and would then doubtless be preoccupied with Alexander, so I thought I might make the most of a quiet morning to explore the school grounds, the Devon coast, and to take a few photographs.

I was looking forward to an easy day.

∽ ∼

Relaxed and resolved, armed with my camera, and slowly but surely beginning to uplift myself with quantities of tea and tobacco, I wandered back towards the main school building in the early morning sunlight and wondered about the difference the day made: in contrast to its forbidding features the night before, All Souls now appeared a place benign and wondrous. The turrets and gables sang and soared rather than grappled towards the sky, and the meadow down towards the clifftops and the sea glistened in the morning light. It was also as quiet as a monastery, which I knew could mean only one thing: breakfast. From reading the position of the sun in the sky – a trick taught me by Morley – and from my years of experience, I guessed that the traditional hour of porridge was upon us, and so I followed my nose into the school, which might have been every school: the murky sea-green paint, the clanging of cutlery, the stench of unwashed boys, and disinfectant and sewage. I could almost hear the porridge pots bubbling on the stove.

And sure enough, the dining hall, where only the evening before two dozen of us had feasted upon fine food and wine, was now packed with boys, perhaps three hundred of them, of assorted shapes and sizes, some of them seated and silently tucking in to their thin, gruel-like provisions, others queuing for theirs from a couple of cooks who stood guard over a cauldron of porridge and a jam pan full of steaming tea.

The sight of three hundred expectant faces turning towards me made me feel instantly queasy, and took me back to my own wretched schooldays, which had been characterised by all the usual privations and difficulties: the usual slaps and kicks and punches, the usual punishments and raggings, all the usual sadism and torture, the pointless endless public school jolly japes and roundabout of violence. It has of course become fashionable now to denigrate our great public schools, but in my experience they are – or certainly were – places more than worthy of such denigration. I remember there was one particular boy at our school, an Italian Jew, Levi, who we had tormented ceaselessly and mercilessly from dawn till dusk and from his first day to his last, excluding him from games and activities, staff and students alike, taunting him, beating him with even more than the usual ferocity. 'Jew, Jew, a smoggy smoggy Jew' was the rhyme. And then one day in assembly we were singing a hymn and Levi laughed at something we were singing – something to do with Jesus, meek and mild. He actually laughed out loud: I suppose it must have been all the pressure and tension building up inside him, a kind of release of tension. And the headmaster, who was also our divinity teacher, rushed down and pulled him from the line by his hair and started beating him there and then, in front of the whole school, and we were all laughing, it was so shocking. We didn't know what to do. And then the head-master dragged him out of the school hall and I don't know what happened next but Levi simply never returned. He dis-appeared from our lives. And we never asked why. Nor did we care. It was the natural order of things.

Several of the teachers – including my German friend, Mr Bernhard – beckoned me from my reverie and over towards the high table, where they suggested I join them for break-fast, but there was no sign there of Morley, or indeed of the headmaster, or of Miriam, or Alexander, and with the hungry eyes of both teachers and pupils upon me I excused myself, explaining that I needed to go and take some early morning photographs of the school estate.

Relieved, I made my way out of the front of the building, gasping in the fresh air, and strode swiftly on past a gate-house, and then down a long, steep, wooded, winding dirt road – which must have been the road we had taken in the car the previous night with Miriam. At the bottom of this road was what appeared to be a water-pumping station – not something I had noticed the night before, an odd, incongru-ous redbrick lump of a building in a patch of trees – and then the road abruptly stopped, and there were the cliffs, over which and upon which we had almost sacrificed ourselves the night before.

The sun was now blazing, burning off any early mist, and in the autumn morning light I saw that there was a perilous pathway cut down and through the cliffs, with ropes attached as handrails to the rocks, and below that – somewhere, five hundred feet or more below – the beach. I finished my cigarette, slung the camera across my back, and clambered slowly down.

And there on the beach, astonishingly, was Morley, standing by a mound of twisted black metal, which appeared to have recently been a car.

And neatly laid out next to this wreckage was a body – the body of a boy, a boy horribly mangled, carefully arranged.

Morley had his back to me and was busy making notes. He did not look up.

'Ah, Sefton. Good of you to join us.'

The scene was distressing: Morley, as usual, was calm.

'What . . .?'

'Indeed, that is the question, as our friend Hamlet might say. I was walking down here early this morning and discovered this poor blighter, who seems to have made the same miscalculation as us last night. Did what I could, but nothing to be done.'

The boy's limbs were horribly twisted, his face contorted in a grimace, as though he had stared at Death itself.

'Horrible,' I said.

'Quite. Now, could you hold this?' Morley held out a tape measure. 'The police will be here with their cameras and dusting powders in short order, I have no doubt, but in the meantime . . .' He paced over towards the cliff, measuring the distance, then strode back and began poring over the wreck of the car, as if it were an ancient manuscript, or a book contract.

'Come on then, photographs. Straight documentary, if you please. None of your artistic touches.'

'Yes, Mr Morley.' I had no intention of aestheticising the scene. And I had no intention of taking any photographs: it would have been a desecration.

But then, automatically, almost without thinking, while Morley busied himself with more measurements and calculations, I took up the camera and took the required photographs, attempting to record every detail as accurately as possible. We worked in silence for perhaps fifteen minutes.

One of Morley's very last books is about photography, *On Photography* (1940): he has a theory about it, obviously. I have no such theory. All I do know is that a horrible scene like the one that was laid out before us on that bright Devon morning is something that – alas – demands a witness. Morley always spoke of the purpose of *The County Guides* as a form of witness. 'This is here,' he would sometimes say, in explanation of the books. 'This is what this place *is*. What these people *are*. These are its glories.' And these, I might add, are its horrors and its ruins: *The County Guides* tells one story about England and Englishness; my photographs, I suppose, tell another; they are perhaps the negatives of Morley's words. Or the shadow.

I could not have described our work as such then, of course. What struck me most about the scene on that awful morning was the smell – precisely because there was no smell. There was just the smell of the sea, vast and thorough and entire, erasing everything, the waves crunching against the pebbles on the shore as though intending to devour the earth entirely – and I snapped back with the camera.

Then above the noise came another sound, and I looked up to see Dr Standish arriving with Alexander, their faces solemn.

The headmaster was dressed in the same clothes as the day before but Alex was the sort of man who likes to dress differently for different occasions. That morning he was sporting an outfit suitable for a stroll: a cap, a tweed jacket, plus fours and sturdy boots.

'Good grief,' said the headmaster. 'What's this?'

'Ah,' said Morley. 'Good morning. Out for your morning constitutional?'

'What?' As they approached closer the headmaster was speechless. Alex seemed unperturbed.

'Good grief. It's . . .'

'One of yours?' asked Morley.

'I . . . It's . . .' The headmaster was too disturbed to speak.

'Michael Taylor,' said Alex. 'Well well.'

'Michael?' said the headmaster. 'Not Michael!'

'Stolen a car and taken a wrong turning, eh?' said Alex.

'Really?' said Morley. 'That's what you think?'

'Oh yes, he is – was – a terribly inquisitive sort of child, Michael. Forever fiddling around with things, poking around where he didn't belong. Taking things apart, failing to put them back together. You know the sort of thing. Engines, all sorts. Isn't that right, Headmaster?'

'Is that right, Headmaster?' asked Morley.

The headmaster was lost for words. He was down on his knees by poor Michael Taylor. All the colour had drained from his already ashen face, giving him the appearance of a ghost that had caught sight of itself. He touched the back of his hand to the dead boy's face. The grey sea continued to spit pebbles up the beach towards us. He blinked several times in disbelief and then turned to stare at Alex, who in turn stared out to sea. Morley continued to fuss around the vehicle. And I stood with my camera, waiting.

And suddenly the headmaster became animated: it was like seeing a man regain his strength after having been knocked down, like a boxer getting up from the canvas. He stood up and strode ramrod straight over towards Alex, but then seemed to change his mind, and turned instead towards Morley, gripping him by the elbow and whispering something in his ear, taking him by the arm and leading him away from the vehicle and over towards the cliffs. I smiled weakly at Alex, who smiled confidently back. Though they were now some little distance away we could both still hear Morley and the headmaster speaking above the sound of the sea.

∽ ∾

'This is rather difficult ... You understand of course that parents are going to be arriving all morning?'

'Yes.'

'Well, I wonder ... if we might not mention this ... immediately to the boys? It might cause distress.'

'Distress, yes.'

'And panic, even.'

'Panic?'

'Well ... A tragedy like this. At this time. It would be very difficult for—'

'For the boys.'

'Precisely.'

'What about the boy's parents?'

'Whose parents?' said the headmaster.

'The dead boy's parents, Headmaster. Michael.'

'Michael is . . . was . . . one of our orphans.'

'You take in orphans?'

'Their fees are paid for by some of our benefactors. It's an arrangement we have. For boys who show exceptional promise, but who . . .' He stared at the boy's body lying motionless on the cold grey rocks. 'Well. It would just be better if we could . . . Do you understand, Morley?'

There was a long lingering pause then as Morley hesitated before answering.

'I understand,' he said.

'So might we keep this . . . for the moment?'

'Between ourselves,' said Morley. 'But the police will be notified of course.'

'Directly. Yes. Of course. But the boys, the parents, the staff . . .'

Morley glanced in our direction, and he looked for a moment lost.

'Yes. I think we can keep this to ourselves.'

～ ～

The two men then walked back towards us.

'Gentlemen,' said the headmaster.

'We're to keep it between ourselves,' said Alexander.

'Yes,' said the headmaster.

'But wouldn't it be better to postpone the Founder's Day—' I began.

'Good, that's understood then,' said the headmaster, ignoring me.

'A tragic accident,' said Alexander, 'and to have occurred at this time seems particularly unfortunate.'

'But—' I started again.

'Exceedingly,' agreed Morley. 'Yes, I quite agree.'

'Perhaps you'd like me to remain here, to explain matters to the police?' asked Alex.

'No, no,' said the headmaster. 'I would prefer to stay, and if you wouldn't mind taking Mr Morley and Mr Sefton up to the school and making a call to the local police station that would be most helpful, thank you.'

'Certainly,' said Alex. 'The police will be here shortly, Headmaster.'

Wherever we went, in those years, there were always – eventually – police.

Morley glanced at me. 'OK, Sefton?' he asked.

'Fine,' I said.

And so we began the long climb back up to the school. As we reached the point from where the car had driven over, Morley bent down to examine the tyre tracks. Alex continued on ahead.

'What do you notice, Sefton?'

'Tyre marks.'

'Several tyre marks,' said Morley, pointing to a writhing mass of lines and marks.

'Yes. Presumably where we also got stuck yesterday, Mr Morley.'

'Presumably so, yes. Presumably so.'

A disturbing scene

We walked slowly and in silence back up to the school.

'I do hope this won't put a dampener on your speech, Mr Morley,' said Alex.

'I see no reason why it should,' said Morley. 'As you say, a tragic accident.'

'With any luck we'll have the matter all cleared up by this afternoon,' said Alex.

'I'm sure we will,' said Morley. 'I'm sure we will. But do tell me more about poor Michael Taylor.'

'Not much to tell,' said Alex. 'Perfectly pleasant young boy. Nothing wrong with him. Mischievous, I would say. Accident-prone.'

'Really?'

'Well, clearly, given his unfortunate demise.'

'Assuming it was an accident.'

'I can hardly see any other explanation.'

'Perhaps not,' said Morley. 'Perhaps not.'

'I know he was a great favourite of my brother.'

'Yes,' agreed Morley. 'Clearly.'

'Your brother?' I said.

'The headmaster,' said Alex.

'You're brothers?'

'That's right.'

'I thought you knew, Sefton?' said Morley.

'No,' I said. 'I had no idea.'

'Yes.'

'Younger brother,' said Alex, smiling.

'I met Dr Standish, what was it, around 1917, I suppose?' said Morley. 'You were away at the war, Alex.'

'For my sins,' said Alex. 'Hence' – he held up his left hand, which, I suddenly realised, was lacking a thumb.

'Cause you much pain?' asked Morley. 'We have a handy-man who lost his arm. A kind of ghost pain. Causes him terrible agonies.'

'Mustn't grumble,' said Alex. 'It's nothing really. One learns to manage these things.'

'Of course,' said Morley. 'Though of course some pain never goes away.'

Reaching the top of the cliff, I looked back and saw the headmaster standing at the edge of the water, staring out into the distance, the waves dashing over his feet, for all the world like he was Canute, driven to the edge of his kingdom and his authority.

CHAPTER 8

THE SCIENCE MISTRESS

As the three of us approached the school, in a silence that can only be described as deadly, we came upon a group of four or five boys about some business behind the tennis courts, a group of four or five boys whose business it clearly was not to be behind the tennis courts. They were, inexplicably, but as boys do, beating one poor chap about the shins with wickets and apparently trying to force him to drink some doubtless horrible concoction from a cup. Innocent horseplay, no doubt. Catching sight of them in the distance, Alex slowly, quietly and deliberately increased his pace: it was like watching one of Rousseau's strange lions stalk its prey. Each silent step grew longer and more terrifying and then, when he was almost upon them, he called out in his deep, sepulchral, confiding tones – that might easily have been confused with a snarl – 'Boys!' The boys froze, like startled animals, and stumbled up against the fence surrounding the courts. They were cornered.

Alex strode over to them with such controlled and yet such obviously boiling fury that if not exactly murderous it might easily, clearly and most properly be described – as Morley was later to describe it to me – as 'slaughterous'.

'Boys?' he called again, now just inches from them.

All colour had drained from Alex's face and his fists, or fist, rather, was clenched tight; one could feel him about to pounce. I almost went forward to restrain him, but Morley held out his arm to hold me back and as he did so Alex spoke again, even quieter this time, up so close to them that he might almost have whispered, although what escaped his mouth was in fact more like a deep animal growl. 'Boys.'

They looked, simply, terrified. Morley still held me back.

'Yes, sir?' piped up one poor little fat lad, in a terrified, adenoidal squeak.

I rather wondered what kind of punishment might now be meted out to them. One teacher at my old place of work, the Hawes School, had specialised in knocking heads together, the boys face to face: more than one boy had had his nose broken being subjected to such cruel punishment. Another teacher would have disobedient boys stand up at the front of the class while others were made to paste over their mouths using glue and strips of paper; I had seen boys faint from pure terror at the mere prospect of this punishment. Another colleague kept in his class a range of tools for disciplining that could really only be described as instruments of torture: a birch rod, which he kept planted in a pot of water, in order to keep it pliant; a cat-o'-nine-tails; and a set of battledores of various sizes made of thick sole leather. Yet another, a Scotsman, delighted in a technique he called 'Kick the Can', in which boys were instructed to kick their miscreant classmates as they crawled on their hands and knees beneath the desks. Alex's chosen form of punishment, I had no doubt, would be equally and appallingly violent.

'Don't. Do. That,' he said. 'Do you understand?' He raised his thumbless hand. I thought for a moment he was about to strike out with it, but then he simply reached out and put his hand on the shoulder of the fat boy.

'Yes, sir. Very good, sir,' said the boy. 'It won't happen again, sir.'

'Go,' said Alex, turning his back towards them. And they went.

～ ～

'Well, you certainly seem to have them under control,' said Morley admiringly, when we caught up with Alex, whose temper seemed to be entirely and instantly restored.

'One does one's best,' he said, with a pleasant smile.

'Restraint,' said Morley, 'is a virtue. *Aequam memento rebus in arduis servare mentem.*'

'Indeed,' said Alex.

Morley picked up the abandoned cup, the contents of which the boys had been trying to force upon their companion. The liquid had been spilled on the ground. He sniffed at the cup.

'Mmm. What do you think, Sefton?'

I took a sniff. It smelled to me of sea water – and something else. Something indefinable. I recalled from my own schooldays some of the noxious liquids we had tried to force upon one another.

'Harmless prank, no doubt,' said Alex. 'Anyway, Mr Morley, perhaps you need time to work on your speech?'

'Yes, I rather think I do,' said Morley. 'And I have a couple of articles to send off this morning. A history of the alphabet, something on keeping tortoises as pets, and a review of this book *The Hobbit*? Have you come across it?'

'I can't say I have, Mr Morley, no.'

'Curious thing. By some man, Tolkien, Professor of Anglo-Saxon at Oxford.'

'Really?'

'Dragons and dwarves and what have you.'

'It sounds fascinating.'

'Yes. Clearly based on the *Edda*s. Some sort of allegory about England, I fancy. Need to think about it. Have to have it written and sent by noon, along with the others.'

'Well, I can certainly make arrangements for your articles to be picked up and sent. We have post collected three times a day from the porter's lodge.'

'Excellent. I was rather concerned that I'd have to travel into town somewhere.'

'No need, no. We're not as cut off here as some people think.'

'Clearly. Well, that would be very kind of you, thank you.'

'And you have everything else you require?'

'I think so,' said Morley. 'Perhaps some barley water and a pot of strong tea? I am well provided with writing requisites.'

'Very good. I'll have those sent up to you.'

'And you'll know where to find me, when the police arrive?'

'Indeed. And you, Mr Sefton?'

'Me?' I was still thinking about the body on the beach. I was in no state to plan a day's work.

'We need photographs, Sefton,' said Morley. 'For the

book. Some local colour. Interviews. You know the sort of thing. Mustn't let things slip.'

'No shirking,' I said.

'No shilly-shallying.'

'No funking.'

'Precisely.'

'I'll get about gathering local colour then,' I said.

'Good man!' said Morley. 'Good man you are!'

We had now reached the school buildings, where the day had begun in earnest.

'Now, gentlemen,' said Alex, assuming authority, 'you'll perhaps excuse me. I shall telephone the police immediately about our tragic little accident.'

'Excellent,' said Morley. 'As I say, if we're required you'll know where to find us.'

'Thank you, your cooperation is much appreciated.'

Alex strode away, and Morley disappeared off to write. I entered the school alone through the back corridors.

The place was buzzing with activity. Boys were rushing around, carrying furniture under the instruction of the staff, who attempted to steer them round other boys who were washing and rubbing and scrubbing at floors. There were boys with buckets and boys with brushes – stiff brushes, small brushes, long feather dusters. Boys arranging flowers, and boys cleaning mirrors. Boys buffing brass, and boys dusting shelves. Wall scuffs were being wiped, windows washed, and cracked old floorboards were being coated with wax. Patches of rush matting were being watered from a can. Rugs were beaten and curtains shaken. It was a tornado of activity, like woodworms at a mighty felled oak. I recalled a phrase from *Morley's Manual of Housekeeping:*

A Practical Guide to Everyday Home Maintenance and Cleaning (1929): 'The upkeep of our houses and their contents is both a Christian duty and a privilege afforded to the homeowner or householder. As Christian householders we might take our motto from Corinthians 14:40. "Let all things be done decently and in order."' Indeed we might. We might also take our motto from Matthew 23:27. 'Woe unto you, scribes and Pharisees, hypocrites! For ye are like unto whited sepulchres, which indeed appear beautiful outward, but are within full of dead men's bones, and of all uncleanness.'

As I watched all this hectic human activity I thought of poor Michael Taylor lying down on the beach.

Picking my way among stacked tables and chairs, a piano, statuettes, tea chests, boxes, I made my way to the main entrance to the school. Outside on the gravelled forecourt stood a liveried van, which announced that it was from Potbury and Sons in Sidmouth, along with another small lorry that apparently belonged to a Mr Perry, a haulier from Sidford. While Messrs Potbury and Perry were unloading their vans – a marquee, more tables – yet another lorry arrived, loaded with logs, and then yet another, a Mr Roberts' coal lorry.

My friend Mr Bernhard the mathematics master stood, waving his arms around like a conductor, shouting instructions at schoolboys, porters and lorry drivers, consulting all the while with a man in a flat cap with a clipboard.

'Ah, Mr Sefton, Mr Sefton!' He waved me over. 'Come, come, come!'

'You're running quite a delivery depot,' I said.

'Yes,' he said.

'Organised chaos?'

'No, no, no, not chaos at all.' His attention was then caught by a boy who was struggling past with a large ornamental pot plant. 'Careful, Evans! Careful!' Evans looked as though he were about to burst into tears. 'Go slowly!' It was difficult to imagine how Evans could go any more slowly, or more forlornly. 'Everything is going very smoothly, actually, Mr Sefton. Very very smoothly. Our tasks will be completed by noon.'

'Well, jolly good,' I said, lighting a cigarette.

'And this is Mr Potbury, from Potbury and Sons,' announced Mr Bernhard, introducing me to the man with the clipboard.

'Roit,' said Mr Potbury, vigorously shaking my hand.

'Cigarette?' I said.

'You're a gentleman, sir, don't mind if I do, sir,' said Mr Potbury. 'Proper job,' he added. 'Many thanks.'

'Mr Bernhard?'

'No, thank you,' said Mr Bernhard. 'No time.'

Mr Potbury and I smoked for a moment in silence, watching Mr Bernhard expertly conduct the scene of hurrying and scurrying before us.

'You're flat out, then?' I said.

'Like pushin' an 'andcart up 'ill backwards, sir,' said Mr Potbury. 'Terrible lot to do.'

'We will have everything in order and in place by noon,' said Mr Bernhard, confidently.

'Of course,' said Mr Potbury. 'He's keeping us on our toes,' he said to me, adding more quietly, 'German. Terrible lot of foreign teachers. What's wrong with our home-grown English teachers, eh?'

'I . . .'

'My wife's a teacher, she'd have loved a job here. You here for Founder's Day?'

'No,' I said. 'I'm just here visiting.'

'Mr Sefton is here to write a book about Devon,' explained Mr Bernhard, between instructions to a group of boys who were carrying what appeared to be a rock-solid mass of bunting, 'with Mr Swanton Morley.'

'Really?' said Mr Potbury, impressed. 'The People's Professor?'

'The very man,' I said.

'I read him every week. Our boys love his *Children's Newspaper*.'

'I'll tell him. He'll be delighted.'

'Where would you suggest they visit, Mr Potbury?' said Mr Bernhard.

'Round here?' Mr Potbury took one final drag on his cigarette and then pinched out the tip with his fingers, and pocketed the stub. 'Well, they should definitely get down to Beer, shouldn't they? See the old underground caves.'

'Yes, I've heard about the caves,' I said.

'No, no, no!' cried Mr Bernhard, hurrying over to redirect some poor chair-carrying porters who were about to enter the main entrance. 'Round the back, please. Round the back.'

'They are creepy,' said Mr Potbury. 'The caves.'

'Really?'

'My wife doesn't like them. Too dark.' He nodded towards the camera strung around my neck. 'Taking photographs as well then?'

'Yes, I am.'

'You know they've got a whole what's-it-called set up downstairs?'

'A darkroom? Yes, I heard.'

'You should see it. I arranged the deliveries from London a couple of months ago when they first moved in. Never seen anything like it.'

'I might take a look actually.'

'You should. Just go downstairs, it's next to the science room. You can't miss it. Anyway, I should probably get on here or I'll be in trouble with the Kaiser. No rest for the wicked, eh?' At which he got on, Mr Bernhard continued on, and I finished my cigarette.

A police car pulled into the forecourt. I rather thought I might make myself scarce. I went down the stairs to have a look at the darkroom: as always, I was seeking distractions, from myself and from the task at hand.

I found the science room and peeked in – the door was conveniently open. This presumably was what had at one time been the building's cellar: there were no windows, and the place felt damp and solid; I was conscious of a kind of brooding underground presence. The room was not dark, however – or not entirely dark. Row upon row of bare bright light bulbs hung down over the many desks, giving the place the appearance rather of a subterranean operating theatre, or an amphitheatre. I could barely make out the dimensions of the place: outside the bright glare of the lights, shades and shadows substituted for walls.

A woman I had seen at the dinner the previous night but had not met was busy moving around the room. She was, I assumed, the science mistress. In the strange, vast, lit space of the room she appeared to be perfectly tiny – almost like an apprentice or puppet version of herself – and she looked as dark-featured as a Kalderasa. As I observed her unnoticed for a moment it occurred to me that she seemed deeply unhappy, although perhaps this was merely because she was preoccupied: Morley was always sceptical about trying to read people's emotions and characters from their features. (Contrary to the claims in a number of biographies, indeed, Morley could not abide what he sometimes referred to as the 'party trick' methods of fictional detectives. In his celebrated article, 'Against the Red-Headed League', with which many will doubtless be familiar, he wrote a long, *long* rebuttal of Sherlock Holmes's supposed methods, in Conan Doyle's famous story, in which the master detective makes the claim, based on a moment's observation, that a man worked in manual labour, took snuff, was a Freemason, had been to China, and had recently done a considerable amount of writing. Morley's argument in the article was both highly refined and utterly self-defeating, proving the very thing he set out to decry: a characteristic of his style as both thinker and writer.)

Nonetheless, if one were judging the science mistress by appearances alone, as of course one should not, one might have made certain assumptions about her and might have thought twice about accepting an invitation to tea: she had jet-black hair, and wore a black dress buttoned high at the throat, and boot-black boots, and was enveloped in a black cloak made of some modern, synthetic material that was presumably designed especially for protective use by science mistresses. She was also cursed with odd, uneven features that made it look as though her head might at some time have been pressed in a vice, or as if she were being seen through a distorting mirror. To my naive and untrained eye she looked like the sort of woman who might at any moment cast a spell upon you, toss you into a cauldron, and then fly off into the night on a broomstick. It was partly circumstances, of course: the science room was filled with a strong smell of both sulphur and ammonia, as though the devil himself had recently appeared, and someone had obligingly cleaned up after him. But whatever the reasons, and in spite of all prejudice, the overall impression, as I say, was rather forbidding.

'Yes?' she said. I was clearly not, as I had assumed, unobserved. 'You're too early for the tour.'

'The tour?'

'You're a parent?'

'No, I'm here with Mr Morley, who's giving the Founder's Day speech.'

'Of course.'

'But I'd love to have the tour,' I said, rather obligingly, still hovering at the door.

'The tour is for the parents.'

'Yes.'

I stepped into the room at this point, drawn towards her and also towards a glass tank set on a bench by the near wall that contained a hive of small, writhing creatures – Morley had something very similar back at St George's. I tried to remember what it was called. He had his aviary, his apiary, and his formicary – for his ants – but this was a . . .

'Vivarium,' she said, without even a glance towards me.

'Yes. That's it. A vivarium. I'm sure it must take some considerable upkeep and maintenance?' Morley taught me over the years to ask obvious questions and to let people talk about what interested them: he claimed this was his technique, though I have to say that I never once saw or heard him use it; he was so busy talking at people that he often failed to hear or understand the simplest of statements.

'Not particularly,' said the science mistress. She continued furiously moving things around. 'The digestion of lizards is very slow.'

'Right.'

'No need for frequent meals.'

'Ah.'

'And they hibernate in cold weather and in winter hardly need feeding at all; flies and insects, a bit of turf; no artificial heat.'

'A bit like schoolboys.'

'Ha,' she said, clearly unamused.

'What are they?'

She came over towards me. 'Lizards,' she said, with a tone of contempt.

'Yes, I rather meant, what ... kind of lizard are they?' They were big and they looked scary.

'South American lizards. *Tupinambis merianea, tupinambis refescens* and *tupinambis teguixin.*'

'Very good.' I knew as little about lizards as I knew about birds. I glanced around the room. 'You've got it all set up rather wonderfully.' I wandered over towards the long bench at the front of the room, behind which was a large blackboard, flanked by two doors, one open and one closed. 'And what's through there?'

'Nothing,' she said. 'My office. Why?'

'It's just, I'm looking for the darkroom, you see.'

'The darkroom?' She stiffened in her manner rather.

'Yes.'

'Sorry, what was your name again?'

'Stephen Sefton,' I said, offering my hand.

She stared at me, lopsidedly, her arms folded. 'And?'

'I'm here with Mr Morley. We're writing a book about Devon.'

She unfolded her arms and adjusted her voluminous black cape about her shoulders, with a fierce, unnatural rustling that suggested she might at any moment take off. She did not in fact take off, but proceeded instead with her work, shifting around the room as we spoke.

'And why do you want to see the darkroom?'

'Alex mentioned that he had established a darkroom here.'

'Did he?'

'Yes.' I held up my camera. 'I take the photographs for Mr Morley's books.'

'I see.'

'So . . .'

She brushed back past me and disappeared through the door into her office. 'It's locked,' she called from inside the room. 'The darkroom. It's locked.'

'Right. I don't suppose you have the key?'

'No.'

'And you don't happen to know where he might keep the key?'

'No,' she said, emerging from the adjoining room carrying a large box filled to the brim with all sorts of metal instruments – scissors, forceps and scalpels – which rattled as she moved.

'Here,' I said, moving towards her. 'Do let me help you with that.' As I reached out for the box, I noticed that under the gaping black cloak she was wearing a chain around her neck, attached to which were a number of keys.

'No, thank you,' she said, snatching the box away from me, and placing it noisily on the long demonstration bench at the front of the room.

'If you're sure.'

'Quite sure, thank you. If you want to gain access to the darkroom you'd have to speak to Alex himself, I'm afraid. He has the keys. And I am really very busy.'

'Very well. Well, thank you,' I said, and, turning away, went towards the door. I had almost gone, when she called out after me.

'While you're here,' she continued, 'you might want to make yourself useful. If you really want to help.'

'Certainly,' I said, turning back.

'You can help me set out the dissection equipment.'

'Yes, of course, by all—' and before I had finished she had disappeared back into the adjoining office and appeared again with another box, a large sealed cardboard box, which she handed to me.

'Right. You're planning a dissection then?' I asked.

'For the parents. So they can see what their money has bought them. Over here, please,' she said, gesturing me towards the long demonstration bench, which was set out with various flasks and bottles, enamel trays of instruments, and a dish containing small balls of some damp, strong-smelling cotton-wool wadding.

'And what are you dissecting?'

'Frogs.'

'Really.' I saw no sign of frogs. 'And where do you keep the frogs?'

'There.' She nodded towards the box in my hands. I realised with a shock that the box was not only rattling, but humming with the most curious sound, like cattle lowing.

'Frogs?' I said, dropping the box.

'Careful!' she said.

'Sorry, I . . .' I was remembering an incident in Spain, when I had awoken one night in our tent, which we had pitched in a forest, to find it filled with tiny, wailing, vivid frogs spotted all over and with feet like talons.

I bent down, picked up the box of frogs, stood up – and as I did so, in a swift flowing movement, the science mistress produced a small flick-knife from the pocket of her dress, flicked it open, and came suddenly towards me, which caused me almost to drop the box again. Staring directly at me, she sliced perfectly through the string and tape that secured the lid of the box, and then with equal swiftness reached in and removed a frog from the box, grasping it with one hand by its long writhing legs, and reaching with the other hand for a cotton-wool ball soaked in chloroform, which she pressed over its mouth.

'Keep it shut, please,' she said, nodding towards the box. I frantically shut the lid of the box. 'Good. There,' she added, proffering me the now deceased frog.

I wasn't entirely sure what to do with it.

'One on each desk. Every boy'll get a frog they're going to demonstrate.'

'Right.' I placed the box on the bench, and took the frog to a desk, and we repeated the procedure until there was the sound of no more rattling and humming, and only the smell of chloroform.

'All done,' I said.

The strange Mrs Standish

'Yes,' she said, scowling.

'Well . . . I'll perhaps go on then.'

'Yes, that's all now, thank you,' she said.

'Right, well, I'll . . .'

She turned her back to me.

'Sorry,' I said, 'I didn't catch your name.'

'I'm Mrs Standish,' she said, as she disappeared into her office.

'Oh,' I said. 'Standish?'

'That's right,' she called.

'It's a common name around here?'

'Not as far as I'm aware,' she said.

'So you're . . . married to the headmaster?'

She appeared at the door of the office, and smiled at me, baring her tiny teeth. 'No!' she said. 'I am not married to the headmaster! I'm married to Alexander. The other Mr Standish.'

'Oh. Yes, of course . . .'

'Thank you for your assistance. Goodbye.'

∽ ∼

A bell rang as I made my way up the stairs away from the dark science room and the strange Mrs Standish and towards the light, dozens of boys rushing down past me.

CHAPTER 9

EVERYTHING IN HAND AND UNDER CONTROL

DESPERATE FOR FRESH AIR and some semblance of normality, I walked up and straight out the front of the school – and almost into the arms of the law.

Bernhard was still there with his clipboard. He was talking to the two policemen who had arrived earlier. He seemed to be directing them towards the beach. I was not inclined at that moment to speak to them, or indeed to anyone else, so I hung back until they passed.

'Ah, Sefton,' said Bernhard, spotting me. 'All well?'

'Yes, all fine,' I said. 'All fine. The police, they're here to ...?'

'I'm not sure. Something to do with Founder's Day? They've seen Alex. They are looking for the headmaster.'

'Very good,' I said. 'And you don't know where Alex is?'

'He was here a moment ago.'

'Well, I'll leave you to it.'

'I'll see you later, at the speech?'

'Yes, of course.'

The lorries were still being unloaded of their tables and chairs and I strode briskly up the lane towards the farm buildings where I had spent the previous night. I was going to smoke, perhaps take a few photographs, clear my head, and forget about the morning's grisly events. I was tired of people – all of them, the living and the dead. Mrs Standish. The headmaster. Alex. The dead boy. Everyone.

Just before the farm buildings there was a gate on the right into a field and at the gate were gathered a trio of forlorn-looking farm labourers, and Mr Gooding, with an expression of gap-toothed despair.

'Good morning, Mr Gooding,' I said. 'Gentlemen.' One of the labourers I recognised as Abednego, the man who had been out watching the school the night before.

Mr Gooding looked at me uncomprehendingly, as if he'd never seen me before.

'Stephen Sefton,' I said, 'you're kindly putting me up, in the farmhouse?'

Mr Gooding continued to look blank and forlorn, just as the headmaster had looked on the beach. The gathered labourers looked at me suspiciously, and in utter silence.

'Father's lost a donkey,' said Abednego eventually.

'Lhost a donkey,' said Mr Gooding.

'Oh dear. I'm sorry to hear that.'

'Lhost a donkey,' said Mr Gooding again.

'You're sure you've lost it? Don't they wander, donkeys?'

'Not our donkey,' said Abednego. 'He's been safe tethered in that field for thirty years.'

'It's them boys,' said one of the other men. 'Stuck-up bunch of good-for-nothings, the lot of them.'

'Well, I'm sure they're not all—' I began.

'What would you know about it?' continued the other man. 'We never had any trouble before the school came. I tell you what I'd do if I got my hands on one of them. I'd—'

'Bhoys!' said Mr Gooding.

'Sorry, we've not met,' I said to the angry man, trying to calm things down. 'My name's Stephen Sefton. And you must be . . .'

'Shadrach,' he said.

'Meshach,' said the other.

'And Abednego,' I said. 'Yes, of course.'

'We've never lost a donkey before,' said Abednego. 'In all our years.'

'And you've been here a long time?' I asked.

'We've been farming here sthince the Chivil War,' said Mr Gooding.

'And this was always a good farm,' said Shadrach.

'And good land,' said Meshach.

'And we never had any trouble,' said Shadrach. 'It's them bloody boys.'

'Forgive his language,' said Abednego.

'Of course,' I said. 'He wasn't sick, your donkey? They're not like elephants, where they—'

'There wasn't nothing wrong with my donkey.'

'Father took him to Sidmouth every summer, for the children,' said Abednego.

'He was a good donkey,' said Mr Gooding. 'Didn't take much to look after him. Half an ounce of tobacco to get him moving and a half-pint of cider when he'd done. Children loved him.'

'We lost a goat last month. And then the chickens. And now the donkey. What's next?' said Meshach.

'You want to take some photos of this,' said Shadrach, nodding towards my camera, stepping away from me, turning and pointing behind him towards a large empty donkey field, and beside it a chicken run, protected by wire, which was entirely empty of chickens. 'Plymouth Rocks, Minorcas, Brahmas, Dorkings – good all-round fowls. And they're all gone! Gone, the lot of them. Go on! Take a photograph of that!'

I wasn't sure that it would make a particularly interesting photograph, but nonetheless I took up my camera and was about to take a few photos of the missing hens when there came the characteristic sound of the Lagonda: 'the call of the wild', according to Miriam; 'the sound of a puma', according to Morley. I turned to see the car coming thundering up the lane.

Miriam was at the wheel and I was astonished to see that sitting in the passenger seat beside her was Alexander, a homburg mounted on his head like a helmet. I recognised an excuse to get away from my donkey conversation with the labourers and went to wave Miriam down – 'Sorry, gentlemen,' I said, 'I'll be back in a moment' – but at the sight of me Miriam showed absolutely no sign of stopping. Instinctively, before I knew it I found myself in the middle of the lane, making it impassable, with Miriam violently honking the horn and the vehicle continuing to bear down upon me.

I stood my ground. Miriam looked at me. And I looked at her. She blinked first. The car came to a halt a mere three or four inches from my chest.

I took a deep breath of relief.

'Going for a spin?' I asked, when Miriam turned off the engine.

'And what business is it of yours?' she demanded.

'Is it not rather . . .' irregular, I was going to say, but everything at Rousdon was beginning to strike me as irregular. In the context of the morning's events, Miriam's driving around with a married man was perhaps not the strangest thing that could have happened, but it seemed disturbing and inappropriate nonetheless. Not least because Alexander surely had important police business to attend to.

'Miss Morley expressed a desire last night to see the caves at Beer,' said Alex.

'The caves at Beer?'

'Indeed. And I happen to have some business in Beer this morning so I thought I might ask her to accompany me there. Instead, she has very kindly agreed to take us both in the Lagonda.'

'Really?'

'Yes, Sefton, really,' said Miriam. 'Now—'

'But what about—' I began.

'The other matter is already in hand, thank you, Mr Sefton,' said Alex, glancing away.

'What other matter?' said Miriam.

'Just, preparations for Founder's Day,' said Alex.

'Very good,' I said.

'If you wouldn't mind letting us past then, Sefton. We are of course deeply touched by your concern and interest, but—'

'But shouldn't you really be here?' I said, still standing firm round at the front of the car. 'Helping . . . Mr Morley prepare for this afternoon? Rather than going on a jaunt?'

'First,' said Miriam, clearly getting ready to refute and rebut. (I had long since learned to recognise the signs of her refute and rebut manner, a manner that involved a pursing of the lips, a twitching of the nose, and a very slight but nonetheless discernible tossing of the head.) 'As well you know, Sefton, Father requires very little assistance. And second, it is not a jaunt we are embarked upon. It's for the book. It is educational. And so, if you wouldn't mind . . .'

'Everything's in hand and under control,' said Alex, staring ahead. 'Everything in hand and under control,' he repeated.

'There, you heard X,' said Miriam, smirking.

'X?'

'Alex,' she said. 'Everyone calls him X.'

'Really,' I said.

'Everything's in hand, Sefton. And under control. Did you want anything else?'

'Actually,' I said, stepping round towards the driver's door.

'If you wouldn't mind excusing us for a moment, Alex – X – *Mr Standish*? I wonder if I could have a word, Miriam?'

'About?' said Miriam.

'It's a . . . personal matter, actually.'

'Really!' said Miriam. 'A "personal matter"? I do sometimes wonder who brought you up, Sefton. It is really the height of bad manners. I'm sure that whatever it is you need to "have a word" with me about can wait till later, and in the meantime . . .' and she went to switch on the engine.

'No,' I said, grabbing her wrist as she was about to turn the key in the ignition.

'Sefton! Take your hands off me!'

'Sorry. I—'

'What on earth do you think you're doing?'

'Actually,' I said, changing tack, 'I thought I might come with you.'

'To the caves?'

'Yes. I've heard so much about the caves at Beer.'

'Well, thank you but no thank you,' said Miriam. 'No need. We'll be fine.' She moved to switch on the engine again. And I grabbed her wrist again. She glared at me. And I stared at Alex, who was staring straight ahead.

'For the book,' I said. 'I really must take some photographs of the caves at Beer, for the *County Guides*.'

'Inside the caves?' said Miriam. 'They'll not be very interesting photographs, will they?'

'They are very dark,' said Alex.

'Exactly,' said Miriam. 'They're caves, Sefton. Dark caves. You don't have any lighting equipment with you, do you? Not that I'm aware of.'

'No,' I said. 'But I rather thought . . . Outside the caves. That would make a wonderful photograph, I think, wouldn't it?' The hesitation seemed to have secured my passage. I opened the back passenger door of the Lagonda and leapt into the back. 'Let's go then,' I said.

Miriam glanced around and glared at me. Alex glanced at her. She started the engine, and we sped off down the lane, Mr Gooding, Shadrach, Meshach and Abednego staring after us.

'Really, Sefton,' called Miriam from the front, 'your quarrelling and tiresomeness is quite appalling.'

'Don't mind me though,' I called from the back. 'You just carry on there. Imagine I'm not here.'

'Really!' began Miriam again, clearly about to launch into another series of complaints.

'Actually, you are very welcome to join us,' called Alex from the front. 'It's probably wise to take three, in case one of us gets lost.'

'Do people get lost?' asked Miriam.

'It's certainly happened before.'

'I would love to get lost!' said Miriam.

'I'm sure,' I said.

Miriam glanced around again and gave me another of her stares. 'I do hope you're not going to be a killjoy. Sefton is a terrible killjoy, I'm afraid, X.'

'I'm sure he has his reasons.'

I leaned forward to touch Miriam on the shoulder. 'Miriam, I do wonder if we might have a word.'

'Not now, Sefton. My God, man, will you not take no for an answer?'

I cleared my throat. 'In private. It's a rather . . . thorough conversation.'

'A thorough conversation? Certainly not! Never!'

We continued in this back and forth bickering manner, with occasional contributions from Alex, all the way to Beer, through narrow lanes shadowed by the great dark trees that stood weeping and brimming over the roads.

 ∽ ∼

Beer itself, I must admit, was rather an idyll: fringed with thatched cottages leading down towards a tiny harbour, several of the cottages displaying examples of intricate lacework in their windows and outside.

'Oh, how delightful!' said Miriam, spotting the lacework. 'It's absolutely exquisite!'

'Queen Victoria's wedding dress was made here,' said Alex.

'Really?'

'Or Honiton.'

'Gateway to the south,' I said.

'Here or Honiton,' continued Alex.

'Perhaps both?' said Miriam.

'Precisely,' said Alex. 'The true origins and whereabouts of the making of Queen Victoria's wedding dress are rather like tales of the origins and whereabouts of the relics of Christ, I fancy.'

'Ha, ha, ha, ha!' snorted Miriam, unnecessarily.

'It was said, I think, to have cost a thousand pounds.'

'Worth every penny, I'm sure,' I said.

'Ignore him,' said Miriam. 'He's just trying to be provocative.'

Unlike Miriam, I was not trying to be provocative.

A swarthy-skinned woman who looked like a gypsy, or a Spaniard, was sitting outside one of the cottages and waved to us as we approached, clearly recognising Alex. She was smoking a small clay pipe, and wore an intricately embroidered shawl.

'If you might stop here,' said Alex.

'Certainly,' said Miriam.

'I'll only be a moment,' said Alex, getting out of the car.

This was my opportunity. 'A word then, Miriam, if you don't mind,' I said.

'Oh, Sefton!' said Miriam. 'Absolutely not!' And she leapt up from her seat, and went to join Alex and the woman.

I sat, stranded rather, in the car. There was some kind of exchange between Alex and the woman, with Alex possibly handing over some money, though with no noticeable exchange of any goods. And as Alex had promised, the exchange, whatever it was, was over in moments, and he and Miriam returned to the car.

'They're terribly skilled lacemakers,' said Miriam.

'Really?' I said.

'They're producing some work for the school,' explained Alex.

'Lace?' I said. 'For a boys' school?'

'They do work of all kinds,' said Alex. 'Sewing, embroidery. We could stop and look around the village at some other examples, if you'd like'.

'Oh yes, let's!' said Miriam.

'We do have to be back at the school by lunchtime,' I cautioned.

'Will you ever stop being a killjoy?' asked Miriam. 'Particularly when I've asked you not to.'

'I'm just saying that we need to—'

Alex consulted his watch. 'Actually, Miss Morley, Mr Sefton might be right.'

'I do hope not. How tiresome. Surely we have enough time, don't we? The caves are not far, are they?'

'There's an entrance to the caves about a mile along the road here,' said Alex. 'But once we're there some of the passages to the larger chambers are rather long. And torturous. And treacherous.'

'Well, I certainly don't mind torturous and treacherous,' said Miriam. 'Do you, Sefton?'

I coughed loudly.

'We should probably press on,' said Alex.

'I blame you,' said Miriam, to me.

'I do think you'll enjoy the caves,' said Alex.

'I'm sure I will,' said Miriam, clambering back into the Lagonda.

'They're really quite extraordinary. I think I can safely say that you will never have experienced anything quite like the caves at Beer.'

'Beer: Cliff and Cove'

CHAPTER 10

THE CAVES AT BEER

'I just think so much of life is terribly terribly dull, don't you, Alexander?'

'I do indeed, Miriam. Terribly dull.'

'And most people also, don't you think?' Here Miriam shot a glance in my direction.

'Is it Nietzsche,' said Alex, 'who claims that most people who appear to be alive are in fact already dead, because they have never been awakened to the powers and possibilities of their own life, and the opportunities for thrill and pleasure?'

'Sounds like Nietzsche,' I said, though I had not, admittedly, at that time, ever read any actual Nietzsche. My German was not quite up to my Latin – which itself was not entirely up to scratch. But everything I had heard about Nietzsche, even then, did not endear him to me.

'The human spirit yearns for thrill and pleasure,' said Miriam, tossing her head back in what I imagined she imagined was a Dionysiac fashion.

'Yes,' agreed Alex, rather keenly.

'Such a shame that not everyone is of the same opinion.' At which Miriam shot me another withering glance, and I wished, not for the first or last time, that I had left them to their Nietzschean adventure alone.

～ ～

We had parked at the side of the road, next to a large sign that announced that the caves were shut and that trespassers would be prosecuted. Miriam and Alex took no notice of the sign and continued in their flirtatious and confiding conversation.

I got out of the car and pointed at the sign. 'Trespassers?' I said, interrupting them. 'Prosecuted?'

'And?' said Miriam defiantly, also getting out of the car.

Alex simply ignored me and started walking over towards a stile that led into a wood. I grabbed Miriam by the arm. I was determined this time not to waste my opportunity by prefacing my remarks.

'He's married,' I said bluntly.

'What?' she said. 'Who?'

'Him,' I said. 'Alex. I met his wife this morning.'

'And?' said Miriam. 'That affects me how, exactly?'

'Well, don't you think it's . . . rather . . . foolhardy to go off with a married man to some caves when . . .'

'When what?'

'Did he tell you about . . .'

'About what, Sefton?'

'The incident.'

'Oh, the accident?' she said. 'The poor boy in the car? Oh yes, yes, he told me all about that. Terribly sad, but the police are there already. It's all being sorted. So.' She folded her arms. 'And?' She cocked her head in her customary challenging fashion.

'Well. It's just ... Doesn't it seem like rather bad form to—'

'Bad form? Sefton, you may be bound by considerations of what you consider to be "bad form" but some of us like to think we're rather beyond such pettiness in human affairs. This is 1937, I think you'll find, not 1837.'

'Well, I hardly think the death of a child, in any age, at any time, could be considered a "pettiness", could it?' I said.

'You're merely being obtuse now, Sefton.'

'Obtuse?'

'Yes. Obtuse. And otiose. And obfuscatory.' She was not Morley's daughter for nothing. 'Clearly I would place the highest value on human life – unlike you, perhaps? – but I hardly see in this instance what on earth this tragic accident has to do with anything. Except that you seem to be using it as an excuse to suggest that I'm some sort of woman of low morals who can't be left alone for one moment with a married man.'

'Of course that's not what I'm suggesting' – it was exactly what I was suggesting – 'but—'

'But nothing, Sefton. Married or not, Alex is a very charming and intelligent and witty companion. Unlike some people I could mention. You're more than welcome to accompany us to take some of your pointless photographs for Father's book, or you can stay here at the car. Frankly, it matters to me not one jot.'

At which point Alex conveniently returned to the car and

– pretending not to hear our conversation – noisily pulled a couple of lanterns from the back seat.

'So?' he said. 'Ready?'

'Or iota,' said Miriam, to me.

'Mr Morley's speech is at 3 p.m.,' I cautioned.

'We know,' said Miriam.

'We shan't be long,' said Alex.

'Precisely,' said Miriam.

'The path is reasonably clear. As long as you don't mind a little trespass.'

'Sefton prefers to stick to the tried and tested routes, I think you'll find,' said Miriam. 'But I am certainly interested in a little trespass,' with which she defiantly took Alex's arm and walked off with him in a purposeful fashion towards the path to the caves. Assisting Miriam over the stile, Alex glanced back in my direction with a blank, emotionless stare.

I followed after them.

The path through the wood was overgrown, but Alex swept all before him, kicking and thrashing away at brambles with a ferocious energy. After perhaps five minutes of hacking our way along the path the bracken gave way and we entered a gloomy clearing. There were birds high up above in the trees, and the rustling of creatures in the brambles all around, and another sign: this one featured a skull and crossbones and read simply, 'Keep Out. Danger'.

'It's safe then?' I asked.

'Really, Sefton! I wouldn't have thought you'd have been deterred by a few warning signs,' said Miriam. 'Having been in Spain.'

This remark caused Alex to smirk rather, and excited in me such a terrible bitterness that I decided to hang back a little further, and leave Miriam to her fate, whatever it might be. As if she somehow knew that she had been abandoned, she for the first time expressed some slight hesitation.

'Are we in danger?' she asked Alex.

'Not at all,' he said. 'There's an adit into the mine right here. The sign's just a way of keeping people out.'

'So it's perfectly safe?' I asked, from a distance.

'It's perfectly safe if you know what you're doing,' said Alex.

'And you do?'

He did not reply.

He and Miriam stood at the entrance to the mine, an opening carved out of the rock and steadied with stout timbers and iron. Alex lit his lanterns.

'We could share?' he said, offering a lantern to me.

'Sefton will be fine,' said Miriam.

'Now, Miriam, it is *very* dark in here,' said Alex melodramatically. 'Are you prepared to face total darkness?'

'I am,' said Miriam, her voice rather husky with fear.

'Come on then, let's get on with it,' I said.

And we walked into the narrow passage.

'Watch your footing,' said Alex; to my surprise the ground sloped upwards as we entered. 'We have to go up before we go down. For the purposes of drainage.'

For a moment there was light behind us, and then we slipped into the still, cool slurry dark of the caves at Beer.

An account of the caves can be found in *The County Guides: Devon*, wherein you can read all about the history of the quarries, which were first worked by the Romans, and which have supplied stone to the great cathedrals through-out England and beyond. You can read all about how the stone was quarried by hand, in vast blocks weighing four tons or more, and how it was then carted on horse-drawn wagons or by barges from Beer beach to its destination, sometimes involving journeys of hundreds or thousands of miles. You may read how the freshly quarried Beer stone is ideally suited to fine-detail carving, saturated as it is with water and with very few fossils, and how it has always been much prized by stonemasons. You may read how the stone is found in a thick twenty-foot seam running north to south below other chalk layers, and how on exposure to the air it dries a rich, thick, creamy white and becomes almost indestructible, enduring for centuries. You may read about the difference between chalk and limestone, and the history of rock formations in the British Isles.

You can read all this and still you would have no idea about the caves at Beer.

As far as my memory serves, they are like this.

I remember first the puddles of water – splashing through them, my shoes becoming soaked. And I remember the low passages – banging my head against solid rock.

'Mind,' said Alex. 'The passages are rather low, but the chambers are only a hundred yards. I'm not taking you too fast, am I? Would you like me to go slower?'

'No!' said Miriam. 'Not slower! Come on, Sefton, keep up.'

I remember shuffling forward, bent and wet-footed, with Alex and Miriam up ahead, the sound of them talking quietly between themselves, accompanied by the sharp sound of rocks crunching underfoot, so that the entire rhythm of our short journey was of murmurs, splashes and crunch.

'Father would love this!' said Miriam. 'He's a very enthusiastic mycologist, you know.' She sounded nervous, I thought, as though speaking for reassurance.

The darkness deepened and all of the usual indicators of space and time seemed to disappear: there was nothing to orient us. When Alex spoke his voice came echoing as if from nowhere: it was difficult to identify the exact source of the sound. Without a human face or body to identify it, his voice seemed rimless and all-encompassing, like the voice of the place itself, speaking somehow from beyond life.

'Here we are,' he said. 'The caves at Beer.' He held his lamp up high, illuminating his face, which – to my astonishment – seemed to glow, with a phosphorescent-like glow, orangey and yellow. It was most extraordinary: absurd and unbelievable, like a pantomime ghost, and yet also undoubtedly impressive and inexplicable. All the anger I had felt towards him seemed to have disappeared. There was no doubt that here, he was in charge, he was to be obeyed. Something brushed past my ear and I let out a gasp.

'Bats,' said Alex.

'Bats?' cried Miriam.

'The caves are populated by greater and lesser horseshoe bats. They use the caves to hibernate. We shan't be too troubled by them.' His voice was full of reassurance. 'Follow me,' he said, and we followed him as he revealed a secret world to us.

It was almost as if we had stepped out of the darkness into a pale sunlit morning. The underground chamber we were standing in was glowing with light: immense, serene and profound. I put out my hand to touch the rough walls.

'Well?' said Alex.

'It's amazing!' said Miriam, and for once I had to agree with her. It was the most extraordinary sight, as if the world had somehow been reversed.

'Extraordinary is it not,' said Alex, 'that something so dark should yield such light?'

'Extraordinary,' said Miriam, entranced. In the lamplight her face seemed to be surrounded by a halo, her dark eyes glaring out at me.

'Like a darkroom, Sefton, is it not?' said Alex. He was right.

In the years that followed, in all my work with Morley on the *County Guides*, I spent many hours in darkrooms, sitting on a stool by the developing tanks, endlessly repeating the slow mechanical gestures that produced the miraculous development of an image. It took years for me to master all the equipment and the techniques of photography. Many of my early efforts were poor by any standards – the images ill-conceived and ill-staged, the execution poor. Sometimes I accidentally exposed entire rolls of film: most of Essex, for example, I recall, was wiped out in its entirety and I had to return to take more photographs. Half of Cumberland and most of Westmorland similarly went missing. I amassed more and more equipment: tripods, a light meter, various filters and shutter-release cables. And I bought more and more beautiful cameras. An AGFA 6x9. A Voigtlander. A Rolleiflex. But the most pleasurable part of the whole process remained the simplest and yet the strangest and most profound: the transformation of the negative from dark to light, and from light to dark. The taking of great photographs, I realised after many years, involved somehow capturing the very deepest parts of something, those depths where people and places are their very opposites, or their other selves, and eventually I came to understand that this paradox applied not only to my subjects but also to myself. When I pressed the shutter I was indeed capturing something, but that something was not them, out there: it was me, in here. The darkroom was the laboratory of my soul.

～ ～

'Yes,' I said involuntarily to Alex. 'It is like a darkroom. Thank you.'

'No need to thank me,' said Alex. 'This place is a place of truth. It is a place of revelation. It is in places like this where we as humans truly begin and end. We live in a flicker of light, but the darkness was here yesterday and today, and will be for ever. The dark places of the earth are from where all good issues.'

This little speech, for all its rather strange and stagey qualities, seemed to me at that moment to be utterly truthful and profound. Words that I would have found ridiculous to have been uttered up above seemed somehow perfectly acceptable here. In a place where all the usual assumptions were reversed, perhaps anything was acceptable. Alex was simply making the darkness fathomable.

'Now,' he continued. 'I must show you some of the other

chambers. They say that there are chambers here that have not been visited since the time of the Romans.'

'Perhaps we will discover one ourselves!' said Miriam. 'Something that no one has ever discovered before!'

'Perhaps we shall,' said Alex, 'perhaps we shall.'

And so we pressed further and further on into the caves, through narrow low passages, discovering new aspects of darkness. There were rooms of light and rooms of darkness, but the chamber where everything happened I remember most clearly because of its smell: the caves throughout smelled curiously dry and clean, but this place had a stale, rank smell, mixed with something richer and darker, almost like sweat.

'There,' said Alex, raising his lantern. It was a small cave entirely filled with hundreds, perhaps thousands of small, stinking, suffocating mushrooms, their pale flesh a horrible admonishment to the dark.

This time it was Miriam's turn to gasp. It was like witnessing a forest of tiny grasping fingers and thumbs.

'For centuries the locals have used the caves for the cultivation of mushrooms—' began Alex.

'They look like ...' interrupted Miriam, who was, for once, lost for words.

What they looked like were the dead, imploring, desperate and pleading.

It was like a scene out of one of my nightmares from Spain. We had come across a church, a beautiful small white chapel, and it was a cold, dark, wintry night, and we were seeking shelter, and the doors of the chapel were swinging open, and so we went inside and inside were women and children who appeared to have been starved to death. And then there were the men – their men? – piled up beside them, shot in the head, shot in the back. And one woman lay, emaciated, with a baby still suckling at her breast and her mouth was wide open, and her eyes squinting, as if she were looking up in joy or in amazement, perhaps at the expectant return of her husband, or at God, or justice, or at planes high up in the blue dark sky above, dropping bombs. And they lay there in the dust and the dirt, their fantastic poor white-dark skin shining in the night, and we lay down beside them, gathered together for warmth, and we drank and drank and swore vengeance. And we wreaked vengeance. An eye for an eye. And even now sometimes in my dreams I see the church and sometimes I even see Franco himself, parading across the vast dark mortuary plain of Cadiz towards us, screaming out his achievements, and us cowering in fear and destroying one another.

I was overcome with this terrible memory then, lost in the chambers and passages of time, sunk in the stench, and I have no idea how much time passed – it could have been a minute, it could have been an hour – before I realised that I'd lost Alex and I had lost Miriam and when I called out there came back only the echo of my own voice.

For a moment I stood perfectly still, my breathing shallow, and then I panicked and started to run, through the blank space, and through the darkness, yelling out. Spiders' webs swept across my face, chastening my every move, and water splashed up around my ankles, and the faster I ran the closer I seemed to come towards the very darkest and furthest and earliest places of the world, and the very darkest and furthest and earliest places of my being. The air became warmer and thicker, my breathing slower and more sluggish until eventually it felt almost impossible to walk, and impossible to move. The darkness became all-powerful. Vast chaotic empty landscapes of nothing seemed to stretch out into the recesses of the gloom and it was impossible to tell whether I was standing in some vast chamber or on a narrow path above some yet deeper and darker depths. It was as though I had been utterly abandoned, on a river or on the ocean, cut off from all civilisation and all hope of rescue, and drifting away fast from everything I had ever known towards oblivion. As I stumbled through the caves and passages there were moments when my past loomed up inside me, in the shape of dreams and horrible flashes of memory – my parents and grandparents, floating towards me in the dusk, there to greet me and to warn me – and it was as if someone had removed the shutters on life and I was able to see inside myself and the world and its meaning for the first time. I felt as though the inner truth of things had been revealed. And the inner truth was darkness.

When I eventually emerged from the caves, panting and frantic, and made it back down the path towards the car, I found that it had gone. Miriam and Alex had left me behind. I looked at my watch. I had been lost for no more than fifteen minutes. But I felt utterly abandoned. I sat down by the side of the road, alone, and wept.

CHAPTER 11

SCIENTIA POTENTIA EST

RESCUE CAME IN AN UNLIKELY FORM, as rescue often does. In one of his books of homiletic sayings, *Morley's Words to the Wise* (1930) Morley includes a little phrase, one of his favourites, that he always claimed was from the Yiddish – though frankly his sources were often unreliable, and anyway I suspected him of making up at least half of what he claimed to know. Anyway, the phrase is this: 'The unexpected should always be anticipated, but never relied upon.' Whatever its provenance it is certainly not an unuseful saying, particularly for those who might find themselves out on a limb, lost, abandoned, or otherwise at one of life's crossroads.

Having recovered my composure I began walking along the road back to Rousdon. After only a short distance an old woman riding a pony and trap drew up alongside me. She asked where I was going and I told her that I was headed for All Souls. 'Climb aboard!' she said – and her words were not issued as an invitation. They were an instruction.

She was the sort of elderly country woman – almost

entirely disappeared now from England – who issues only instructions and reprimands. She belonged indeed to that irrefutable and irrefusable class of person whom Morley sometimes referred to as 'the Great Great-Aunts of England', the sort of Englishwoman – we met them on our travels again and again, more numerous than the proverbial English rose, and twice as prickly – whose opinions were forthright, whose energies formidable, and whose prejudices terrifyingly fierce. Her clothes were likewise: she wore a pair of creamy yellow plus fours, an old brown pair of men's boots, a long crimson velvet coat rubbed shiny with use, and a large round fluffy tam o' shanter, set at a rakish angle upon her head, that promised at any moment to fly off and begin to self-seed. She was also of such a profound yet uncertain size, in both breadth and height, that she visibly wobbled as she issued her edicts: the entire effect was of a vast, fearsome blancmange.

'Do you like cats?' she asked.

'Yes,' I said, hoping that this might be the answer she was looking for.

'Good.'

This was my part of the conversation concluded. In the remaining half-hour that we spent wobbling together in the pony and trap I discovered much about Devon ('Not the county it was!'), the people of Devon ('Not the people they were!') and much else besides (horses: 'Not what they were!'; bishops: 'Not what they were!'; and butter, cider, cream and Honiton lace, all of them not what they were). At one point in the conversation, as we bounced up and down in the trap, she was denouncing one or other aspect of Devon society with such force that as she threw back her head her false teeth flew out, all in one piece. Somehow she caught them in her right hand, whipped the horse to go faster, and continued talking as though nothing had happened. This was revolting yet also undoubtedly impressive, demonstrating a mental and physical agility quite remarkable for a woman of her age and size: she was most definitely what she were.

She eventually slowed as we approached the school gates.

'You can drop me here,' I offered.

'I will do no such thing, young man,' she said. 'I shall drop you at the school, as I said I would.'

'Thank you,' I said. 'It's really very kind of you.'

'Kindness is not what it was,' she lamented.

'No,' I agreed.

As we turned in past the school gates she drove the pony harder with her whip until we were actually racing along the driveway, which was now flanked by cars stretching all the way down to the school, some of them guarded by their chauffeurs, who stood in suspicious little groups, smoking in the fashion preferred by chauffeurs, and servants and poachers, and all other men who have to hide the habit, the cigarette cupped in sheltering palm, the burning ember hidden from the gaze of bosses and employers. I shall never forget this long line of hunched, apologetic smoking men staring at us with astonishment as we blazed confidently past, with perhaps the greatest ever of the Great Great-Aunts of England waving with one hand in triumphant greeting as we thundered down upon them.

We drew up sharply at the doors to the school in a spray of gravel.

I adjusted myself with relief in my seat.

'There.'

'Well,' I said. 'Thank you, it was really very—'

'Unnecessary,' she said, waving me off, preoccupied with arranging the reins in her lap, and waving away half a dozen cats who had appeared as if from nowhere upon our arrival. 'Run along now.' I wasn't sure at first if she meant me or the cats: she meant me.

'My name is Stephen Sefton by the way,' I said, putting out my hand.

'Jolly good,' she said, neither shaking my hand nor even glancing in my direction. 'I'm Marjorie Standish.'

This caught me off-guard. 'You're . . .? Sorry?'

'Marjorie Standish,' she repeated. 'Are you deaf?'

'No. I see. And so . . . Are you . . . related by any chance to—' I was interrupted before I could get to the end of my question.

'Related? Ha! Dear boy. I'm the mother!'

And with that she struggled out of the carriage and wobbled off slowly into the school, accompanied by the cats, a porter immediately arriving to lead away the poor exhausted pony.

I was of course long accustomed to schools functioning like primitive tribes, where everyone knows everyone, and is beholden to everyone, and is therefore unable to break the bonds of fealty and filiation: this explains many of the great strengths and very obvious weaknesses of the British public school system. But All Souls was not like a primitive tribe:

All Souls was more like a family. An actual family – and blood is of course thicker than water. Or, rather, as Morley might put it, eschewing the obvious in favour of the obscure: 'For naturally blood will be of kind / Drawn-to blood, where he may it find' – a couplet he often liked to quote, presumably from some second-rate poet from *Morley's Complete Collection of Minor English Verse* (1929).

Outside in the courtyard stood the two policemen I had seen earlier in the day. They were talking between themselves. I nodded to them and hurried into the school. I assumed – as Alex had insisted – that everything was in hand.

Inside, everything was now shipshape and shining – not least because the boys and staff had given most surfaces, including the paintings, and very likely the crockery and the cutlery also, a thick coat of coach varnish, the smell of which obscured, though did not entirely hide, the reek of yesterday's cooking and the ever present stench of schoolboy sweat.

I sidled into the back of the hall, which had undergone another transformation: now, instead of being set with tables and chairs for breakfast, or for a grand meal at high table, it was arranged as for a concert: row upon row of seats, occupied by expectant parents and fidgeting sons. The fires had been lit against the early autumn afternoon chill, and waves of perfume and brilliantine were beginning to swirl and coil in the heat. Floral displays flanked the dais. There was an air of expectation. Up at the front the teachers were gathered like a jury, or like the Greek gods deciding on the fate of Odysseus and his men, and seated at the very back, like a sentinel, was Alex. So he had got back safely. I looked around for Miriam – no sign. I was keen to talk to her. Leaving me inside the caves may perhaps have been an accident. Leaving me outside the caves was clearly intended to provoke.

Proceedings opened with a poorly prepared but thankfully extremely short excerpt from the school's recent production of *A Midsummer Night's Dream*. Theseus was played by an effeminate boy who looked as if he might struggle to tie his own shoelaces, never mind to found Athens, and his bride Hippolyta was a gibbon-featured young chap with ginger hair, glasses and freckles. Theseus gabbled – 'NowfairHippolytaournuptialhourdrawsonapace-fourhappydaysbringinanothermoonbutOmethinkshow-slowthisoldmoonwanesshelingersmydesireslike toastep-dameoradowagerlongwitheringoutayoungmansrevenue' – while Hippolyta drew out every single syllable, pomping hard on each fourth or fifth word, presumably in the hope that such words, simply by virtue of the rules of English grammar, might be significant nouns or verbs and so might magically convey the sense and meaning: 'FOUR days will quickly STEEP themselves in night; / FOUR nights will quickly DREAM away the time; / And then the MOON, like to a silver BOW / New-bent in HEAVEN, shall behold the NIGHT / Of our solemnities.' In *Shakespeare for Schoolboys* (1935) Morley expresses the opinion that gobbets of Shakespeare should be learned by heart by schoolchildren entirely without the aim of understanding – in the same manner as Bible passages and the long poems of Tennyson – 'in the hope and expectation one day of understanding'. The boy players of All Souls certainly seemed to have taken this principle to heart.

After this theatrical opening number there was a brief fanfare of ill-tuned trumpets, a mumbled prayer by the school chaplain, and then the headmaster got up, thanked various parents and donors who had assisted with the move to the new school, and proceeded to introduce Morley.

'Here at All Souls,' he intoned, rather dustily, in that dusty age-old manner of all intoning headmasters, 'we believe that whether a man starts his life in a grand castle or in some modest cottage he should have an equal opportunity to rise to the top.' I looked around the room at all the fur coats and the diamonds, and the pinstripes and the vicuna overcoats and it seemed to me unlikely that many of the boys here had started life in some modest cottage, or indeed in a great castle. Nonetheless. 'Here at All Souls we like to think of ourselves as intellectual aristocrats.' Again, I had distinguished no such signs of intellectual distinction during my time at the school. Anyway. 'Our motto, as you know, is *Scientia Potentia Est* – Knowledge is Power, the words of course of the great Francis Bacon, and no one of my acquaintance is more powerful in this sense, no one perhaps exemplifies the aristocracy of the intellect more than my dear friend, our Founder's Day speaker this year, Mr Swanton Morley.'

There was some shuffling at this point, as the audience expected the headmaster to conclude. But he went on, and on, providing a more than generous summary of Morley's various achievements.

'Mr Morley and I could not have come from more different backgrounds. While I was lucky enough, like you boys, to enjoy the benefits of an English public school education, and a number of years of higher learning at Cambridge, Mr Morley had to make his way in the world entirely by dint of his own efforts. Leaving school at fourteen, he began working as a copy holder for his local newspaper in Norfolk. At twenty-five he was the toast of London, and the editor of the *Westminster Gazette*. He is a member of the Royal Society, the Linnean Society, and is the founder of the Society for the Prevention of Litter. He is also the author of more than one hundred books, and he is currently embarked on a project to write a guidebook about each of the English counties. He is, in short, and without doubt, one of the most brilliant men I have ever met. We will doubtless all have much to learn from our speaker today. So, ladies and gentlemen, boys, please welcome our Founder's Day speaker, Mr Swanton Morley, the People's Professor.'

So, ladies and gentlemen, boys, finally to Morley.

He was seated not with the teachers up on the dais but with the local dignitaries down at the front of the hall, and as the headmaster beckoned him forward he at first rose slowly and stepped haltingly towards the stage, but then, with a discernible twinkle, he suddenly sprang up the few steps in a manner that could only be described as theatrical. This tendency to the theatrical was perhaps a weakness of Morley's and has been remarked upon by a number of his critics, though one might also claim in his defence – and in the case of Morley one might surely be permitted to make the claim and the comparison – that it was simply his way of honouring one of his great heroes, Charles Dickens. In his popular book on Dickens – *Dickens At Work* (1930), part of his multi-volume 'Writers At Work' series, in which he details the working lives of writers, from Shakespeare to Milton to

Trollope, noting their working routines and habits, their earnings from both book- and non-book-related activities – he devotes several chapters to the subject of Dickens's reading tours. These chapters reveal much, I think, about Morley's own habits and interests as a writer and I can perhaps do no better – rather than attempting to analyse and describe the complex motives for his own incessant public speeches, and readings and tours and promotional activities – than to quote what he writes about Dickens in the famous chapter, 'Dickens on Stage':

Charles John Huffam Dickens was, therefore, as we know, and as we have seen, and as I hope amply to have demonstrated, a *great* writer. Indeed, one of this nation's very greatest, the inheritor of Chaucer, and of Johnson and of Shakespeare himself. An immortal, one might say, even among the immortals. Yet Dickens was also, more than any of them, a performer. Indeed, I believe, and I hope to convince you, dear reader, that Dickens was a great writer *because* he was a performer. A great performer. Charles John Huffam Dickens is the great example in English literary history of the writer *as* performer, or the performer *as* writer. His page is a stage, and his stage a page. As a young man it is said that Dickens took lessons with one of the great comedians of his time, and it is perhaps possible to imagine him, our greatest prose stylist, as a music-hall act: Charles Dickens, Miles of Smiles! A keen amateur theatricalist, shall we say – Dickens himself surely drives us towards such terms of invention – in 1858 he became a true professional. In 1858, aged forty-six years old, a man in the very midst of life, a man who has published no fewer than eleven novels, works of extraordinary range and vitality, *The Pickwick Papers* (1836–37) and *Oliver Twist* (1837–39) and *Nicholas Nickleby* (1838–39) and *The Old Curiosity Shop* (1840–41) and *Barnaby Rudge* (1841) and *Martin Chuzzlewit* (1843–44) and *Dombey and Son* (1846–48) and *David Copperfield* (1849–50) and *Bleak House* (1852–53) and *Hard Times* (1854) and *Little Dorrit* (1855–57), a man who is also editing a weekly magazine, and who has helped to establish a home for fallen women, and who has a wife and children, a man who by any standards, even by his own extraordinary standards, is a busy man, embarks upon an extraordinary new project, a project for which he will be remembered almost as fondly as for all his other works and endeavours!

In 1858 Charles John Huffam Dickens takes to the stage. In 1858 he embarks upon his first great reading tour of the cities of Great Britain and Ireland. It was of course a risk, as all great enterprises are a risk, but everywhere throughout the land Dickens found himself greeted by rapturous houses. The question for us perhaps is why? Not why was he adored: the evidence is there for all to read in the books. The question is rather, why take the risk? Why, if your home is on the page, why attempt to make another home on the stage? I think perhaps the answer lies here: for Dickens, it was simply not enough that he was writing his novels, and his articles, and editing his magazines, and agitating on questions of political reform. For Dickens, above all the great English writers, needed to be *with* his readers. To be actually with them and among them. For Dickens, there was a need, a hunger, a desire to be loved, a simple human need for human company and the thrill of other people.

For Dickens, read Swanton Morley.

He stood at the lectern in silence for what seemed like a long time, long enough for everyone in the audience to examine him closely: the thick tweed suit, the bow tie, the moustache, the brogues, the costume: his writer's habit. 'My harlequinade,' he once described it to me. 'My costume and disguise.' And then, and only then, when the teachers' eyes were upon him, and the boys' eyes were upon him, and the parents' eyes were upon him, then and only then, when he had everyone's full and undivided attention, did he begin to speak.

'Boys,' he began. 'Boys, boys, boys. I am shocked.' He paused. For a long time. This was certainly an arresting opening. I saw that several of the young fellows, whose hunched shoulders already indicated the beginnings of boredom, straightened appreciably. The headmaster also adjusted himself slightly in his seat – perhaps concerned that Morley might mention the morning's tragic accident. He had nothing to fear. 'I am shocked,' continued Morley, 'to have had this honour bestowed upon me.' There was a slight huff of amusement and relief among the parents. 'But I am also disappointed.' Again, a pause for dramatic tension. 'I am disappointed in myself.' It was clear that this Founder's Day speech was going to be interesting.

'Traditionally, you will know, the Founder's Day speech begins in Latin. And so I intended to begin my speech today here at All Souls, in this magnificent new school, perched as it is on the very edge of England, *a fronte praecipitium a tergo lupi*, as it were. But anyone who is a scholar would say of my Latin and my Greek what Johnson famously said of Milton's two Tetrachordon sonnets: that the first is contemptible and the second not excellent. I have decided therefore to address you, if I may, this afternoon, on this special occasion, boldly and directly, in our own dear mother tongue.'

Disparaging looks were exchanged among some of the teachers up on the dais, but one could feel a palpable sense of relief among the boys and their parents, who could at least look forward to understanding something of what was said. Morley was of course being falsely modest: his Latin and Greek were neither contemptible nor perhaps excellent, though they were certainly eccentric, as far as I could tell, as were his Afrikaans, his Armenian, his Yiddish, his Vietnamese, his Czech, his Esperanto, his Pitman's shorthand, his Braille and, very often, his English.

'Life, boys, as many of you will doubtless already be aware, can be difficult. In fact, not only *can* life be difficult – it *is* difficult. It *will* be difficult – and it will sometimes be difficult for *you*, as it has doubtless been difficult for your parents.' Appreciative nodding among the parents here. 'At times, boys, you will find your loyalties divided. Or perhaps you will find yourselves cast down, or cast among those who do not have your best interests at heart. You will at times have to face the dark and stifling interiors of the human mind: your own and that of others. Perhaps you will find yourselves placed under what might seem to be intolerable pressures and strains, and it will seem to you, to quote the unforgettable Noddy Boffin in *Our Mutual Friend*, as though society were merely a matter of "scrunch or be scrunched".' Morley here theatrically relished the scrunching sound of 'scrunch' and 'scrunched'. The speech seemed to be drifting rather towards a challenge.

'It is my belief, boys, however, that life's difficulties can often be overcome – both the little difficulties, and the larger difficulties. It is my belief that one can, as it were, "unscrunch" the tangled mess of our lives, that one can face up to one's responsibilities and overcome those forces and individuals, however powerful and forbidding they might seem, who seek to cast us down into darkness. All of us, boys, have a choice. And you have a choice in particular, in these magnificent new school premises, to make it a place of safety, a place of calm, as well as a place of learning.'

Up on the dais, Alexander remained impassive. The headmaster seemed to give a little sigh, whether of deep appreciation or of despair I could not tell.

'I would like this afternoon, if I may, ladies and gentlemen, to take as my text Captain Scott's famous last letter. This letter, you will recall, was composed by a man who was facing a situation in real life as strange and as terrible as any fiction that ever occurred, a situation as extraordinary as any sprung from the imaginations of Aeschylus or from Sophocles or from Shakespeare. A truly desperate situation. This was a man upon whom the Fates had truly been let loose.' He stared hard out at the audience – as though summoning the Fates himself. '"Things," writes Scott, "have come out against us." The art of English understatement, ladies and gentlemen! Scott and his men are stranded and alone, their deaths imminent. "Surely misfortune could scarcely have exceeded this last blow. We arrived within eleven miles of our old One Ton Camp with fuel for one last meal and food for two days. For four days we have been unable to leave the tent – the gale howling about us."' I felt a sudden chill in the hall, as though a ghost had walked past. '"I do not think human beings ever came through such a month as we have come through, and we should have got through in spite of the weather but for the sickening of a second companion, Captain Oates, and a shortage of fuel in our depots for which I cannot account, and finally, but for the storm, which has fallen on us within eleven miles of the depot at which we hoped to secure our final supplies."

'And this, boys, is what Scott wrote of the valiant Captain Oates, who had fallen sick: "He was a brave soul. He slept through the night before last, hoping not to wake; but he woke in the morning. It was blowing a blizzard. He said: 'I am just going outside, and may be some time.' He went out into the blizzard, and we have not seen him since. We knew that poor Oates was walking to his death, but though we tried to dissuade him, we knew it was the act of a brave man and an English gentleman."

'Be in no doubt, boys – despite all that has been said and written about it – that Captain Scott's adventure was a failure. It failed to achieve its objective, and it failed for all the reasons that we ourselves fail in life. A lack of planning, a lack of preparation, a lack of foresight. A lack of leadership.' Was it the case that the headmaster gave another, deeper sigh here? I am perhaps remembering falsely. But Morley went on. (The text of the speech is available in *Talking to Boys*, 1938.) 'But did this mean that Captain Scott and his men were themselves failures, boys? Were they fools to embark on this adventure? Was the expedition a mistake? The answer to these grave questions of doubt, I believe, is an emphatic no. Captain Scott and his gallant band were seeking knowledge – not riches, not power, but a deep knowledge of the mysteries of the human world, and such knowledge is always worth the sacrifice. The quest for true understanding is a quest that takes us beyond ourselves into the realms of the dangerous, the unknown and, perhaps, into oblivion.' Alexander, I noted, was nodding in agreement.

Morley continued, and as speeches go I thought it was pretty good. I wondered subsequently if he was perhaps subtly indicating that something was rotten in the school – though the deep-rooted nature of the rot I did not then understand and even he, I fancy, was at that time unaware of exactly what was wrong, and how wrong, and besides, we had simply had no time to think about it or to investigate it further. We were caught up and caught out. After the speech Morley was whisked away by the headmaster to be proudly paraded before the boys of All Souls and their parents – all the boys, that is, except Michael Taylor.

Founder's Day fun and games

CHAPTER 12

OUT ON THE LAWN

WE WERE IN A MARQUEE out on the lawn at the back of the school, by the tennis courts. Where this morning the boys had been fed gruel they were now fortified with sticky buns, cucumber sandwiches and lemonade, while their parents were treated to tea, coffee, fino and oloroso. The older boys circulated with the sherry, their circulation becoming steadily more uncertain as the afternoon wore on. I rather suspected that they might be helping themselves when out of sight. Morley found himself, as always, in a throng, with parents and boys asking him to autograph books and pamphlets, and quizzing him about his various writing and campaigning activities, and his opinions on various matters of great public import. What did he think of the National Government? What about the abdication? What about Spain? Mr Hitler? The state of the novel? The state of the nation? And what was his advice on removing stains from rugs and carpets? The usual tiresome sort of questions, which, to his credit, he never tired of answering.

A father – a big bluff, heavy-handed sort of chap, with the

look of a West Country cattle-dealer – shuffled forward with his son, who might as well have been the cattle. Big-boned and slow, with decidedly bovine features, the boy stood sullen by his father's side, as though awaiting the butcher's blow.

'Mr Morley,' said the father, tipping his hat.

'Sir,' said Morley, respectfully adjusting his bow tie.

'I wonder if you might have some advice for our budding young writer here?'

'Budding young writer, eh?'

'Well,' said the budding young bovine writer, blushing.

'What is it you would like to write?'

'Erm.'

'Tell him,' said his father, nudging him sharply.

'I would like to write poetry.'

'Ah, poetry,' said Morley. 'The spontaneous overflow of powerful feelings, eh?'

The boy's father looked rather uncomfortable. 'So any advice, Mr Morley, on how he could break into the business?'

'My advice, sir,' said Morley, addressing the boy but not the father, 'would be not to attempt to break into the poetry "business". For in literature there is no "business". If you want to write, write. And if not, don't. That's all.'

'That's all?' said the father, clearly disappointed.

'If he must, he shall,' said Morley. 'And if he can, he will.'

'That's it?'

'I'm afraid so, sir. I wish there were more to it.'

Having delivered this devastating insight Morley then returned to signing books, swiftly, with his quick and much practised flourish, insisting on talking to each person at great length about their life, opinions, hobbies and interests, often far beyond the point at which they had lost interest in talking about it themselves. During our time together I gradually learned how to extricate him from such encounters: 'Now, now, Mr Morley, don't forget there is a queue,' or 'Thank you, sir/madam/young man/young lady, I'm sure you have many things to do,' but most effective of all, 'Come, come, Mr Morley, we are running behind time.' I was officially employed as Morley's assistant but I often felt more like a flesh and blood barrier between Morley and the endless needs and desires of his many fans. Fortunately the book signing that afternoon continued in a reasonably orderly and predictable fashion – until the elderly Mrs Standish arrived, escorted by the headmaster.

Mrs Standish was clearly not one to stand on ceremony and she simply walked past the assembled children and parents to the head of the queue and presented herself before Morley. Since having delivered me back to All Souls earlier in her pony and trap she had, thankfully, removed her tam o' shanter – which was presumably her version of a flying helmet, or a motoring cap – and had donned a long fluffy grey woollen shawl. She now stood before Morley, smoking from a long cigarette holder, her steel-grey hair sleek upon her head. In the light of the afternoon I noticed she had distinctly downy jowls, which, combined with her vast size, and the grey shawl, and her steaming cigarette, gave her a profound animal presence – as though she were only part human and mostly mammal, a presence further suggested because her slightest move was followed by a posse of cats, the same posse, I assumed, who had greeted her earlier, and who now stood around her as if on show, or on guard, their tails erect. The circus had most definitely come to town.

'The famous Mr Morley, I presume?' she said.

'Yes, madam.' Morley stood to greet her.

'I'm Marjorie Standish, mother of the two boys.'

'Hardly boys,' said Morley. The headmaster looked rather sheepish. 'The headmaster and Alex must be—'

'Do you have children?' asked Mrs Standish.

'I have a daughter and I had a—'

'Then I would have expected you to understand, sir. One's children always remain one's children.'

'Of course they do, madam.'

'I've heard a lot about you, Mr Morley.'

'All of it good, I hope?' said Morley.

She ignored the question.

'Actually, I wonder if we've met before, Mrs Standish?' continued Morley.

'I don't believe so, sir.'

'No? You're not a fellow writer, perhaps, Mrs Standish?'

'Mother likes to paint, don't you, Mother?' said the headmaster.

'Do you know the least beautiful part of the female anatomy for painting, Mr Morley?'

'I don't, no, Mrs Standish, no,' said Morley.

'The breast.'

'Ah.'

'But for photographing? Magnificent! Ironic, is it not?'

'A different medium, I suppose, Mrs Standish. We must allow for these differences.'

'There's a subject for one of your little newspaper essays, Mr Morley.'

'Indeed.' Morley examined her features very closely. 'There really is something very familiar about you, Mrs Standish.'

'I have an excellent memory, Mr Morley, and I can assure you that if we had met before I would be able to recall it.'

'Well, perhaps not then – which makes it all the more pleasurable to make your acquaintance now.'

'Indeed.' The cats quivered expectantly around her feet.

The small queue of boys with their parents stuck behind Mrs Standish, meanwhile, were becoming rather restless. The headmaster turned and apologised to them, and then attempted to move his mother on.

'I think Mr Morley is rather busy at the moment, Mother, signing books and what have you. Perhaps we'll speak with him again later?'

Mrs Standish had begun rifling through her large hand-bag.

'It's your school, isn't it? These other people can wait for five minutes, can't they? What's wrong with them? Train to catch?'

'I'm sure they can wait, but—'

'Do you like cats, Mr Morley?'

Never one to be thrown by an unexpected question, Morley had an instant response.

'I'm afraid, madam, I'm the kind of cat-lover who likes them best when they bark,' he said.

'I adore cats,' said Mrs Standish, producing a paper bag full of fish heads, tails and entrails, which she proceeded to toss to the felines gathered around her. 'Fresh this morning from Sidmouth,' she said. 'I go at least twice a week for supplies.'

'Excellent,' said Morley.

The boys in the queue, like Morley, were unperturbed but some of the parents expressed their shock and disgust at

Mrs Standish's outlandish behaviour. Sensing the beginnings of a commotion, Alex arrived to assist, with Miriam. He took instant control of the situation.

'You've met Mr Morley then, Mother?'

'Clearly,' said Mrs Standish. 'And who is this?'

'This is Mr Morley's daughter, Mother,' said Alex.

'I see,' said Mrs Standish. 'Pretty little thing. Have you ever met the Duchess of Richmond?' she asked, entirely irrelevantly.

'I don't think so,' said Miriam.

'You would enjoy the Duchess of Richmond! Utterly charming.' Miriam would also so enjoy, apparently, Freya Stark, Nancy Mitford, and Lord and Lady Londonderry.

'We should perhaps allow him to continue with his book signing,' said Alex.

'I have already said we should go,' said the headmaster.

'Very well,' said Mrs Standish, shaking the remaining fish parts from out of her paper bag. 'You're a literary man, Mr Morley,' she said as a parting shot. 'Have you ever read Bulwer-Lytton?'

'Of course, madam.'

'*Pelham*? *Godolphin*?'

'Indeed. And *The Last Days of Pompeii*. Rather too brilliant for his own good, I always thought,' said Morley.

'Really?' said Mrs Standish.

'Come on then, Mother,' said the headmaster.

'Can one be too brilliant for one's own good?'

'Biographies of the great and the good certainly seem to suggest such,' said Morley.

'I always wonder who it is who reads biographies,' said Mrs Standish. 'I find them terribly infra dig.'

'Then infra dig I am, madam,' said Morley.

'Clearly,' said Mrs Standish.

'Mother was a great friend of Bulwer-Lytton, weren't you, Mother?' said Alex, having taken her firmly by the arm and attempting to steer her away from Morley and towards one of the refreshment marquees.

'Indeed. I was blessed to have been acquainted with him. He was a genius.'

'I am always rather wary of the term genius,' said Morley.

'Father,' said Miriam.

'Inferior people often are,' said Mrs Standish.

'We can all have a nice chat later, Father,' insisted Miriam.

'The term I think is often misapplied,' continued Morley regardless, 'to those who have been blessed with time and money rather than with the artistic gifts that we assume are their natural talents. It is a mistake to confuse good luck with genius, I believe, though certainly it makes us feel better about the injustices of this world.'

'Bulwer-Lytton was an entirely exceptional man,' said Mrs Standish.

'I think I'm right in saying he spent the final years of his life in Torquay, is that so?' said Morley.

'That's correct, sir.'

'Perhaps it is easier to appear exceptional in Torquay than it is elsewhere?'

'Goodbye for now, then, Mr Morley,' said Alex, heaving his mother away.

Morley returned to signing books and I was introduced by the rather shamefaced headmaster to some of the governors and benefactors of the school: a natty, foxy little man with blue eyes and a boyish figure, who wore a white waistcoat and sported a red carnation in his buttonhole; another man with glassy, fish-like eyes, which darted around as he talked, giving him a rather sinister appearance; and another, Mr Dodds, who I later discovered had made a vast fortune from the sale of underwater paint to the German navy, and who had cornered me up against a post in the marquee. He was a small round adamant sort of man in an unwise pinstripe suit, clutching a schooner of sherry with a determination that suggested he had no intention of ever giving up either on the sherry, or on his point, which was something to do with hunting.

'Snuff?' he asked, pausing in his conversation for a moment, and blowing his nose with a large bandana handkerchief.

'No, thank you,' I said.

He sneezed. 'Excellent stuff,' he said. 'Now, where were we?'

'Kenya?' I said. For this was where our conversation had led. 'In 1932?'

'Exactly! So I took out my trusty side-loading carbine, came out of the tent, and all I could hear was the roaring of the lions. Ever heard the roar of a lion, man?'

'I can't say I have, sir, no.'

'Makes your blood run cold. Like ice!'

'I'm sure.' I attempted to edge away and back towards Morley, but the small round adamant Mr Dodds shot out his sherry arm to restrain me.

'So, off we go, with the guide, local chap, darkie, perfectly pleasant, eventually come upon the carcass of an antelope. Ever seen the carcass of an antelope?'

'I can't say I—'

'Horribly mutilated, but still plenty of meat on it. So we know they're coming back for more. "They'll be back for more by dawn," says our guide, and so there's nothing for it but to hide ourselves and wait for the blighters to return, and blow me – blow me! – if our chap wasn't exactly right.' He took a swig of his sherry, and I made a quick lunge to escape, but was again too slow. 'Three of the blighters!'

'Three?' I said. 'Antelopes?'

'Lions, man! Lions! Three—'

'Of the blighters.'

'Precisely. Aimed at the first, fired, bam, and she dropped. Loaded another cartridge in the rifle, fired—'

'Bam?'

'Bang, and the second lion she gives a roar but damned if she doesn't keep advancing upon me! Rearing up, more like a horse.'

'Like a horse?' I said.

'Exactly like a horse, except a lion. And I can tell you this for certain, man – if it wasn't for our guide I wouldn't be here today. Won't have a word said against the dark races. Wonderful people. Terribly loyal.'

'Good, well I'll—'

'So anyway, there's the lion' – he made an impression of a lion rearing up, baring its teeth, with a schooner of sherry in its paw – 'and he takes the shot and brings her down. Three lions within no more than about three minutes. What do you make of that, man?'

'Very impressive,' I said.

'Have them all as rugs now down at our place in Budleigh. Ever eaten a lion steak?'

I had not – and indeed never have – eaten a lion steak. They are delicious, apparently. The multiple rug-owning Mr Dodds then prevailed upon me to promise to join him stag hunting in November. I explained that I wouldn't be in Devon in November, and attempted to excuse myself, but he was extremely adamant.

'Tiverton Hunt, best in the West Country. Come down.'

'I might, thank you.'

'You shall!'

'I would be very glad to.'

'Good. Good.'

Despite my further attempts to extricate myself from his stories he then proceeded to tell me in great detail the high-lights of some of the Tiverton Hunt's most successful runs of the past few years. 'Finest beam of antlers I've ever seen,' he was saying, when his wife hove into view. I have rarely been so relieved.

'Darling, I hope you're not boring this gentleman with tales of your conquests?' asked his wife, a woman whom I already knew to be greatly long-suffering.

'No, no, not at all. Fellow enthusiast.'

'Really?' She raised a quizzical eyebrow. 'Well, would you mind awfully going and bagging me a drink?'

'Your wish is my etcetera,' he said. 'Excuse me, dear fellow. Off on an adventure!'

'I do apologise for my husband,' she said, as he moved out of earshot.

'No need,' I said. 'Your husband certainly enjoys hunting.'

'Yes. And you?'

'Not big game, no.'

'You prefer other pursuits.'

'Yes,' I said. 'I suppose I do.'

'I'm sorry,' she said, holding out her hand, 'we've not been introduced, have we?'

'No. My name's Stephen Sefton.'

'And I'm Valerie Dodds.'

'It's very nice to meet you, Mrs Dodds. Do you have children at the school?'

'No,' she said. 'We have ...' She waved a hand in dismissal of her own thoughts. 'My husband likes to support local schools. Education is one of his passions.'

I somehow doubted this very much.

She must have been twenty years younger than her husband, and perhaps ten years older than me. Where her husband was bald in his adamant pinstripes, she was all subtle silk and abundant Pre-Raphaelite hair. She was rich, thin and bored – which meant also of course that she was dangerous. I should have paid more attention to the warning signs.

'And what brings you here?' she asked. She spoke with a kind of feline tone and diction, so much so that she seemed almost on the verge of actually purring. 'You're not a teacher, are you? I think I've met most of the teachers. Son at the school perhaps?'

'No, no. I'm here with Mr Morley, I work for him.'

'The chap who gave the speech?'

'Yes.'

'Really. Didn't quite know what to make of him. Terribly charming, I'm sure. But ... Bit of a chip on the shoulder, perhaps?'

'He is certainly very passionate about education.'

'Quite.' Like her husband, she took no real interest in what I had to say. 'Sorry. Do you smoke? It's a terrible habit, but on these sorts of occasions it does give one something to do with one's hands.'

'I do.'

I offered and lit a cigarette for her, and we stood together in silence, gazing around the room, like Pocahontas and John Smith, waiting for our captor to return. But before her husband made it back, Alexander came walking purposefully towards us.

'Mrs Dodds,' he said.

'Alex,' she replied.

And then turning to me he said, 'I just wanted to say, I am so terribly sorry about this morning. We waited for as long as we could, but Miriam was very keen to get back for her father's speech. You do understand?'

'Of course,' I said.

'I'm afraid we left Mr Sefton rather stranded this morning when we went to visit the caves at Beer,' he explained.

'Ah,' said Mrs Dodds.

'But you made it back OK?'

'Evidently,' I said.

'So no hard feelings?' He put out his hand.

I shook it, reluctantly. 'None at all,' I said, lying.

Miriam then made towards us as Alex was about to leave.

'We waited for as long as we could, Sefton.'

'So I understand,' I said.

'Alex had to get back for Founder's Day, you understand?'

If there is anything worse than being lied to, it is being lied to by two people, neither of whom is aware that the other person has been telling a different lie.

'Yes,' I said. 'He was just explaining.'

'Good. Well, what did you think of Father's speech then?'

'Very good,' I said. 'Very good indeed.'

'I thought it rather odd,' said Miriam.

'Precisely what I was saying,' said Mrs Dodds, who had been eagerly examining Miriam. 'Hello.' She took Miriam's hand in her own. 'I'm a friend of Alex's. Just like you.'

Miriam seemed rather taken aback by the older woman's appraisal. 'He's just escorting me to the lemonade tent,' she said.

'Perhaps you'd like to join us, Mr Sefton? Mrs Dodds?' offered Alex.

'We hardly need provide a chaperone – even for you – to the lemonade tent,' said Mrs Dodds. 'Do we?' Alex simply nodded in acknowledgement of the obvious slight. 'We are perfectly fine here, thank you.'

'Very good,' said Alex.

'Lead on, Macduff,' said Miriam.

I watched them closely as they disappeared off to the lemonade tent.

'Don't worry,' said Mrs Dodds, lightly touching my arm.

'Worry?'

'You look concerned.'

'Do I?'

'Is she a friend of yours?'

'No,' I blustered. It was difficult to say exactly what Miriam was. 'No. Not exactly. She's Mr Morley's daughter.'

'Ah. Pretty young thing. Don't worry. Women always fall in love with Alex.'

'Really?'

'Oh yes. All the time.'

'I see. You too?'

'Once, perhaps.'

[161]

'But no longer?'

'Definitely no longer.'

'Not your type?'

'Not my type at all, no.' She let the words hang in the air, and breathed slowly through her nostrils while looking me up and down. Then she ground out her cigarette under her heel.

'Well, it was a pleasure meeting you, Mr Sefton. I should go and retrieve my husband – he's doubtless bagged another innocent listener. I do hope you'll be joining us this evening?'

'This evening?'

'At the fancy dress ball?'

'The?'

'Fancy dress ball?'

'I didn't realise there was going to be a fancy dress ball.'

'Oh yes. It's tradition, after Founder's Day. A chance for everyone to let their hair down. Well, a recent tradition. Alex introduced it a couple of years ago, at the old school.'

'He is a man of many talents,' I said. 'A party organiser also?'

'Yes. Rousdon's very own Trimalchio.'

'Indeed. And you his Fortunata?'

'Ha!' At this she laughed.

I was rather proud: it was a riposte worthy of Morley himself. (In fairness, it was a riposte of Morley's. I had recently, fortuitously, been reading *Morley's Rome and the Romans for Beginners* (1930). His appalled description of the feast in the *Satyricon* was one of the only parts I could recall.)

'And you must come in costume. No excuses.'

'I don't have a costume with me,' I said.

She looked me up and down again as she departed, with

[162]

what one might describe as a male gaze. 'Well, I'm sure you'll think of something. I hope to see you later.'

'Of course.'

'I'll see if I can find you, shall I?' she said. 'In your disguise?'

'If you wish.'

'I wonder if you'll be able to find me?'

I escaped from the marquee and wandered over towards a group of boys who were gearing up for a game of croquet. Morley of course was in the thick of it, and was busy explaining to them the rules of a game called stoolball. 'Think of it as a vigorous game of rounders,' he was saying.

'Stoolball, Sefton? You must know stoolball?'

I was not in fact familiar with stoolball.

'No, Mr Morley, I'm afraid not.'

'We'll maybe get it set up tomorrow. We need some sort of wooden boards, about ten inches square, fixed to poles. Make a note, Sefton.'

I rather begrudgingly took out a notebook, while Morley dictated the rules of the game to me, and the necessary equipment.

'. . . and then we set them facing each other about twenty yards apart. A bowler and batsman, the bowler attempting to hit the board.'

'Anyway,' I said. 'Mr Morley, could I—'

'Anyway indeed, Sefton. We're about to move on to croquet, if you don't mind. We're running our own amateur Olympics.'

'Aren't the Olympics already amateur?'

'An amateur amateur Olympics then,' said Morley. 'Are you in?'

'I think I might skip this actually, Mr Morley.'

He had got hold of a croquet mallet.

'Excellent mallet,' he said, swinging it wildly. 'Wood, brass, lignum vitae. A fine piece of Great British precision engineering, boys. Now, here's a question for you: what wood would you say this is?' He swung the mallet up aloft.

'Willow?' suggested one boy.

'Ash?' suggested another.

'It's not a cricket bat, sir,' said Morley. 'Sefton?'

'Oak?' I suggested.

'Oak? Oak?' said Morley. 'Come, come. Hickory, gentlemen. The best wood for a mallet. Look at this. Quite marvellous. And all the more remarkable' – he brandished the mallet now as though it were a club – 'since croquet is in essence such a violent game. Much more so than most people realise. The aim, you see, is to destroy one's opponent. To crush them utterly.' At which he pretended to pound one of the young boys about the head with the mallet.

After more monkeying around the game eventually began, and Morley, to my surprise, knocked his ball not towards the first hoop, but rather off towards the east boundary of the court. There was a reason for this, though for the life of me I cannot now remember what it might be. He tried to explain to me many times the rules and the sequences of roquets, croquets and hoops and I have since read his introductory book, *Croquet: A Guide for the Perplexed* (1938) which, frankly, left me none the wiser. Suffice it to say, the knocking of the ball off towards the boundary is a classic opening move. To quote *Croquet: A Guide for the Perplexed*: 'The chances of running a hoop from six yards with a margin of error of only an eighth of an inch are very slight indeed. In croquet, it is by indirection that one finds out direction.'

A boy, attempting to imitate Morley, then promptly knocked his own ball so hard it flew out of the boundary, and rolled away down the steep lawn leading towards the woods and the cliffs.

'I'll get it,' I said, bored already, and went off to retrieve the ball. I thought I might also take the opportunity for a smoke.

It had rolled away quickly into the undergrowth, but I soon spied it, along with a group of boys busy making mischief.

Two tall, stout boys stood in silence apart from the group, scoffing party food – one of them a brace of sandwiches, the other what appeared to be an entire game pie. The poor things reminded me rather of Morley's dogs back in Norfolk: the way they took sharp, sudden bites, snapping at their vittles, all the time looking around as if they might be discovered. Beyond them, deeper in the undergrowth, and with their backs turned to me, was a larger group of boys, who seemed to be poking with sticks at something or someone lying on the ground. The two scoffing boys had clearly been appointed as lookouts, but in their frenzy of eating they had forgotten to do much looking out, and so were shocked and terrified when I suddenly approached them from amid the dense vegetation. I had picked up the croquet ball and as I walked towards them I held it aloft as a sign of peace, and put my finger to my lips. They stopped chomping, and stood with eyes and mouths wide open – pie and sandwiches momentarily suspended, a look a terror upon their faces.

I went slowly and quietly towards the larger group and

stood at the shoulder of one of the boys who was vigorously prodding with a stick.

'Stay here,' I said, in the sternest voice I could muster. 'All of you. Understand?'

The boys nodded in mute agreement.

And then I went to fetch a policeman.

CHAPTER 13

BASIC PSYCHOLOGY

'WELL, THIS IS RATHER DISTRESSING,' said Morley. 'Photographs, Sefton?'

'We have requested your assistant not to take any photographs, sir,' said one of the two policemen who had arrived to investigate the death of Michael Taylor, and who had now taken charge of events. They had indeed requested me not to take any photographs, though the request had been couched in rather more direct – shall we say Anglo-Saxon – language.

'My assistant is a professional photographer, Officer,' said Morley. This was, in fairness, something of an overstatement: I was then and remain now at best an enthusiastic amateur. Morley sometimes jokingly referred to me as his 'Cartier', but I was alas no Bresson and anyway I was not particularly inclined at that moment to take any photographs – particularly not photographs of a mutilated cow.

The poor thing seemed to have had its stomach split from top to bottom, and its head had also been brutally removed: it was the head that the boys had been vigorously prodding with their sticks, making quite a mess of it in the process. The bloody head sat staring at us now, set apart from the carcass, as though bizarrely illustrating some complex Cartesian point about the division between mind and body: the kind of illustration indeed that Morley himself might have included in one of his books on philosophy for children. (*All Cretans Are Liars: Philosophical Puzzles, Conundrums and Quizzes for Use in Schools, Colleges and at Home*, for example, published in 1932, includes a rather odd, jumbled appendix of diagrams and doodles – featuring teapots, razors, lions, tooth fairies – all apparently intended to illustrate Zeno's Paradox, the Gordian Knot, the Problem of Evil and etcetera, though in fact, to my mind at least, they simply confused matters further. It was not perhaps his most successful book.)

'Hmm,' continued Morley, surveying the scene of butchery. 'Distressing. But very interesting.'

Thankfully, by the time I had alerted the police to the mystery of the poor dead cow, Founder's Day was coming to an end, parents were drifting away, boys bidding them farewell, and so this latest All Souls' scene of distress – down in the bushes, beyond the croquet lawn – seemed to have gone unnoticed by those not directly involved. The two policemen had quickly and efficiently taken statements from the boys who were present at the cow-prodding, and I had explained to them the matter of the disappearance of the chickens – and the goat and the donkey – from the farm.

'Disgusting,' said one of the policemen, who was in possession of an extraordinary pair of jug ears and a menacing stare. 'Should be ashamed, the lot of them,' he said, raising a fist towards the boys, who remained gathered around as though awaiting their own horrible execution.

Left to his own devices I rather think the jug-eared policeman might well have begun dispensing summary justice: I feared serious consequences for the boy or boys who were found responsible for the cow's slaughter. But fortunately, having bid all the necessary farewells, the headmaster had also joined us: he looked grief-stricken, but was clearly a restraining presence upon the long arm of the law. Morley, meanwhile, and in contrast, seemed rather blasé about the whole thing.

'Interesting,' he said. 'Very very interesting. Gentlemen, might I make a suggestion?' He drew the headmaster and the policemen towards him with a wave. I also gathered closer. 'Talk among yourselves,' he instructed the boys; and they did: he always had the knack of command. 'Gentlemen,' he continued, lowering his voice rather. 'I wonder if we might ... at least ... attempt to make a silk purse out of our proverbial sow's ear here, as it were – if you forgive the mixed metaphor.'

'What?' said one of the policemen.

'I'm afraid I don't understand,' said the headmaster.

'I think if we are rather practical-minded there might be an opportunity here ...'

'Practical-minded, sir?' said the policeman.

'Yes, I rather wondered,' said Morley, hesitating, 'I rather wondered if you might let me have the head?'

'Which head?' said the headmaster, clearly alarmed.

'The cow's head, sir?' said the jug-eared policeman.

'Yes. That's right. I thought it might make an interesting lesson for the boys.'

'A lesson?'

'Yes.'

'What are you planning to do, Morley?' asked the head-master.

'To cook it,' he said, staring at the cow's head staring back at us. It did not look like a head that wanted to be cooked.

'You want to destroy the evidence?' said the police-man.

'No. No. I want to *use* the evidence,' said Morley, who was carefully watching the boys as we spoke. 'To see if we can . . .'

'To see if we can what?' asked the policeman.

'Well, it's certainly not a lot of good to you or anyone else lying there, is it?' He indicated the vast head, which continued to stare blindly up at us from the dirt, and which continued to look distinctly unappetising. 'The carcass is the thing, surely, in terms of evidence, since it seems to have been rather particularly mutilated. The head has simply been hacked off. Wouldn't you agree?'

'What on earth are you thinking, Morley?' said the head-master.

'I'm thinking that what we really need is a gunny sack . . .'

'A gunny sack?'

'Yes.'

'For what—' began the headmaster.

'It's an extremely odd request, sir, if you don't mind my saying,' interrupted the non-jug-eared policeman.

'Not at all. I just thought it might be a useful distraction for the boys, in the rather distressing circumstances. And I wonder also if it might help us to flush out the culprit.'

The two policemen glanced first at one another and then over at the nervous huddle of boys.

'Flush 'em out, sir?'

'Basic psychology, gentlemen. You're familiar with Freud?'

'Is it a place?'

'I'm familiar with Croyde,' said the jug-eared policeman. 'My wife's sister's husband's family come from Croyde—'

'Freud, Viennese. Fashionable among my daughter and her friends.'

'I have read *The Interpretation of Dreams*,' said the headmaster.

'Not his best,' said Morley. 'I would direct you rather to *The Psychopathology of Everyday Life*: rather revealing. Anyway, gentlemen, in very crude Freudian terms I wonder if what we might be faced with here are certain forbidden wishes and desires being thwarted, as it were, going underground – subterranean, yes? – leading to unexpected but related outbursts of violence and sexual perversion, like hot springs bubbling up from a secret system of caves and conduits.'

The two policemen looked at one another.

'I don't like the sound of that, sir, if you don't mind my saying so.'

'Indeed. But this is the very nature of civilisation, according to Freud.'

'Not as I know it, sir.'

'No, perhaps not,' agreed Morley.

'Nor I,' said the headmaster. 'Thank goodness.'

'Did you say he was from China, this Crude?'

'Freud,' said Morley. 'Viennese, not Pekinese. So what we are witnessing with this spate of attacks is perhaps the surfacing of repressed emotions, guilt and what have you, that

[171]

are literally bubbling up and popping out.' He made a literal popping and bubbling noise.

The two policemen looked at one another again: you could tell they were beginning to think that Morley was actually deranged.

'So perhaps,' said the headmaster, saving the day, 'if we closely observe the boys' reactions as we deal with the cow, we might be able to discern their innocence or guilt?'

'Yes, the long and the short of it, Headmaster.'

Again, the two policemen looked at one another. One of them nodded to the other and they took themselves off to huddle and converse, casting suspicious glances towards us.

'It's not a bad idea,' said one of the policemen, returning.

'It's—' began the other.

'It's just that we would need a gunny sack,' said Morley.

'A gunny sack, sir?'

'Potato sack, grain sack. Something used for gardening or seeds, perhaps? And some clay. Wood for a fire. Get the boys to organise it.'

The policemen conferred again.

'Very good, sir. If you proceed as you suggest, we shall observe the boys' reactions.'

'Excellent!' said Morley. 'Excellent. By indirection we shall catch the conscience of the king, eh?' This again perplexed the policemen rather, but Morley continued. 'And also it is important that one learns in life that anything can be transformed. Waste not, want not, eh?' He nodded back over towards the boys, who were looking at us expectantly.

The jug-eared policeman gave a final consenting nod, accepting what was – I thought, and even by Morley's standards – a ludicrous enterprise.

'Excellent! Now, boys, boys!' he called and the boys came hurrying over. 'The police have given us permission to use the cow's head here for an experiment.'

The police stood by a tree and surveyed the wide-eyed boys.

'What sort of experiment?' said one boy.

'That will emerge as we proceed, boys,' said Morley. 'Like the meaning of life itself. Now, first we need some good clay. Any ideas?'

'We use clay in the art room, sir.'

'Of course you do! Run along then, young man, and bring us back a good bucketful of clay.'

The policeman looked for a moment as if he were going to protest.

'I hardly think the boy is going to run away, do you, Officer?'

'No, sir.'

'Are you likely to run off, boy?' asked Morley.

The boy looked terrified.

'No, Mr Morley, sir.'

'Good. What's your name?'

'Shipman, sir. But the masters call me Captain.'

'Well, Captain, my captain, we also need a gunny sack. Think you could pick something up on the way?'

'A gunny sack, sir?'

'Potato sack? Something similar?'

'Yes, sir. I can get something from the kitchens, sir.'

'Excellent, excellent. Run along then, Captain.'

The boy ran off towards the school as fast as he could.

'Good. Now, we also need a sharp knife.'

The policeman now looked extremely disconcerted.

'Come, come, boys,' said Morley. 'Sharp knife anyone?'

One of the boys – a plump little thing – looked silently up at the tall, thin pale white boy standing next to him. The tall, thin pale white boy looked as though his features had been whittled from a tall, thin pale white whittling stick.

'Knife?' said Morley.

The plump boy swivelled his eyes up at his tall thin pale companion.

'Come along now, gents,' said Morley, holding out his hand. 'We need a knife. For our experiment.' He walked up and down before them. And then again. And again. 'Can't proceed without a knife, alas.'

The plump boy nudged at his companion and the tall thin boy sheepishly produced a long Bowie knife which he had concealed down his trousers.

'Super,' said Morley. 'Thank you.' The policemen looked on in astonishment. Morley took the knife and examined it. 'Excellent,' he said. 'What's your name?'

'Hughes, sir.'

'Best keep it in a sheath in future, Hughes, eh?'

'Yes, Mr Morley.'

'Give you a nasty nick otherwise.'

The policemen were now frantically making notes.

'And finally, a shovel. Anyone got a shovel?'

None of the boys had a shovel, obviously.

'A shovel?' said the policeman.

'There's the gardener's shed over past the tennis courts,' said the freckled, ginger-haired scrap of a boy, who had played Hippolyta in the little Founder's Day playlet, and who looked as though he might at any moment float away.

'Hie thee to the gardener's shed then, Ginger,' said Morley.

'Hie, hie, hi!' And the ginger-haired boy hied, as he was told. 'And you' – Morley then indicated a burly-looking lad, who was sniggering at Ginger's eager departure – 'when Ginger returns, I want a pit dug, six foot by six? Understand?' The burly boy nodded, no longer sniggering. 'Good. In the meantime,' continued Morley, 'I think the police might need a word with some of you, perhaps? Hughes?' He nodded towards Hughes and his plump accomplice. 'And the rest of you are going to build a fire. Sefton, if you wouldn't mind taking charge of the fire?'

'Very good, Mr Morley.'

While I organised a group of boys to gather firewood and to make a mountain of branches and twigs, Morley and the policemen took Hughes and his friend to one side. After twenty minutes or so of questioning, the policemen escorted the boys away and Morley and the headmaster came and stood by our fire-to-be.

'All well?' I asked.

'All shall be well, and all shall be well, and all manner of thing shall be well,' replied Morley.

'Julian of Norwich,' said the headmaster.

'Precisely,' said Morley.

'The police are dealing with the matter,' said the headmaster.

'For better or worse,' said Morley. 'Now, tell me, boys, who on earth has set this fire?' he asked, staring at our little mountain of sticks and branches.

'We did!' cried several of the boys.

'He did!' said several others, pointing at me. I had, admittedly, taken charge of the fire-setting.

'Sefton?'

'Yes, Mr Morley?'

'Boys I can forgive, but Sefton, you really have no idea how to set a fire?'

I rather thought I did know how to set a fire, but clearly I was mistaken.

'What on earth is being taught to our young people, Headmaster?' Morley proceeded to kneel down and started picking off sticks and twigs, one by one. 'You know, sometimes I wonder if we might benefit from a curriculum that applied across the whole of England, that we might all enjoy the same privilege of understanding.'

'An impractical undertaking, I would say, Mr Morley,' said the headmaster.

'Nothing is impossible, Headmaster, unless we decide it is so. My curriculum – a national curriculum, shall we call it? – would include cookery, gardening, practical household skills, the memorisation of texts. And the setting of fires. What do you think, boys?'

'Yay!' cried the boys.

He straightened up. 'No. No good. We'll have to start again, I'm afraid.' He kicked aside what remained of the pile of wood we had gathered. 'Also, we need the fire in the pit, Sefton. How's our pit?' he asked the burly boy, who was busy digging with the spade that had been returned by Ginger.

'Nearly done, sir,' puffed the burly boy.

'Good. Now, perhaps a demonstration? How to set a fire. Step one. First things first. What's the most important thing in setting a fire, boys? Any suggestions?'

'The wood, sir?' said a small blond smirking boy.

'Precisely!' said Morley. 'But what wood? Which wood?'

'Whatever wood one is able to find, sir?' said the boy.

'A beginner's mistake!' said Morley. 'There is wood, young man, and there is wood.'

I sensed the beginning of a lecture. Which indeed came.

First he picked up a small branch. 'Elm, as you know, boys, when lit, is inclined to smoke. A lot.' He tossed the elm branch away.

'Ah,' said the headmaster.

'All wood is possessed of different qualities in this crucial regard. Lime, for example. Anyone know what lime does when set alight? Sefton? Lime, when alight?'

'I'm not entirely sure, Mr Morley.'

'Lime smoulders, gentlemen. Smoulders like a goddess of the silver screen.' He tossed away a lime branch.

There came a slight tittering from some of the boys.

Morley then began kicking through the remaining twigs and branches. 'Elder, oak, robinia – all terribly acrid. Poplar? Very bitter. Larch and Scots pine – they crackle too noisily and throw out sparks at such a great distance that you almost have to wear protective equipment. But the best for heat, boys, hands down?'

'Spruce?' I said, keen to get the questions and answers over with.

'Spruce, Sefton? Spruce? Apple, man! Boys!' he said, pointing at me with both hands. 'Boys! Behold a man who does not know how to set a fire!' The boys looked at me rather pityingly. 'Do you want to end up like this, boys?' There was a general shaking of heads. They did not want to end up like me. 'Apple,' continued Morley, picking up a small branch admiringly. 'Wonderful wood for burning. Wonderful. Little flame, great heat and burns down to a beautiful white ash. Hazel also good.' He picked up another branch. 'Holly –

rapid burning but good. Cherry, slow to kindle, but excellent once alight. But . . . Aha!' He bent down and took a branch from the ground like a prospector discovering diamonds while panning for gold. 'Ash, gentlemen, ash for a fire – ash is the king of woods! Burns green as well as dry. You are of course familiar with the saying "Ash that's green is fire for a queen."' The boys nodded, as if they had heard the saying – which they certainly had not. 'Beautifully clear-flamed. And beech is good. Juniper wonderful for scent. Lilac almost a rival to sandalwood. Walnut also. Larch. The good old Weymouth pine . . .' He seemed to have gone into a reverie.

'So, Mr Morley?' I interrupted.

'So?'

'What would you like us to do with the wood?'

'I'd like them to go and collect some wood we can burn, Sefton. As I had originally hoped they would. And pile it in the pit. How's our pit?'

'Deep, sir,' said the hard-labouring burly boy, now up to his knees in a hole.

'Excellent! So, what is the king of woods, boy?'

'Ash!' came the chorus.

'Very good. And the queen?'

'Apple!' called a couple of lone voices.

'Excellent!' said Morley.

'And elm and lime the jack and ace?' I said light-heartedly.

'No, Sefton. No. Did you not listen, man?'

At which moment the boy Captain came hurtling out of the woods towards us, bucket of clay in one hand, large sack in the other.

'Perfect timing, Captain, perfect!' said Morley. 'Half of you then – you half – off to scavenge. The others, stay here with me. We have other work to do.' Half the boys scurried off, the rest of us remained.

'Now,' said Morley. 'What we need to do is this.'

Rolling up his sleeves, he then led the boys through the final stages of the experiment. First, they larded the sack with clay. This took some time: it was a messy job. The boys who arrived back with branches, meanwhile, were instructed in the correct method for laying the fire, which soon was blazing in the fresh-dug pit, and as the flames began to leap in the dark and damp of the dusk there was a gathering sense of anticipation among the boys, as though they were participating in some profound ancient ritual.

Finally, as we stood gathered in the heat and light, Morley produced his pocket knife – 'A knife, some string and a pencil stub,' he liked to say, 'should be enough to see a man through the darkest day' * – and he instructed the boys in the delicate art of removing a cow's horns from its head, though this proved rather easier said than done, and the severance was only eventually effected – with surprising strength and gusto – by the small ginger boy, brandishing the shovel. The horns went, in the end, with a crack. We then placed the

---

* This is obviously not entirely true: a knife, some string and a pencil stub are not sufficient to see a man through the darkest day. In recent years many readers have contacted me for copies of an article originally written by Morley for his friend Baden-Powell and published in the magazine *The Scout* in April 1931. The article is titled 'Swanton Morley's Tobacco Tin Survival Kit'. I reproduce it here in full, with the kind permission of the Scouting Association.

poor dehorned cow's head inside the larded sack and Morley held up the grisly thing in the gathering gloom, like Perseus having bagged his Medusa.

'Shall I be mother?'

The fire now having burned down, he popped the sack into the pit full of burning ashes, the top of the sack almost level with the ground. The boys then piled more ashes from the fire on top and proceeded to build another fire above it.

'I do hope you'll be able to join us for breakfast?' Morley said to the headmaster. 'It'll need a little finishing off in a skillet, but I can guarantee you'll never have eaten brain and tongue quite like it.'

SWANTON MORLEY'S TOBACCO TIN SURVIVAL KIT

I remember first trekking with Baden-Powell some time after his return from Africa in 1904. We enjoyed a number of walking and climbing holidays together in Scotland and in Cumberland and Westmorland. I learned much on these trips from B-P's skills as an explorer, backwoodsman and frontiersman. On our trips we would often discuss the bare essentials necessary to survive in the wild. B-P would of course be able to survive only with a knife but it was clear to me that for the rest of us a small number of other tools and equipment would be necessary. Hence my devising the tobacco tin survival kit, which I present now as a useful tool kit for the worldwide Scouting movement. My own survival kit is contained in a handsome blue Edgeworth High Grade Plug Slice tin, given to me by my gardener, Mr George Haynes some time around 1906. On one of our walks together B-P admired my ingenious device and I later presented him with his own survival kit, contained in a Super Black Cat Craven A tin. **It is important to note that the use of a tobacco tin does not and should not encourage the use of tobacco.**

This proved too much for a couple of the exhausted, dirty boys – who had doubtless earlier been scoffing pies and sneaking sherry – who promptly vomited, copiously, into the bushes.

'Excellent!' said Morley. 'Now, where were we? Weren't we playing croquet?'

Knife: This is unlikely to be contained in the tin but is obviously the most important item to carry. Buy the best you can and keep it sharp and clean.

Matches: As many of the strike anywhere variety as possible. Consider a minimum of 20.

Flint and Striker: This is essential for when you run out of matches. Note: using a flint and striker requires practice.

Candle: When you light a match, light a candle, which will save you lighting other matches.

Wire Saw: Used to cut wood, bone and metal.

Brass Wire: For snaring and improvising pot hangers.

String: Kite string is strong and lightweight.

Needle and Thread: For threading gut.

Fishing Kit: Some fishing line, swivels, split shot and hooks.

First Aid Supplies: As much as possible.

Mirror: For signalling, rather than personal hygiene.

Whistle: I never leave home without one.

Wrap the outside of the tin with tape and elastic bands which can be used for spring traps.

CHAPTER 14

RURITANIA

IT WAS FAR TOO LATE FOR CROQUET. The boys were ushered to bed and as dark night descended and the smoke steamed steadily from the fire, Morley and I plunged back towards the school and yet further into the strange: it was time for the Founder's Day fancy dress party.

The party had already begun, weirdly, and in earnest, in the school's ornamental garden, which featured a Japanese rock pool and stone toadstools, the sort of sham garden features that were then enormously popular, and which Morley himself railed against in his book *In the Garden with Swanton Morley* (1929): 'In the garden, as in life, the natural is always to be preferred over the ornamental. The first garden, the Garden of Eden, was a place of plenty: it was not a place of excess. The gardener's motto should be *multum non multa*. Much not many.' What we had endured that day, frankly, was already too much and too many. But there was still more to come.

Lanterns and streamers had been hung from the trees, which gave the party an air of the exotic, though the exotic gone slightly sour or off: the garden's roses and gardenia were long past their best, and vast moths hung lazily around the lanterns, their wings the colour of old cracked celadon. It made for a rather shady, brazen, haunting scene – as though the party were itself throwing a party for its own sad passing.

'We seem to have washed up on the shores of the Acheron,' said Morley as we arrived. 'Certainly a scene for the book, eh?'

'Yes,' I agreed.

'"Devon's Nightlife"? A little chapter? Though it's perhaps not entirely representative.'

'No.'

'The fleshpots of Torquay we might need, for that. Worth an excursion. Anyway, do make an effort and mingle, Sefton, while we're here. I have to speak to the headmaster and the police.'

As Morley disappeared my German friend Bernhard approached. He had – to my astonishment – blacked up and was wearing sandals, a turban and an Arab-style robe that he explained to me was called a jibbah.

'I have come as a sultan,' he explained.

'Really.'

'But Mr Sefton, you seem to have come in your civilian clothing! Come, come!'

'It's been a long day,' I said.

'And tonight will be a longer night! You really must be dressed for the party. It is a fancy dress party.'

'I'm fine thank you.'

Bernhard called over to a female teacher, who was wearing a beard and a long dark flowing robe.

[183]

Devon's Nightlife

'Katherine!' he called. 'Katherine!'

Katherine approached.

'Tolstoy?' I said.

'Rasputin,' she replied through her beard.

'Katherine,' said my German friend. 'Do you have something suitable for Mr Sefton here to wear?' And then turning to me he said, 'Katherine teaches the boys English and drama. She is our chief costumier!'

'I'm sure I can find something,' said the bearded Katherine, fingering my clothes. 'Get you out of these old rags, eh?' And then she winked. No one wants Rasputin to wink at them.

'Good luck!' cried Bernhard. And Katherine/Rasputin led me inside the school to change.

～ ～

Fortunately, she left me to make what I could from the clothes trunks and I soon emerged back into the party in full costume. I was feeling rather self-conscious, but then again some of the male teachers were in dresses and full make-up, and there was everywhere a profusion of sarongs, cowboy chaps, Highland wear (including full kilts), feather boas and gangsterish suits. One chap wore nothing but a large green felt fig-leaf attached to a pair of long johns, which was not a pretty sight. There was a Sioux chieftain, a Mad Hatter, a toreador, a pirate, several army and navy officers, and much sporting of eccentric headgear, including sombreros, stovepipes and helmets. Alex's wife, Mrs Standish, was dressed as a ghost. In comparison, I was soberly attired.

A makeshift bar had been erected in the marquee, with

bottles of beer, wine, gin and various cordials, plus a steaming hot punch, and hot chocolate 'for the ladies', explained one of the porters, who was transformed for the night into a barman. The ladies were in fact mostly drinking the punch, and helping themselves also to the light supper that appeared to be the afternoon's high tea, rather thinly disguised.

The police who had been there all day were now relaxing, chatting to staff. There was a sense of us all being at the very edge – or at the end – of something.

'Sefton!' cried Bernhard, spotting me. 'Wonderful! Now the party can begin!' He pressed a glass of something upon me. 'Bloody Mary?'

It would have been impolite to refuse – and so there I was, standing by the makeshift bar drinking a Bloody Mary when Miriam spotted me.

'What on earth are you drinking, Sefton? Bull's blood?'

'It's a Bloody Mary, Miriam.'

'I know it's a Bloody Mary, silly. I mean, why?'

'Nice and weighty,' I said. 'Meal in itself.'

'You should try Alexander's cocktail.'

'Really?'

'Oh yes, it's amazing!'

'I'm sure. What's in it?'

'I don't know. He calls it the Kubla Khan.'

'Of course he does.'

'I think I'll have a glass of the punch, though, thank you for not asking,' said Miriam. 'More than two Kubla Khans and one's an absolute goner . . .'

It was difficult to determine how far she had already gone. I caught the eye of the barmaid and procured Miriam her punch.

'Well, here's mud in your eye,' she said; like Morley she tended to adopt a cod-American vocabulary for social occasions.

'Having fun?' she asked.

'Not particularly, no.'

'Oh, I love it here!' she said. 'You are a spoilsport, Sefton, you know. But I do like your uniform.' My costume was an absurd, tight-fitting military uniform that had presumably been used in a school production of a Gilbert and Sullivan. 'I rather like you in a uniform.'

I ignored the remark.

'Are you a marquis?'

'I think I'm an officer of the law in some Ruritanian country.'

'Ruritania, possibly,' said Miriam.

'Quite.'

'I hope you're not going to arrest me and drag me off to some horrible prison or dungeon?' Miriam had come as Emmeline Pankhurst. She wore a sash emblazoned with the words 'VOTES FOR WOMEN'. I had no intention of arresting her and dragging her off – though I wish I could have done so for many of the partygoers.

The only two people who seemed not to have taken leave of their senses entirely were Morley and the headmaster who sat at a table outside the marquee, deep in conclave. They had been joined by Mr Gooding, the gap-toothed tenant farmer, dressed in a long black coat, presumably in mourning for his chickens, his goat, his donkey, and now – I assumed – his cow.

Music was playing on a gramophone, the lanterns were

swinging in the evening breeze, and then Alex arrived, accompanied by his dog, a small black Pomeranian.

'Hello, sailor,' he said.

I offered no greeting in return and the dog growled at me in an unfriendly fashion.

'My familiar,' explained Alex, who had swept back his hair, in his Valentino fashion.

'And you have come as?' I asked.

'Oh, I merely preside, Mr Sefton,' said Alex. 'I don't dress up for fancy dress.'

'He's gorgeous!' said Miriam enthusiastically, kneeling down to pet the dog. 'What's he called?' she asked.

'Nietzsche,' said Alex.

I stifled my guffaw.

'Oh, how adorable!' said Miriam.

'And do you also have a cat called Kant?' I asked.

Alex simply smiled his seraphic smile.

Miriam was stroking the dog when suddenly he started growling, irritated. And then – just as suddenly – he clamped his jaws around her finger.

'He's—' she yelled. 'Alex!' Her cry quickly turned into a scream, which turned into a bellow as the dog held tight, and instinctively – without thinking – I kicked at the damned thing until it released its bite and began snarling at me. Everything happened quickly: as I kicked the dog, Alex struck me violently out of the way and grabbed both the dog and Miriam by the wrist.

'He bit me!' yelled Miriam. 'He bit me!'

'Are you OK?' I asked.

'Sefton!' cried Miriam. 'You brute!'

'Me?'

'You brute!' she yelled again and pushed me back as I moved towards her. Silence had descended upon the party: all eyes were turned upon us.

'That's most unlike him, I must say,' said Alex.

The school nurse, the eager Miss Horniman, dressed as a jolly jack tar, hurried over. 'Come, come, my dear,' she said to Miriam. 'We'll go and dress your finger. And are you unharmed, Alex?'

'Yes, thank you,' said Alex.

Miriam allowed herself to be led away, scowling at me the whole time.

'We tend not to treat our animals roughly here,' said Alex, as I got up from the ground, before turning and following Miriam and the nurse.

I stared around me: Morley and the headmaster looked on passively while the other partygoers returned to their conversations and their drinks. I had been humiliated once again.

∽ ∾

The night wore on. Miriam and Alex and Miss Horniman returned, laughing among themselves. Alex's wife, dressed as a ghost, led people in various games, many of which involved the intimate passing of coins, balloons and other objects from person to person. I stood the whole time, drinking rather than participating, watching as the teachers fanned paper kippers, floated feathers and hunted for a thimble. The games gradually, inevitably, became more boisterous: there was much slipper-slapping, and various games involving forfeits, blindfolded crawling and stalking,

[189]

and chaotic piggy-back races. A game of Are You There, Jenkins?, which was new to me – two players lie face down on the floor, blindfolded, grasp at one another's wrists with one hand, while attempting to beat each other with a rolled-up newspaper in the other hand – resulted in the French mistress and the music teacher writhing on the floor in an energetic embrace. This was then followed by a rather physical game of blind man's buff, involving much rampaging and blundering around, with members of staff blindly grabbing at one another to guess who they were.

Miriam was busy showing off her bandaged finger to anyone who wished to see it, while Alex strode around authoritatively talking to everyone – except me – and taking photographs. I observed him observing others and it struck me that the camera for him worked in the opposite way that it worked for me. I came to adore the camera because it allowed me to disappear. Alex seemed to wield the camera as an instrument of power, an assertion of himself.

I was about to retire to bed – it was by now approaching midnight – when Alex's wife announced that for the last game of the evening we were all to play sardines. There was a general scattering of people. Alex disappeared. Miriam disappeared. Miss Horniman. My German friend. Everyone, until I found that I was left entirely alone by the bar. Morley and the headmaster remained deep in conversation.

I thought I might take the opportunity to go and explore the darkroom. Into the school, through the corridors, and down the stairs to the science rooms.

'Well?' said a voice.

I turned around, half expecting Alex's wife in her ghost costume.

It was not Alex's wife. It was Mrs Dodds, the benefactor's wife. She was dressed, as far as I could tell, as a courtesan in the court of a French king. Her hairstyle was as vertiginous as her décolletage was plunging. Her heels were staggering. She looked like Clara Bow, or perhaps Louise Brooks. I found it rather hard to concentrate on what she had to say.

'Your costume is . . . very fetching,' I said.

'I'm Madame de Pompadour.'

'Of course.'

We stood close together in the dark.

There were noises from within the darkroom. I looked at Mrs Dodds. She raised an eyebrow.

'That's the darkroom,' I whispered.

'I know.'

'I don't suppose you happen to have a key?'

'No, I'm afraid not.'

'I'd like to get in there.'

'Now? Why?'

I heard more noises. I was about to bang on the door when I realised what the voice was saying.

I looked at her. 'Alex?' I said.

She shrugged. 'I think we need to talk,' she said.

'I think we do,' I agreed.

There was the sound of footsteps creeping down the stairs. There were others about to join us. Mrs Dodds leaned in closer and whispered in my ear.

'My husband will be away tomorrow night. I'll meet you in Sidmouth. At the Mocha Café. At seven.'

And then she stepped out into the light of the corridor.

'Aha!' came a voice. 'We've got you!' It was Bernhard.

We all returned upstairs and out to the party. I hurriedly fetched myself another drink.

∽ ∾

Morley was absorbed in conversation with Mrs Standish, Alex's wife, still in her ghost costume. I wondered if she had any idea what the darkroom was being used for.

'Ah, Sefton. I was just discussing with Mrs Standish here my recipe for making pot pourri. I use the moist method, but Mrs Standish swears by the dry.'

'I see.'

'Mrs Standish is quite a talented young chemist.'

'I wouldn't make any particular claim to expertise,' said Mrs Standish.

'Nonsense!' said Morley. 'Chemistry is a fine profession for a young woman. I foresee a time in the future when women will dominate in all fields of the sciences. They have all the necessary qualities: diligence, persistence, intelligence. Do you have a preference, Sefton?'

'A preference for what, Mr Morley?'

'Wet or dry method?'

'For?'

'Pot pourri, man.'

'I can't say I do, Mr Morley, no.'

'I know Mrs Standish disagrees, but I have to say I think the moist method produces a much more fragrant result.'

'Really?'

'Yes, have you not smelled the odour throughout the school?'

'Ah, yes.' I thought I had smelled something odd.

'Though in the end – wet or dry – it all comes down to the amount of rose petals of course. We both use Atkinson's Violet Powder, as it happens.'

'Well well,' I said.

'Terribly good. Sweet geraniums, bay leaves, lavender, add some salt, pop it all in a stoneware jar and bob's your uncle.'

'Fascinating,' I said.

'Yes. And it turns out we both have our frogs delivered from the same place on St Martin's Lane.'

'Really.'

'Yes. They're terribly good.'

'The frogs?'

'Yes. They send them in a box with damp moss and a few slugs – seems to do the trick.'

'Mr Sefton assisted me with the frogs this morning,' said Alex's wife.

'Ah, very good. Nice and fresh, I hope?'

'Excellent,' said Alex's wife.

'They delivered me some bees once: that was less successful,' said Morley. 'I like the little French frogs the best, you know the green tree frogs?'

'Oh yes, they are excellent.'

'They make excellent barometers. Much more interesting than an actual barometer. Brilliant green in moisture. Very dull when dry.'

The headmaster approached, having been in conversation elsewhere.

'It's been a pleasure talking to you, Mr Morley,' said Mrs Standish. 'But I'm afraid I should excuse myself.' And she ghoulishly disappeared.

'Ah,' said the headmaster. 'Mr Sefton. Still with us at the shenanigans then?'

'Yes, though I think the party is drawing to a close,' I said.

'Good,' said Morley. 'Before the women break into the cordax, eh?' I had no idea what the cordax might be – unless it were something like a foxtrot.

The headmaster was chuckling. 'Now that I would like to see!'

'Might we include Sefton?' Morley asked the headmaster.

'I think we might,' said the headmaster. 'Reliable sort of chap, isn't he?'

'Absolutely,' said Morley. 'None more so.'

'Include me in what, gentlemen?' I asked, taking a long sip of what I fancied was going to be the first of several stiff drinks.

'The headmaster is understandably rather worried about all this unfortunate business with the animals.'

'Not to mention the business of Michael Taylor?' I said.

'Quite,' said Morley. 'Seems to be getting rather out of hand.'

'That's an understatement.'

'Anyway, Sefton, the police have interviewed all the boys involved in the incident with the cow earlier this evening, but they're all claiming they have nothing to do with it.'

'Perhaps they don't,' I said.

'Perhaps,' said Morley. 'Though working on the balance of probabilities I think we would have to conclude—'

'Alas,' said the headmaster.

'Indeed, that they do. So the question is, Sefton, how might we catch our miscreants?'

'How?'

'We are going to set a trap,' said the headmaster.

'A trap?' I said. 'What sort of a trap?'

'We're going to go to the fields and wait for them,' said Morley.

'I'm not sure that's—'

'Of course we're not going to go out into the fields to wait for them, Sefton! It would make absolutely no sense.'

'No sense,' agreed the headmaster.

I glanced around at the party: the teachers in their peculiar costumes; the lanterns hanging from the trees; the vast grey school looming up behind us; the faint drift of woodsmoke from our smouldering pit of fire down below the tennis courts; what Morley would have called the minacious ocean beyond; and the memory of the poor dead boy down on the beach. None of it made any sense.

'The best mousetrap, as you know, Sefton, is a simple mousetrap,' continued Morley.

'Indeed it is,' said the headmaster.

'I was talking to Mr Gooding earlier this evening—'

'Very upset,' said the headmaster.

'Indeed, and it was he who gave me the idea. To catch a mouse one might best use a simple Figure of Four trap.'

'A Figure of Four trap?'

'Yes. Which consists of course of a pair of slates and three thin slivers of wood.'

'Of course.'

'Mr Mouse goes in search of the morsel set under the slates, and crunch.' Morley made the most of the 'crunch'. 'Deadly on mice, does no harm to birds.'

'You're going to make a mousetrap?'

'Of course not,' said Morley. 'But you are familiar with the Book of Daniel?'

'Some of it,' I said, rather doubtfully. 'I might just get myself another drink.'

'You shall not,' said Morley.

'There has been a terrible decline in scriptural knowledge,' said the headmaster.

'Quite so,' said Morley. 'But even you, Sefton, will be familiar with the story of how the King of Persia was tricked by the priests of Baal, who persuaded him to leave out food every night for their god Baal to eat.'

'I have a vague memory of such, yes,' I said; exactly how vague was my memory I did not say. It was vague to the point of being indistinct.

'Then you will recall how Daniel exposed the lies and tricks of the priests of Baal?'

'Er.'

'He spread ashes on the floor one night and was able to show the king that it was in fact the priests themselves who were coming to eat the food.'

'We have ashes,' said the headmaster.

'From our fire,' said Morley.

'Jolly good,' I said.

'And so we thought we might make use of them.'

'I really think I might need another drink actually,' I said.

'Nonsense,' said Morley. 'No shirking, no shilly-shallying.'

'No funking,' said the headmaster.

'Precisely,' said Morley. 'A long complex tale has been written in the snow before us, Sefton, and it is our job to find out where it leads.'

'Fine,' I said. 'When?'

Morley consulted his watches – the luminous wristwatch, the non-luminous wristwatch, the pocket-watch – and, I had no doubt, would have upended his egg-timer also if it had been to hand.

'Now?' he said.

CHAPTER 15

LEX TALIONIS

AND SO AT ONE O'CLOCK in the morning I found myself with Morley and the headmaster in the long corridor outside the boys' dormitories. All was quiet as we shook warm grey ashes onto the cold red lino floor. The idea was that we might be able to identify whichever boy then crept out of bed to go and attack Mr Gooding's animals – an utterly ludicrous plan, in my opinion, though Morley and the headmaster were convinced that their trap would work, and that the mystery would be solved, that we would discover who was harming the animals, and so order would be restored to All Souls. To me the entire enterprise seemed a distraction from the rather more serious matter of poor dead Michael Taylor. I did not believe for one moment that any boy would be foolish enough to emerge from the dormitory that night. I said as much to Morley, quietly, when the headmaster absented himself for a moment, in order to fetch some blankets and a sustaining flask of tea.

'There is something very wrong in this school, Mr Morley.'

'Very wrong?' said Morley.

'Yes.'

'Can something be "very" wrong, Sefton? Surely if something is—'

'I just mean that something is wrong,' I said. 'Wrong wrong. As in not right.'

'Well, I quite agree, Sefton. And if we find out whichever boy it is who's causing harm to the animals then I think we'll have solved the problem, don't you? *Cessante causa, cessat effectus* and what have you.'

'I'm not sure that is the answer to all the problems here, Mr Morley.'

'Oh. Well, what do you think is the answer?'

'I don't know, sir. But I do know schools, and I know that this place is not the same as other schools that I've—'

'One would hope not,' said Morley. 'The headmaster is trying to do something different here, Sefton. In these beautiful new surroundings. I've been sharing with him some of my ideas about education, actually, and I think he might be interested in adopting some of the principles for the school – providing the boys with a truly all-round education that will see them fit not only for the professions but for life. It would transform the place, don't you think?'

'I'm sure it would, Mr Morley, but I'm not convinced it would solve the fundamental problems here.'

'Which are?'

'I'm not certain, but ... Don't you think the set-up here is a bit ... odd?'

'The "set-up", Sefton?'

'Well, the headmaster and his brother and their mother and ... They all seem very ...'

'What?'

'I don't know. It's just that . . . I don't know.'

'Well, perhaps when you do know, Sefton, and you've worked it all out, perhaps you could let me know? In the meantime, in the absence of any ideas or plans of your own, could you perhaps help me and the headmaster lay our modest trap?' The headmaster had by this time returned with the supplies – the blankets, a flask of tea. Morley grabbed a handful of ashes. 'Come on, man, for goodness sake. Dare to be a Daniel, eh? Come on, shake!'

So we all shook the ashes and then we drew up chairs to wait. There were two stairways up to the dormitories, and two dormitories, one for the older boys, one for the younger. I was stationed at one end of the corridor. Morley and the headmaster were stationed at the other. A few candles in sconces lit the corridor and the pale ashes lay between us.

We agreed to take two-hour watches. Morley and the headmaster took the first watch at their end of the corridor. I dozed uneasily on the chair, wrapped in the blanket for warmth.

Half asleep and half awake, I found myself plunged once again into memories of the horrors of Spain at night. Not the gunfire, not the ambushes, but worse: memories of the fellow volunteers who would stub out a cigarette on your neck while you were sleeping; and of the men who would steal from you, your cigarettes, your boots, your food; or who would piss on you to wake you. One night I recall I had asked a Frenchman, Gérard – a huge man, famous among all the Brigaders and known as La Bestia, who liked to boast of the battles he had survived, and the men he had killed, and the women he had slept with – who was drinking and playing cards with friends, to quieten down so that I could sleep. They ignored me and somehow through the noise I managed to fall asleep, only to awake to find La Bestia with his hands around my throat, trying to choke me. Fortunately he was so incapable with drink that I easily managed to throw him off, and afterwards we became firm friends, but it was disconcerting, the realisation that one was as much at risk from one's own side as from the other.

And then I wakened with a start when Morley shook me at 3 a.m. It was my turn to go on watch.

I managed to keep my eyes open for I know not how long and when I came to again it was to the sound of footsteps. I opened my eyes. The corridor was empty. The few candles in their sconces were guttering out. A weak moonlight shone through from the single window at the end of the corridor, barely illuminating the dark footprints in the ash. The footprints weren't coming from the dormitory. They were heading towards the dormitory: the younger boys' dormitory.

I silently unwrapped myself from my blanket and quietly tiptoed my way down the tallow-tinted corridor to the dormitory door, stationing myself just outside so that I could grab whoever it was as they exited. All I could hear was the sound of breathing – the boys, asleep – and my own heart beating. From outside there came the sound of an owl hooting.

And then there came the sound of shuffling towards the door.

I braced myself and as the dark figure emerged from the doorway I swung a ferocious punch towards their head, which knocked them sideways and banged them loudly against the door jamb. As they slumped down towards the floor – and before I had properly prepared myself for an assault – another figure came rushing out after them. As they blundered into me I grabbed at them. They gave a yelp and I held tight and dragged them into the dim light of the corridor.

'What on earth?' said the headmaster, who had come rushing down the corridor at the sound of the commotion. 'What on earth is the meaning of this?'

'Headmaster,' said the man I had apprehended.

'Jones?' said the headmaster. It was one of the teachers – Jon Jones the Welshman.

The figure on the floor was groaning.

'What are you doing here?' asked Morley, who had also joined us.

'I might ask you the same,' said Jones, in his challenging Welsh fashion.

'We are here, Jones, to try to get to the bottom of these problems with the animals,' said the headmaster.

'Same as us then,' said Jon Jones.

'Really?' I said.

'Really,' said Jones, staring at me.

'Come on, get this man up,' said Morley, reaching down towards the man on the floor.

'Mr Dodds!' said the headmaster. 'I am so sorry.'

Mr Dodds, the benefactor, gradually rose to his feet, with Morley's assistance. In one hand he was clutching a teddy bear.

'Ah, a Steiff,' said Morley, admiring the bear. 'Very nice. Very nice indeed. Never mind your Siemens: German engineering at its best, a Steiff.' Mr Dodds offered Morley the bear to examine. 'Thank you. But why might you be stealing teddy bears from the boys' dormitories?'

'We thought,' said Jones, 'that if we took a few teddies it might teach the little—'

'Children,' said Morley.

'A thing or two,' continued Jones.

'Really?' said the headmaster. 'And teach them what exactly?'

'An eye for an eye, presumably,' said Morley.

'Exactly,' said Jones.

'The old *lex talionis*.'

'It's just a bit of fun,' said Mr Dodds. 'Jones and I were going to set up a few of these little creatures as target practice.'

'What?' said the headmaster.

'Just a bit of fun, Headmaster,' said Mr Dodds, who had clearly been drinking heavily.

'Just a bit of fun?' said the headmaster. 'Creeping into the boys' dormitories in the middle of the night to kidnap their soft toys?'

'Surely you can see the funny side, can't you?' said Jon Jones.

The headmaster looked stern. Mr Dodds barked with laughter.

At the sound of the laughter a group of boys – all of them in their regulation blue and white striped winceyette pyjamas – timidly made their way out into the corridor and gathered around us. They looked terrified.

'Nothing to see here, boys,' said the headmaster. 'Back to bed, please. Immediately.'

'Headmaster,' said one small boy. 'I need to pee, sir.'

'Use the chamberpot, boy.'

'Chamberpot's full, sir.'

Mr Jon Jones, in challenging Welsh fashion

'You'll have to wait until the morning, I'm afraid.'

'Headmaster,' said another boy. 'There's something on the floor, sir. A sort of white powder, sir.'

'Never mind,' said the headmaster.

'What is it, sir?'

'Ashes: someone has spilled some ashes.'

'Headmaster,' said another boy. 'Michael Taylor's not here, sir.'

'No. I know. Michael has ... gone away.'

'Where is Michael Taylor?' asked Jon Jones. 'I didn't know he was away.'

'Is he ill, sir?'

The headmaster ignored the question.

'It's time for bed, gentlemen,' said the headmaster. 'I will deal with you in the morning, Jones. In the meantime, perhaps you'd be so kind as to escort Mr Dodds to one of the guest rooms. Everything's fine,' he reassured the boys. 'Everything in hand and under control.'

CHAPTER 16

THE CIDERIST

AFTER ONLY A COUPLE of hours' sleep Morley and I break-
fasted with the boys on the head of the cow.

A weak sun filtered through the clouds and a heavy dew
lay upon the grass as we squatted around the dirty, smoking remains of yesterday's fire. Morley instructed the boys
in digging the head from out of the ground. The ashes were
like warm sand. The gunny sack was charred, and inside the
clay had baked hard to the skin of the head, peeling it off
to reveal a dark, sinewy meat beneath. The eyes, brain and
tongue had been cooked to a solid jelly. Morley cut away
long stringy pieces of the meat and then warmed them in a
skillet heated in the ashes, distributing them among the boys
until the skull was entirely stripped and every morsel had
either been eaten or discarded.

'Delicious, eh?' said Morley, his mouth full, offering me a
small hot sliver of brains.

I declined. The boys were silent and in awe, as though
partaking in a ritual meal. I could not entirely share their
enthusiasm. The whole thing smelled of Spain.

The day slowly became warm and the school routine began again, as it must. The headmaster had Jones to deal with, and the police, presumably, would be continuing with their investigations. Our experiment with the ashes had not been a thoroughgoing success, but Morley, as always, was undaunted. As promised, he had organised for a few of the older boys to go surfing. He'd hired a charabanc – courtesy of the Sidmouth Motor Company and Dagworth's Ltd., who usually ran trips around Salcombe, apparently – and so we found ourselves sitting, four to a row, in the wide, open-topped vehicle, Morley up front with the driver, who wore a proud white cap, a dark suit and a bold red company tie. It was like a works outing.

Miriam followed us in the Lagonda, accompanied by Alex: I had by now abandoned her entirely to him. She seemed happy enough. She wore her hair swept back from her face, and a man's white shirt knotted at the midriff, a pair of billowing navy trousers – free and natural, uninhibited, quite unlike her usual ensemble. Alex wore a light, almost semi-tropical suit and ancient suede shoes. In the car together they looked Mediterranean, or like a sleek, rich, satisfied missionary couple, setting forth to preach the good news, that the blind might receive sight, the lame walk, the lepers be cleansed and the deaf might hear.

In the charabanc, under Morley's instruction, we played games of animal, vegetable or mineral, sang hymns, and then Bernhard, who was keen to accompany us – surfing not yet having arrived on German shores – led us in a song from *Through the Looking Glass*, a book described correctly as 'a mathematics master's idea of a novel', in Morley's memorable survey of children's literature, *Morley's Children's Classics*

(1932). Bernhard was clearly not familiar with Morley's judgement – alas. The song went: 'Sprinkle the table with buttons and bran, put cats in the coffee, and mice in the tea. Then fill up the glasses with treacle and ink ... Mix sand with the cider, and wool with the wine.' The boys preferred this to the hymns and joined in with gusto. All in all, and combined with Morley's customary and incessant chatter about birds and buildings and fascinating topographical features, the quirky wholesome heartiness had me hankering for a good night out in Soho.

As we drove past Axminster – 'the carpet capital of the kingdom', according to *The County Guides* – we came upon a hand-painted sign, made to look like a giant pointing finger, and underneath the sign, in an uncertain, splotchy, paintbrushed cursive hand, were two fateful words: FARM CIDER.

'Stop!' cried Morley, spying the sign. 'Stop!' he cried again. And the driver of the charabanc pulled up sharply, sending boys tumbling forward. 'Well!' said Morley. 'Here we are then!'

'Oh dear,' said Bernhard, resettling himself in his seat. I rather suspect that he had been gearing up for a recital of 'Jabberwocky'.

'Farm cider!' exulted Morley.

'Is this really a suitable stopping place for the boys?' asked Alex, who had pulled up with Miriam in the Lagonda, and who had come to see what was the problem.

'Suitable?' said Morley. 'Suitable? Farm cider? The oil – the essence, the elixir! – of the West Country!? Suitable! It is more than suitable, sir: it is essential! Come along, boys!' And with that he had us all clambering out of the charabanc and about to proceed up a narrow grassy lane, following the direction of the giant pointing finger. 'Wait here, driver,' he instructed.

'We'll stay here also, I think, Father,' said Miriam.

'As you wish,' said Morley.

I glanced back to see her lounging by the Lagonda, laughing with Alex at who knows what.

∽ ∾

'Now, where one finds cider one will also necessarily find what, my friends?' asked Morley, hurrying on ahead.

'Drunkards?' said Bernhard, trotting beside Morley like a large obedient German dog, boys running along in their wake.

'Wrong, Mr Bernhard,' said Morley. 'Wrong. Where one finds cider one will also necessarily find: apples!'

'Ah,' said Bernhard.

'And a knowledge of the English apple, and its uses, and abuses, is surely an essential part of any Englishman's education, is it not?'

This had clearly not occurred to Bernhard before, and in fairness had probably never occurred to Morley either; his thinking was entirely improvisational: a finger pointing here, a finger pointing there, always a new train of thought, always something new to discover. 'Culture,' he began riffing – I knew by now all the signs – '*cultivar*, same Latin root stock, I think you'll find. And English literature, boys, is of course ripe with—'

'Absolute nonsense?' I offered quietly.

'Apples,' continued Morley, oblivious as always to any

[209]

sense of the absurd about any of his vast and sudden enthusiasms. 'And forbidden fruit, obviously, though apples are not specified in the biblical account, as we know, eh, boys?' The boys nodded. Clearly, they couldn't care less about apples – but the thought of cider! 'If we think about it for a moment, gents: folk tales, fairy tales, Snow White, the myth of Atalanta. We might in fact interpret the world's entire storehouse of knowledge as like a rich orchard – might we not? – ready for us to pluck the little round orbs of goodness from its generous branches. Make a note, Sefton, please. I feel a chapter coming on: "Devon and . . ."?'

'"The Devil's Brew"?' I suggested.

'Hardly, Sefton. "Devon and . . ."?'

'"The Forbidden Fruit"?'

'We'll come up with a title later. Notes and photographs though, please.'

'Yes, Mr Morley.' I produced my pencil and notebook. I had, thank goodness, left the camera in the charabanc.

Morley strode on, the heels of his brogues before us.

'Thomas Hardy, boys?' he asked. 'Have you read Hardy?'

Several boys admitted, rather mournfully I thought, that indeed they had read Hardy.

'Well, there we are, then. Absolutely ripe with apples, Thomas Hardy. Might make a separate article actually, Sefton: "Hardy's . . . Forbidden Fruit"? Now that might work. Make a note.'

I made another note, while the boys barrelled down the lane, making quite a hullabaloo – the thought of the cider! – until we came close to a small thatched farmhouse, where Morley called them all in to show them the low orchards, rather like olive groves, that flanked the lane on either side. He began explaining to them methods of pruning and cultivation.

'Careful pruning, as you see, boys, is essential. And why?'

No one answered: the boys had suddenly grown quiet and their attention seemed to be elsewhere.

'The removal of rot, boys,' continued Morley, 'and scab, and canker. Codling moths. Spot, pox, worms. You name it, gentlemen. I'm afraid, as our friend Hamlet might say, that the apple flesh is heir to a thousand natural shocks.'

'I'm not sure about this, Mr Morley,' protested Bernhard.

'Come, come. I hardly think that introducing the boys to the product of nature will corrupt them, Mr Bernhard. I am myself, as you know, a devout teetotaller, but I see no reason why the boys should not be familiar with nature's storehouse—'

'That's not what I mean,' said Bernhard.

'Well, what do you mean, man?' said Morley.

What Bernhard meant was a farmer who had appeared while Morley was talking, and who had successfully gained all our attention: he was pointing his shotgun at us.

The silence deepened. Morley, sensing that he had lost his audience, eventually swivelled round.

Two barrels faced him.

'Ah!' he said, entirely unruffled. 'Mr?'

The ruddy-cheeked farmer clenched his jaw tight, and his shotgun tighter.

'The ciderist, I presume?'

The farmer looked rather bewildered at being described as a ciderist.

'Mr . . .?' pressed Morley.

'Reeder,' said the farmer angrily.

'Mr Reeder the ciderist, it is an honour to meet you, sir!' Morley went to shake the farmer's hand, ignoring the gun.

'Well . . .' said poor Mr Reeder the ciderist, overcome, like so many before him and so many since, by Morley's bluff good humour and utter lack of normal, sensible behaviour. He'd have made an excellent politician. In the face of such careless, thoughtless, lunatic bonhomie Mr Reeder the ciderist had no choice but to lower the gun and shake hands: in an instant Morley had won him over. The boys looked on in amazement.

'Who are you?' asked Mr Reeder, momentarily regaining some of his powers of resistance. 'All of you? Who are you?'

'Us? Ah. Yes, sorry, we clearly startled you, sir. But we were unable to warn you in advance. Spur of the moment sort of a thing, isn't it, boys?' More wide-eyed nodding from the boys. 'This is a school trip, Mr Reeder! We are introducing the boys of All Souls to the joys of the natural world. We have come, sir, to pay homage to the fruits – literally! – of your labour. Indeed, to paraphrase the poet, to admire your fruits, filled with ripeness to the core – boys?'

'Keats!' cried one learned little chap.

'Correct!' cried Morley. 'And to commune with you, if we may, in your Vale profound. Anyone?' This was an allusion too obscure – but no matter. 'Wordsworth!' concluded Morley. 'Champion of the real language of real men!'

This little speech seemed to prove more than sufficient explanation for Mr Reeder, who had clearly been alerted by the noise of the boys to expect the arrival of barbarian hordes (and in fairness, barbarian hordes and public schoolboys can often be confused). His ruddy features softened.

'Now you're sure you don't mind?' asked Morley.

'We'd also like to buy some cider,' I added. I thought this might prove a more useful sweetener – as indeed it did.

'Very well,' said Mr Reeder. 'But you need to quiet them boys. I've animals.'

'Of course. Did you hear Mr Reeder, boys?'

'Yes!' cried the boys.

'Ssshh,' said Morley. 'Good, now. Let's show Mr Reeder we know our business, shall we? The great cider-producing counties of England?'

'Devon?' said one.

'Obviously,' said Morley. 'And?' Putting people on the spot was rather a habit with Morley: it was not, I think, a form of incivility, as some have claimed, but rather his simple determination always to be finding out more about the world, and encouraging others to do the same.

'Devonshire . . .' prompted Morley. 'Herefordshire and . . .'

'Kent?' said one boy.

'And where are you from, boy?'

'Kent,' he admitted.

'More impressive if you had been from Essex, of course,' said Morley, clearly disappointed. 'But well done, nonetheless.'

Mr Reeder stood with his arms folded, listening.

'Now, boys, the uses of cider?' asked Morley.

'For getting drunk, sir?' piped up one wag.

'One use, of course, boys. But one use only – and strongly to be discouraged, isn't that right, Mr Reeder?'

Mr Reeder's livelihood of course depended on encouraging people to drink cider. Also, he looked like a man who perhaps enjoyed – and perhaps only very recently – a drop or two of his own produce. He remained silent.

'Isn't it good for rheumatism?' I suggested, rather hoping that this might move the conversation forward.

'I rather doubt it, Sefton. Does one drink it, or rub it in?'

'I'm not sure, Mr Morley.'

'It might be more efficacious if imbibed,' he said. 'Isn't that right, Mr Reeder?'

'Can't say,' said Mr Reeder.

'Vinegar I was thinking, Sefton. Vinegar, boys! Cider being made into vinegar by a process of second fermentation. Is that correct, Mr Reeder?'

'I just make cider,' said Mr Reeder. 'Pure Devon cider.'

'There we are, boys. A man proud of his product. Now, if Mr Reeder might allow us, perhaps we might see the cidering process? May we, sir? Might we?' said Morley.

Having gone so far, and having been thus flattered by Morley, Mr Reeder had no choice but to admit us further and he dutifully took us to an old stone barn out behind his farmhouse, which contained sacks and stacked boxes of apples, and various damp, stained clamps and presses that looked like ancient instruments of torture. In the very centre of the barn, like some sort of diabolical altar, was a large round stone trough, crusted thick with skin and pith, a stone wheel attached to a pivot point at the centre: a cider apple slaughterhouse.

'Ah!' said Morley. 'Your cider mill? Smell that, boys.' We all sniffed, expecting apples. There was instead a strong smell of horse manure.

'Horse is out in the field,' explained Mr Reeder.

'Ah, what a pity,' said Sefton. 'It would have been good to see the mill in action. Though I wonder . . .' I detected a disturbing glint in Morley's eye: a telltale twitch in his moustache. 'With your permission, Mr Reeder?' He picked out a dozen boys, and organised them in getting harnessed to the reins of the giant stone wheel. 'There we are, Mr Reeder!' Some further fussing with the harness followed as the boys fought among themselves. 'Whoa, boys!' said Morley. The boys calmed. 'A human horse for you, sir! Do with it what you will.'

Mr Reeder hesitated for a moment but then decided to join in the pretence and proceeded to urge the boys forward: 'Go on, boy! Walk on now.'

'Now, boys,' asked Morley, as they strained at the reins, 'how many varieties are there of English apple?'

'Ten?' said one poor boy, gritting his teeth as he attempted to move forward.

'No.'

'Twenty?' offered another, grimacing with effort.

'No.'

'One hundred?' puffed another.

'No.'

'Five hundred?' offered the most adventurous of all – and suddenly, gaining momentum, the boys and the big stone wheel began to edge forward.

'Thousands, gentlemen! Thousands and thousands. Isn't that right, Mr Reeder?'

Mr Reeder had gone to fetch some sacks of apples, and Bernhard and I joined him in unceremoniously dumping the contents into the stone trough, as the wheel began to make its inexorable way around.

'And what varieties do you use, Mr Reeder, if we might ask? It's not a trade secret?'

'We use everything but an All-Doer,' said Mr Reeder. 'Go on!' he added, urging the boys forward.

'Everything but an All-Doer?'

'All-Doer don't do.'

'I see. An All-Doer is a variety?'

'That's right. Ashton Bittersweet and an Ashton Brown, they're all right. But beggars can't be whatever it's called.'

'Choosers.'

'That's right.'

The stone wheel was moving forward steadily now, crushing the apples in the trough. I had expected crunching, but it was instead a liquid kind of a sound, as though the primitive mill were itself gorging on the apples.

'So you take whatever you can get?'

'That's right,' said Mr Reeder, who was obviously delighted with the boys' work. 'Good Devon apples.' He nodded over towards his sacks and boxes, pointing them out one by one, calling them out as if they were his own children. 'Longstem, Blue Sweet, Hollow Core. Hoary Morning, Slack Ma Girdle, Keswick Codling, Sour Natural, Jacob's Strawberry, Johnny Voun, Johnny Andre, Plumderity, Rattler, Buttery d'Or. Pig's Nose—'

'Pig's Nose?' said Bernhard, concerned.

'An apple?' said Morley. 'I'm assuming, Mr Reeder, rather than a porcine appendage?'

'Pig's Snout,' continued Mr Reeder, regardless.

'Ditto,' said Morley.

'Thin Skin, Limberlimb, Butterbox—'

'Poetry!' exulted Morley. 'Poetry, boys! Did you hear? Plumderity, Rattler, Buttery d'Or. You don't know Ronald Hatton at East Malling, by chance, do you, Mr Reeder?'

'Can't say I do, sir, no.'

'Research centre for the study of fruit trees, absolutely fascinating work. We must visit one day, Sefton. Just remembered. Make a note.'

'Very good, Mr Morley.'

'I think I'm right in saying, Mr Reeder – am I? – that Kentish cider tends to use a higher percentage of culinary and dessert fruit rather than the traditional cider apples, producing a cider rather lighter in body and flavour?'

'I couldn't tell you, sir. I just makes Devon cider. Pure Devon cider.'

The boys had found a rhythm now, and the mill crushed all beneath it.

'Perhaps you could talk us through the process, Mr Reeder, if you wouldn't mind?'

'We make the pulp.'

'This is the pulp?' said Morley.

'That's right. And when the pulp is smooth, then we build the cheese.'

'Cheese?' said Bernhard, who was clearly enjoying this mad, impromptu educational outing, as were we all.

'We build up some reeds with the pulp,' said Mr Reeder, 'so the juice can be squeezed out, and then we trim the cheese and press the cheese, and then we have our cider put into casks to ferment.' He indicated a long row of casks stacked along the other side of the barn.

～ ～

We passed a pleasant hour going through the process in more detail with Mr Reeder and then, eventually, loaded with a sack of apples and a case of cider, made our way back down the lane towards the road.

'Thank you, Mr Reeder,' cried the boys.

'Goodbye,' said Mr Reeder, waving us off.

'Honestly, you two don't know what you've missed!' Morley told Miriam and Alex, as we arrived back at the charabanc and clambered aboard. 'Season of mists and mellow fruitfulness.'

'You too, Father!' said Miriam, honking the horn on the Lagonda as she set off behind us. 'You too!'

CHAPTER 17

ALOHA!

THE BEACH AT CROYDE, according to Morley in *The County Guides*, is 'not only a hidden gem: it is a jewel in Devon's crown'. It is indeed a place of hidden and peculiar charms, lying on a little promontory between the vast stretches of Saunton and Woolacombe, accessible only via a steep route down below a few lonely thatched cottages. The charabanc parked by the cottages and we clambered down to the beach with our provisions, over wet rocks and sharp grass. It was low tide.

'I feel like Chistopher Columbus,' said Morley. He took a couple of his deep pranic breaths.

'Perfect,' he announced, holding his index finger aloft to check the wind. 'Easterly,' he said. 'Splendid!' and then speedily led the boys up towards the north end of the beach.

For anyone who has never taken part in surfing, I should explain. Surfing requires an obsessive concern with detail, a great deal of patience, and an utterly illogical, death-defying determination to pit oneself against the uncontrollable forces of nature. It is, in other words, Morley's ideal sport.

At the far end of the beach great waves came barrelling towards the shore with a shocking ferocity, some of them as much as four or five feet high.

'Chop, chop!' said Morley, chivvying us along. 'Come along, come along. We haven't got all day.' The boys reluctantly changed into their bathing costumes. And Morley changed also, though having done so he then popped a woollen pullover on top, giving him the appearance not so much of a man determined to do battle with nature but rather of a man preparing to use an outside lavatory late at night. The appearance was deceptive.

Morley gathered the boys around down by the waterline and explained his purpose.

'*Aloha!*' he began. 'Which is the Polynesian equivalent – as of course you know – of the Hebrew greeting *Shalom aleichem*, or the Arabic *Assalum Akaylum*.' The boys exchanged glances. Not only did they not know that *Aloha* meant *Shalom aleichem* and *Assalum Akaylum*, they had no idea what on earth he was talking about. 'Repeat after me, gentlemen, *Aloha!*'

'*Aloha!*' the boys weakly chorused back.

'Can't hear you!' said Morley. '*Aloha!*'

'*Aloha!*' bellowed the boys back.

'Good! Anyway, gentlemen, we are gathered here today to pay homage to the wine-dark sea and her overwhelming and intoxicating power, a power governed only by the Good Lord Himself. *Et dominabitur a mari usque ad mare, et a flumine usque ad terminos terrae.*'

Looks of incomprehension once again – I caught the gist only of *terminos terrae*.

'Some of you may already be familiar with the history of

surfing' – again, there were more uncomprehending glances – 'and so to be brief . . .'

He was not brief, of course: he was Swanton Morley. From what I recall his 'brief' history began with an account of ritual practices in ancient Polynesia, continued into the late eighteenth century with the adventures of Captain James Cook, detoured into Australia and ended around the 1920s with a Hawaiian gentleman whose name I cannot now recall but who apparently won some Olympic medal or other and who went on to become a self-appointed ambassador of surfing. It was not an uninteresting tale, but at about ten minutes or more in duration it was at least nine minutes too long.

'Now, gentlemen, I want to show you something.'

Morley often carried with him a knapsack of the kind used by poachers – a dark brown, greasy canvas bag. From this unassuming bag he now produced, improbably, a volume of the *Encyclopaedia Britannica*.

'The *Britannica* is not a convenient pocket companion, boys, but until someone invents either a truly convenient pocket encyclopaedia – a pockepaedia, shall we call it – or a pocket large enough and capacious enough to contain a gentleman's home reference library *in toto*, the *Britannica* it is and the *Britannica* it will have to be. I have brought this volume with me today, gentlemen, in order to show you this . . .' He opened up the book to the entry on Hawaii. 'This, boys, is my inspiration!'

He held the book aloft, showing a photograph. The photograph showed men standing up upon the waves. I had certainly never seen anything quite like it: several boys gasped.

'This is not what is sometimes called belly-boarding, boys. This is not stomach-skimming! This, gentlemen, is stand-up surfing!' He struck a pose, resembling Christ on the cross, on a tightrope. 'By the end of the day, gentlemen, it is my hope that you will all be standing tall, as God intended you to be, cresting the ocean waves! Proud, erect and nut-brown Adams, the lot of you!'

I lit a cigarette and stared out to sea. My own costume consisted of my underwear: it occurred to me that I would make a rather unassuming Adam.

'Now, first things first, gentlemen,' Morley continued. 'This, boys, is a surfboard.' He tapped one of his long wooden boards that the boys had lugged down to the beach. 'Anyone seen one of these before?' No boy spoke. 'As I thought. But it is my contention this morning, boys, that to be in Devon – never mind to live in Devon – and not to surf is like living in Scotland and never to have worn the kilt, or to be in Egypt and not to have scaled the pyramids, or to live in France and never . . . to have eaten snails.' Some of the boys made gagging noises. 'Surfing, boys, is your duty and your inheritance.'

During this speech, Alex, standing behind us, had been assisting Miriam in getting changed. I looked around to see her giggling as he held a towel for her. Some duty.

'My aim today, gentlemen, is to show you the rudiments of surfing, and perhaps to ignite an enthusiasm that will last for years, if not a lifetime. To surf, gentlemen, is to taste freedom. It is to experience knowledge of the world in its most powerful and intimate form: dark, flowing and pro-found. It is to embrace and to be embraced by what I believe Yeats himself . . . Sefton?' – I nodded absent-mindedly in agreement, which was all I was required to do – 'What Yeats himself described as the "white breast of the dim sea". In years to come, gentlemen in England now-a-bed shall think themselves accurs'd they were not here, and hold their manhoods cheap whiles any speaks that fought with us upon Saint Crispin's day . . .'

'Father,' called Miriam from behind us, as Morley looked set to launch into further horations.

'Ah yes,' said Morley, remembering himself and his audience. 'For the purposes of my demonstration my lovely assistant will show you the moves, and will explain them to you. Miriam, would you like to wax the board?'

Miriam strode before us in her emerald-green swimming costume. There was an audible intake of breath among the boys. Alex came and stood beside me, resplendent in his own gleaming white costume, complete with embroidered crest and initials on his chest.

Morley meanwhile had produced from a leather tobacco pouch a small hard ball of wax, which he held aloft.

'This, gentlemen, is beeswax, which I have mixed with a small amount of coconut oil and some standard rosin, in order to assist the surfer to grip the board. Miriam, could you show the boys how to rub the board?'

The talk of breasts and rubbing was becoming too much for some of the boys and there was a sudden outbreak of sniggering. (For a man who adored wordplay and word-games, Morley seemed inexplicably oblivious to all forms of double entendres and bawdy: his book of limericks, for example, *Morley's Limericks for All Occasions* (1930) entirely misses the mark. So dull and so innocent are they, one might almost use his limericks as lullabies.)

[223]

Morley held the board up straight as Miriam proceeded to wax it lengthwise, then crosswise and finally in a circular motion. The slow rubbing motion as she did so clearly caused some excitement and consternation among the boys. One raised his hand.

'Yes?' said Morley.

'Permission to go for a pee, sir?'

'If you must, boy,' said Morley. 'If you must. Now. Note, Miriam has finished her rubbing when small bumps of white wax have appeared on the board. This process must of course be often repeated. When the white wax appears lumpy and dirty it should be scraped off with a long hard smooth edge.' This proved too much for another boy, who also begged permission to pee. Worse was to come.

'Miriam will now demonstrate to you boys the basic techniques for surfing: paddling out to the waves, and standing erect on the board. Miriam, if you wouldn't mind?'

Miriam obliged by lying flat down on the board, her feet dangling over the end.

'First, you lie down on the board, as demonstrated. Not too far forward, not too far back. You will have to manoeuvre yourself into a comfortable position.' Several of the boys were in extremely uncomfortable positions. 'You then begin to paddle, like so.' Miriam made as if to paddle. 'Hands lightly cupped, as you can see. Your hand should enter the water smoothly, sweeping low, almost as if you were caressing the wave. As with swimming, too much splashing is a sign of poor style. So, nice and smooth, just as Miriam is demonstrating. Stroke, stroke. Caress, caress. Stroke. Any questions?'

Silence again, as the boys watched in awe.

'Next, you slide your hands along the side of the board, ready to push up.' Miriam did so. 'And so with your hands flat on the deck, you raise your body off the board into position, thus.'

Miriam was now in a position poised over the board. She resembled Josephine Baker, mid-routine. She looked at the boys gathered in a tight circle around her, her eyes at waist-level. The atmosphere was tense.

'Father,' she said. 'It might be an idea before we go any further for the boys to go and accustom themselves to the water, don't you think?'

'But we're only halfway through the demonstration,' said Morley.

'Bit of vigorous exercise, and a dose of cold water, to get their organs moving,' said Miriam. 'Warm up. Stretch the arms and the shoulders. Essential, I'd say.'

Before she could finish speaking the boys had sped off down towards the sea, where they thrust themselves into the cold comforting waves.

'Well,' said Morley. 'I rather think that could have waited until we were finished.'

'I rather think not,' said Miriam, winking at me and glancing down. 'Sefton?'

I too raced down to the water and doused myself in the waves.

~ ~

Once the boys and teachers had reassembled, Miriam went through the rest of the procedures: up into crouching position, the slide into the stand, arms out for balance.

'Now, anyone like to try?' asked Morley. A dozen hands shot up, for the privilege of being the first to lie down where Miriam had been. Once every boy – and Bernhard and Alex and I – had been through the routine, Morley explained several other manoeuvres that seemed far beyond our capacities.

'Very good,' concluded Morley eventually. 'Now what?'

'Into the sea?'

'Incorrect,' said Morley. 'What we do next is this.' And he promptly sat down, arranged himself into a yogi-like cross-legged position, and stared out to sea.

'No man—' he began.

'Or woman, Father,' said Miriam.

'No man or woman should venture out into the seas without first watching the waves. Are they too big to risk? Are they suitable at all for us to surf? From what direction do they come? As beginners you will prefer the gentle rolling wave to the heavy pounding break, but as your skill increases you will be able to tell what to expect. You will learn to read the waves, as a salty sea dog.' He continued to stare out, yogi-like, for some time. And then he leapt up again.

'Now, Miriam, would you like to demonstrate how to surf?'

Miriam strode proudly down towards the waves, her surfboard carried under her arm. It was a vision as from a dream.

'Note the carrying position,' said Morley. 'Never, under any circumstances, drag your board along, boys. Why not?'

'Because it would damage the board?' said one boy.

'Correct,' said Morley. 'And more importantly and obviously?'

'It would remove the wax?' said another boy.

'*Précisément!*' said Morley. 'Your board needs to remain smooth and waxed.'

Miriam by this time had paddled far out on the board. Waves crashed over her.

'Note,' said Morley, 'the way in which Miriam raises herself up from the board to allow the wave to pass between her body and the board, and then she sinks back down onto the board and continues to paddle out . . .'

Miriam did exactly as Morley described, raising and lowering her body slowly over the foaming surf. The boys were becoming restless again, so it was fortunate that she astonished them with what happened next.

Far out in the surf, she had turned the board and was facing the beach.

Morley described for us what we were witnessing, because none of us had ever seen anything quite like it before.

'Note: the surfer feels the wave – picks up the board – arches her back – tucks her arms beneath her – before pushing up – and then – up, up – see! – into the crouching stance – arms out – bending the legs. And lo!'

And lo indeed: Miriam was now standing on the board, just as in the *Britannica*, her feet apart, arms outstretched, looking shorewards, riding a wave, rushing towards us, grinning.

It was a truly amazing spectacle: the long brown board, the blue-white wave and Miriam in emerald green . . . And as she came washing up in shallow waters it was all any of

The cold comforting waves at Croyde

us could do to prevent ourselves from rushing out into the waves to embrace her. On reaching the shoreline she simply and gracefully dismounted. We all burst into a spontaneous round of applause, which Miriam bowed to acknowledge, before turning and paddling out with the board again. This of course only made the accomplishment all the more impressive. The demonstration continued for several more runs, with variations, Miriam shifting her weight between front and back foot, somehow turning the board left and right.

﹏ ﹏

I felt that I might have watched the same scene, utterly contented, repeated for hours. But I sensed Alex at my shoulder, his pure white bathing costume burning in the sun.

"'Her clothes spread wide,'" he said quietly. "'And mermaid-like, awhile they bore her up: but long it could not be till that her garments, heavy with their drink, pull'd the poor wretch to muddy death.'"

'What?' I said.

'Ophelia,' he said. 'Surely you know Ophelia?'

'Ophelia?'

'A famous woman among the waves,' he said. 'Eh?'

'Now, Sefton?' said Morley, interrupting us. 'Would you care perhaps to take a ride with Miriam?' He placed his own surfboard in my hands.

'I ... certainly would,' I said, looking triumphantly at Alex, and I ran down to the water to join her.

Miriam seemed rather disappointed.

'Oh,' she said, 'it's you. Are you ready?'

'Ready-ish,' I said.

'I suppose that will have to do,' she said. 'Just follow my lead, Sefton. If you can.'

I carefully followed her every move, to the best of my ability: paddling and ducking through the waves until we seemed far out and alone – just us and the waves, and the sun high above us, rocking gently up and down. Alex and Morley and the boys seemed like creatures on another planet. It should have been perfect, but I was surprised: I was nervous, almost panicking.

'Where did you learn?' I asked, trying to steady my nerves.

'Learn what, Sefton?'

'Surfing.'

'Learn?' she said. 'Learn? This isn't school, Sefton.'

'No, of course, but—'

'Like anything worth learning, surfing cannot be taught,' she said. 'Whatever Father says. One learns only by doing, Sefton.' She tossed back her head and smoothed her hair away from her face: she knew of course in that moment that she was beautiful, and that she had me entirely. 'Agatha Christie first showed me how.'

'The lady novelist?'

'Indeed. Excellent surfer. Surprisingly nimble. Friend of Father's. And George Bernard Shaw – though he's a terrible poseur. Takes himself rather more seriously than the surfing: not good. It's the dance, not the dancer, Sefton.'

I felt a swelling beneath me and behind me.

'Now!' cried Miriam. 'This is our wave, Sefton! Follow me! The dance, remember, not the dancer! The dance!'

I kicked frantically with my feet. I felt the wave come from behind and pick me up like the hand of God Himself, and I grabbed the edges of the board and began to kneel and ... Blinded by the spray, unable to breathe, I was immediately somersaulted off, smashing my face onto the edge of the board as it came slicing down through the waves towards me.

My head snapped back and I felt my nose pop and blood come spurting.

Moments seemed like an eternity: I was choking on water, frantically struggling up to the surface, gasping, heaving, coughing. Flailing, turning around towards the beach, I saw Miriam speeding off away from me towards the shore. Somehow this calmed me: I was overcome, simply, by shame.

Some dancer. Some dance.

Defeated, I recovered the board and paddled slowly back into the shallows.

Miriam strode back past me into the water.

'Are you OK, sir?' asked a boy.

'I'm fine,' I said.

'Bad luck,' said Morley, who was acting as umpire, lookout and referee. 'I should have said: it is a dangerous sport.' I pinched my nose to feel the swelling: it was as though someone had hammered a blunt nail directly between my eyes. 'Next?'

And Alex strode forward and grabbed the board triumphantly from my hands.

I turned to watch, the taste of blood in my mouth like bitter metal. Alex followed Miriam and when the right wave eventually came, he managed to raise himself from the board and stood for a moment, before crashing down into the surf.

'Bravo!' cried Morley.

And 'Bravo!' echoed the boys.

～ ～

The day wore on, with the boys throwing themselves into the surfing with total abandon; not one of them suffered a mishap like my own. My bloodied nostrils dried and crusted, the bridge of my nose was wide and soft and sore.

Once everyone had followed Miriam out and enjoyed a turn on the boards, Morley himself gave a demonstration.

Dressed in his woollen bathing suit he lay down on the wooden board and paddled out, then sat, his head bobbing above the waves, waiting for the right moment. And when that moment came he was suddenly, magically, up on the board, arms outstretched, hurtling towards the shore, like some mad bejumpered Jesus on the Sea of Galilee. His moustache hung down wet like an old dog's whiskers.

'That was . . . amazing,' I said, when he made his way up the beach, though my dented nose flattened the 'amazing' into what sounded like 'amusing'.

'Amusing?'

'Amazing,' I said again, though the word caused me pain.

'Want me to set it straight for you?' said Morley, referring to my nose.

'No, thank you,' I said.

'Sure? I've done it before. Had to help fix up Teddy Baldock once after a fight at Premierland. Friend of mine had been training him. Best bantamweight I've ever seen fight. Did you ever see Baldock fight? Pride of Poplar?'

'No, I didn't, Mr Morley.'

'Doesn't look too bad anyway. Gives you a touch of the old Joe Louis, you know.'

'Thank you.' I certainly felt like I'd been beaten to a pulp by a heavyweight.

'The thing with surfing, Sefton,' continued Morley, 'it's like cycling. One never quite loses the knack.'

'Once one has acquired the knack.'

'Quite. But you'll get there, Sefton. You need to relax. Be at one with the waves.'

'At one with the waves?'

'Absolutely. You do seem rather – what do they say? – uptight at the moment, Sefton, if you don't mind my saying so.'

'Uptight, Mr Morley. Really?'

'Yes.'

'Well. I . . . I'm worried about Miriam.'

'Miriam?'

I nodded over to where Miriam was horsing around with Alex and some of the boys.

'I have warned you about Miriam,' said Morley, looking out to sea.

'You warned me, Mr Morley?'

'Several times,' said Morley. 'Untameable.'

'Yes, but . . .'

'I suggest you leave her to her own devices, Sefton. When her mother died, I perhaps slightly lost my—'

'Lunch!' announced Bernhard at that moment, and boys suddenly came crowding round.

'Line up! Line up!' said Bernhard.

We were once again finishing off the remains of yesterday's afternoon tea: cakes and hard-boiled eggs, mostly, plus the rather ornate fresh cucumber sandwiches that had been prepared for the parents: rounds of bread cut with a fluted cutter, and the bread spread unappetisingly with a kind of green butter that seemed to have been concocted from vinegar, egg yolks – and fish. The sandwiches had not proved a great success with the parents yesterday. And they were no more appetising today.

'Capers?' said Miriam, chewing.

'Capers,' confirmed Morley. 'Alas.' He had extremely strong opinions about sandwiches: they most certainly should not contain capers, though he did permit anchovies, with egg, and they should ideally be consumed within an hour of being made, in order 'to prevent the moisture from the filling wreaking havoc with the crust'. (His little pamphlet – one of his self-published *jeux d'esprit* – 'On Making Sandwiches', contains a long prefatory warning about the dangers of confining sandwiches 'in closed receptacles' and instructions on how to make one's own muslin sandwich bag, to allow the sandwich 'the freedom to breathe'.)

The boys were equally unimpressed with the sandwiches, some of them defiantly spitting them up, forming them into little green balls, and hurling them at one another.

'Boys!' cried Bernhard, utterly ineffectually.

'Boys!' said Alex quietly – and the sandwich spitting immediately ceased.

'Time for a game, perhaps?' said Morley.

'Beach cricket?' said Alex.

'Good idea!' said Morley.

'Allow me,' said Alex, getting up immediately. He was the only one among us who had changed back into his clothes, which emphasised his appearance of superiority. 'I have spent the best part of a year trying to inculcate in these young fellows the basics of inswing, but I'm afraid I'm not having much luck.'

'Takes a while,' said Morley.

'Indeed,' agreed Alex. 'But no time like the present. Cricket, chaps, come on! No more mucking around now.'

There was widespread groaning from the boys, but they got up and made their way down the beach in preparation for a game of cricket.

'Can we tempt you to join us, Sefton?' asked Alex.

'No, thanks,' I said.

'Pity. Bernhard?'

'Germany is not a cricketing nation, I'm afraid.'

'Thank goodness,' said Morley.

'I'll sit this out,' said Bernhard.

As Alex departed, Miriam came and sat close beside me. 'He's an Eton blue in cricket, you know.'

'Really?'

'And he gives the boys lessons once a week on the art of swordsmanship.'

'Swordsmanship?' I said. 'Renaissance man.'

'Yes. Epee, sabre. Singlesticks,' she said, licking her fingers clean from the remains of cucumber sandwich. 'Love the nose, by the way.'

'Thank you.'

'Sort of like a snout. Have you ever fenced, Sefton?'

'I can't say I have, Miss Morley, no,' I replied, though I had, to my shame, held a knife to the throat of a man in Spain and threatened to kill him unless he allowed us unfettered access to his larder. Some of our men also helped themselves to his daughters.

'Sport of kings,' said Morley, who was flicking through the pages of the *Encyclopaedia Britannica*.

'Indeed,' said Miriam.

Keen to clear my mouth of the taste of the cucumber sandwiches, and looking for any distraction to avoid having to discuss Alex's endless schoolmasterly accomplishments, I handed round apples from the sack from the cider farm. When I bit into mine there was at the centre a tiny white coiling maggot. I spat out my mouthful in disgust.

'Not you too, Sefton?' said Morley, not looking up from the *Britannica*. 'What's the problem, man? Taste of the old Laodiceans, eh?'

I had no idea what he was talking about.

'"I will spew thee out of my mouth?"' said Miriam, apparently in clarification.

'Correct!' said Morley. 'Book?'

'Of Revelation,' said Miriam.

'Correct! Chapter?'

'No idea, Father.'

'Three, verse sixteen. But no matter.'

'It was a maggot, Mr Morley,' I said.

'Ah. You know what they say, Sefton.'

'What?'

'It's the apple that corrupts the worm, not the worm that corrupts the apple.'

Miriam had wisely cut her apple in half, to avoid any maggot surprise – and she held the pure white cut face towards me on her palm.

'The old apple clock is ticking, Sefton,' she said.

Down on the beach Alex continued drilling the boys on their inswing.

'It's something Father used to say when I was young,' she explained.

'Wonderful sight, isn't it, Sefton?' said Morley, looking up from his book, pure contentment on his face.

'Indeed it is, Mr Morley,' I agreed, though I wasn't sure if he meant the boys, the apple, or the *Britannica*.

'Forms a pentagram, of course,' said Morley, indicating the half of the apple that Miriam had handed him. 'Ancient symbol of the goddess Kore. Persephone, Queen of the Underworld.'

'We could stay here tonight, Father, and go home for breakfast tomorrow?' interrupted Miriam.

'I'm not sure that would be entirely practical,' said Bernhard, who was busy clearing up the remains of the lunch.

'Nonsense,' said Miriam. 'Do us all the world of good. Sleeping out under the stars, as nature intended.'

'I'm not sure that we have come properly equipped for an overnight stay,' said Bernhard.

'Oh nonsense!' said Miriam. 'Father's a famous fresh air enthusiast, aren't you, Father?'

'Oh yes,' said Morley. 'Absolutely. The more fresh air we get the better, obviously. Nothing worse than to be cooped up. One might simply imagine an individual hermetically sealed in a room who breathes and rebreathes his own impurities – it would make himself liable to all sorts of infections, wouldn't it?'

'I'm really not sure,' said Bernhard, gobbling the few remains of some cake.

'Oh come on, chaps,' said Miriam. 'It is a glorious autumn afternoon. The boys are enjoying the surfing and the cricket.

We have enough provisions to see us through. And we could rise early and be back in time for classes tomorrow.'

'I'm really not sure.'

'Well,' said Morley. 'I was rather hoping to show the boys how to collect gulls' eggs. And I did wonder if it might be good to teach them how to make Australian boomerangs . . . Simple to carve, but takes a while. I thought we could use driftwood. Taught to me by the Aboriginals when I was there. All the best Australian boomerangs are notched on both surfaces, you know, almost honeycombed. Like a golf ball. Most curious and I . . .'

I remembered as Morley continued that I had arranged to meet Mrs Dodds in Sidmouth early that evening.

'I think we should probably return,' I said, looking to Bernhard for support.

'We would really have to have checked with the head-master,' said Bernhard. 'It might seem rather reckless other-wise.'

'Reckless?' said Morley. 'Reckless?' Miriam looked at me and raised a victorious eyebrow. 'Reckless? I really do think this is what's wrong with schooling these days, Mr Bernhard, if you don't mind my saying so. The lack of adventure. Lack of initiative. Fear. Where are those who are willing to take these boys and show them what life is really about? Who is willing to stick their neck out and do what's right, eh? What we need are more men like Alex in our schools.'

'Quite so,' said Miriam, clapping her hands together. 'Hear, hear!'

'My ideal school,' said Morley, warming quickly to a theme, 'is a place where boys learn how to milk a cow, shoe and ride a horse, bake bread, grow fruit, keep bees and engage in handicrafts such as carpentry, building and leatherwork. I've been speaking to the headmaster about this. Also, the rudiments of engineering and—'

'That's all very well, Mr Morley, but—' I began.

'Each boy could simply place his blazer on the ground tonight and we could make a big ring,' said Miriam, 'with the fire in the centre, and some large stones for the fireplace, and the boys can collect wood and twigs, and we can surf and then—'

Bernhard suddenly leapt up and gave a cry. He was pointing down at the sea.

For a moment I thought he was pointing at the cricket ball, which was sailing high up into the sky, a small, hard red ball against the vast pale blue. But he was not pointing at the cricket ball. He was pointing at a speck, a splash in the ocean. One of the boys had apparently slipped away from the game of cricket and taken a surfboard, and swum out too far, and gone under. Bernhard had seen the splash – but the boy had not resurfaced. Alex, much closer to the shore, had also seen and was already running down to the sea, plunging in fully clothed, swimming out with a terrific stroke towards where the boy had disappeared. The boys had run down behind him and gathered at the shore. Miriam was crying out.

The boy surfaced for a moment, hand and head, and Alex reached him and grabbed him, but suddenly he too was pulled under, the boy dragging him down.

Miriam screamed again.

I too had run down to the shore but by the time I had reached the water's edge Alex had dragged the boy out and had laid him on the beach, where he tilted his head back, and the boy choked up sea water and then Alex gave him the kiss of life – which had, thank goodness, the desired effect. The whole thing was over in minutes.

The boys whooped and hollered. Miriam wept. Alex stoically shook himself dry. Bernhard attended to the boy, a young man named Louis – and soon we all traipsed our way back to the charabanc, all thoughts of staying the night abandoned.

∽ ∾

'Well, certainly a memorable day,' said Morley, clambering aboard.

'Satisfied now?' asked Miriam quietly, as she walked away towards the Lagonda.

'Satisfied with what?' I asked.

'That Alex is a better man than you? Braver? More honourable?'

There was no answer to this question.

We sang no hymns and played no games: the ride back to All Souls passed in silence.

CHAPTER 18

AN ADEPT

I ARRIVED IN SIDMOUTH more than an hour late for my appointment with Mrs Dodds.

I had the driver of the charabanc drop me off en route to the school, outside the Grand Cinema, with the excuse that I was going to see a film.

'A film?' said Morley. 'Not a bad idea actually. Haven't been myself for at least a week or so. Perhaps we should take the boys?'

'Yes!' cried the boys, whose day with Morley had already involved more incident and excitement than they might reasonably expect to enjoy in an average year.

'No,' said Bernhard strictly. 'We must return the boys to the school now, Mr Morley.'

'That might be best,' I said.

'Hmm. I suppose,' agreed Morley, who was clearly chastened by the day's events. Widespread groaning from the boys. 'What are you going to see, Sefton?'

I had no idea.

'I think there's a new Fred Astaire,' said Bernhard, coming to my rescue. '*A Damsel in Distress*?'

'Yes,' I agreed. '*A Damsel in Distress.*'

'Didn't have you down as a Fred Astaire fan,' said Morley. 'No,' I said.

'With Joan Fontaine,' said Bernhard. 'I am a great fan of Joan Fontaine,' he added.

'A Joan Fontaine fan,' said Morley. 'Can't say I share your enthusiasm. But a rather pleasing euphony.'

'And there is a new Marlene Dietrich,' said Bernhard. '*Angel*? I *adore* Marlene Dietrich.'

'Entirely wholesome?' said Morley, whose favourite film star was Charlie Chaplin, and whose favourite Chaplin was *The Champion*, in which Chaplin famously knocks out the tough guy using his lucky horseshoe in his glove, and then dances around the champ in the championship fight, a scene that might almost have served as Morley's own celluloid emblem (though as any true aficionado will recall, and as Morley himself points out in *Morley's Movies*, Chaplin used exactly the same rigmarole in *City Lights*, an inexcusable example, according to Morley, of self-plagiarism, albeit a fault to which he himself was more than ever so slightly prone).

So they dropped me off directly outside the Grand Cinema. Having claimed I was going to see a film – though I had no intention of going to see a film, and was in fact already late for my meeting with Mrs Dodds – I had no alternative but to go inside.

The Grand Cinema was perhaps rather less grand than its name suggested, though by no means a proverbial flea-pit: there was good brocade, much polished wood and brass, and a general air of tidy efficiency. People were coming and going. Couples were queuing. Tickets were being briskly issued.

For a few moments I loitered, pretending to read the signs and advertisements on the walls: the Clifton Place Private Hotel, at Clifton Place, I discovered, boasts electric light in all bedrooms, and a new Woolworth's store had recently opened in town. I lingered as long as I could. But then – because Morley had become engaged in some complicated conversation with the charabanc driver, and so the boys remained enviously watching and waving at me through the cinema's big plate-glass doors – I had no choice but to join the end of the queue. And then – because Morley and the charabanc driver remained deep in their complicated conversation, and the boys continued watching and waving – I found myself shuffling inexorably forward. And then – still under scrutiny, alas – I found myself, inevitably, at the top of the cinema queue. This was not what I had intended.

'Yes?' said the small plump lipsticked girl behind the counter, without looking up: she was concentrating on filing her nails with an emery board.

I dug deep into my pockets: I had just enough for the price of the ticket, but then I would be entirely broke. Morley wouldn't be paying me until the end of the month. I was always short of money. The boys outside continued staring in. There was no skulking off.

'Yes?' repeated the small plump girl.

I looked up at the posters. There was in fact no Marlene Dietrich or Fred Astaire available: the choice was between some pulpy thing called *Dangerous Secrets* and some odd-looking British film, *The Edge of the World*.

'Hello?' said the small plump girl, finally looking up. '*Dangerous Secrets* or *The Edge of the World?*'

'How about *Dangerous Secrets at the Edge of the World?*' I said.

'Sorry?'

'No, it's a joke,' I said.

'*Dangerous Secrets* or *The Edge of the World?*'

'Have you seen them?' I asked.

'Yes.'

'Which do you recommend?'

'*Dangerous Secrets,*' she said.

'What's it about?'

'The usual,' she said.

'The usual what?' I asked.

'Secrets?' she suggested. 'Dangerous secrets?'

'Sounds perfect,' I said. '*Dangerous Secrets* it is then,' and as I handed over my only coins I looked outside to see the charabanc slowly pulling away.

The girl handed me the ticket – flashing neatly filed nails – which I tried immediately to hand back.

'Actually, I wonder, could you give me a refund?'

'A refund?' She squinted suspiciously at me. 'But you only just bought your ticket.'

'Yes, I know, but I didn't really want to go and see it.'

'Well, you shouldn't have bought the ticket then, should you?'

'No, but I'm not going to see the film and I really need the money, so if you wouldn't mind? I'll just give you the ticket.' I pushed it across the counter towards her. 'And you just give me my money . . .' I held out my palm.

'We don't do refunds.' She turned and pointed to a sign

displayed behind her which said, clearly, and entirely without caveats or clarifications: 'NO REFUNDS'.

There was some impatient jostling from those in the
queue behind me.

'Is there a problem?' asked a young Devonian man in an
aggressively broad flat cap.

'I'm just waiting for a refund,' I said.

'We don't do refunds,' said the plump girl, pointing again
to the sign.

'Are you blind or what?' said the young man in the cap.

'I would hardly be going to the cinema if I was blind,
would I?' I said, my back turned to the young man. I felt him
barge me sharply with his shoulder. The entire weight of the
queue behind seemed to begin to press in on me. I stood my
ground.

'Could I speak to the manager?' I said to the plump girl.

'Fine,' she said. 'Go ahead.'

There was more impatient jostling behind me.

'Come on!' said the young man. 'You're holding us all up.'

'The manager?' I repeated.

'He's there,' the small plump girl said, pointing, but before
I had a chance to follow her directions she hollered, 'Paul!'
and Paul – a slight, balding young fellow with an ill-formed
moustache and a receding chin and who wore a bright red
concierge uniform that matched the colour of the small
plump girl's lipstick and who was manning the doors to the
cinema – came shuffling over.

'Everything all right?' asked Paul.

'Man wants a refund.'

'We don't do refunds,' said Paul, pointing at the 'NO
REFUNDS' sign.

I explained that I simply no longer wished to see the film.

'No refunds,' said Paul. 'Management policy. You've got your ticket. You can see the film, or you can go home.'

'Come on then,' said the man behind me. 'Off you go back home to Mummy. You heard what he said.'

'Yes,' I said, turning to face the young man, flashing my recently broken nose. 'I heard what the gentleman said, but I think you'll find that under law I am still entitled to a refund if I have decided I am not going to partake of the product. The purchase of a ticket is not a binding contract.' Clearly I had spent too long with Swanton Morley: I was talking myself into trouble.

'Have you got some sort of a problem or what?' said the young man.

'No, I don't have a problem,' I said. 'Why? Do you have a problem?'

'Where are you from? Are you one of the ass-trologers from up at the school?' he asked.

'No,' I said, 'I am not an astrologer.'

'Or one of the wizards?' said the small plump girl.

There was laughter from the queue.

'No, I am not a wizard,' I said. 'I'm from London.'

This caused further merriment.

'Go on then. Get out, if you're going, or get on in if you're coming here,' said Paul.

I was definitely going. I pocketed my ticket and walked outside.

Sidmouth, according to Morley in *The County Guides*, is east Devon at its finest: 'With its frowning hills, its quaint shops and buildings, its fine seafront, and magnificent cottage hospital, a man could be born and live in Sidmouth and die content in the knowledge that this, like so many of our wonderful English seaside towns, represents the best of all possible places in the best of all possible worlds.' Frowning and quaint are certainly correct: for all its seaside frivolities, Sidmouth I found to be a rather solemn, serious little town. And I cannot in all honesty recommend the Grand Cinema. Then again, perhaps all our judgements – of people, as of places – are based on such little evidence and incident.

I strolled briskly through the marketplace, past the International Stores, and the new Woolworth's 3d and 6d shop, and Green's the Fruiterer, past the Post Office and down towards the Esplanade, where I went into the Mocha Café, where Mrs Dodds was waiting.

She sat at a table at the very back, hidden almost completely from view behind some giant aspidistras, deep in thought, fingering her pearls. She rose from her seat as I approached: tall, dark-haired, statuesque. And angry.

'I'm so sorry I'm late, Mrs Dodds,' I said. She offered no greeting in return. 'I'm afraid the day has been rather … eventful.'

'I'm not a shopgirl, Mr Sefton. I am not accustomed to being kept waiting, and I can't say I'm much interested in your apologies.'

'No. Sorry.' I felt like someone who had been summoned before a headmistress, or a high priestess.

'I only have fifteen minutes. We'll have to make it quick,' she said.

'Yes, of course.'

'Well, sit down, man, you're making me nervous.'

We settled ourselves opposite one another at the table.

'I ordered you coffee,' she said. 'But it'll be cold.'

'That's fine,' I said, 'thank you.'

'So.' She settled back into her chair – one of those uncomfortable continental café-style things of dark steamed wood and rattan, with a raised rim around the edge that soon cuts uncomfortably into one's thighs. 'Why were you at the darkroom?'

'I just wanted to look in the darkroom,' I said.

'That's all?'

'That's all.'

'There's no other reason?'

'No. Why?'

'You've not heard anything about the darkroom, and you don't know anything about the darkroom?'

'No.'

She sighed deeply. 'Can I trust you, Mr Sefton?'

'I hope so.'

'Hope, in my experience, does not get us very far. Can I trust you?'

'Yes, Mrs Dodds,' I said firmly. 'Absolutely.'

She looked around and then reached out across the table and took my hand. 'Look at me, please, Sefton. Directly. Into my eyes.'

I looked at her. She may have been forty, or perhaps older, but she was perfectly made up: her skin was pale and smooth, her cheeks delicately rouged, her eyebrows dark and arched, her lips a glossy red. And her wide brown eyes were clear and pleading. I was rather keen, at that moment, for Mrs Dodds to trust me.

'You give me your word as a gentleman that what I'm going to tell you will remain the strictest secret?'

'Of course.'

'Say "I do."'

'I do.'

'You swear on your mother's life?'

'I do.'

'And on the Holy Bible?'

'I do.'

If there was anything else she could have had me swear upon I'm sure she would.

'No one must know,' she said.

'No one,' I agreed.

She looked around again – there was no one near us – and then directly at me again and lowered her head slightly and began to speak, quietly but firmly.

'I met . . . Alex only eighteen months ago. My husband had been invited to attend a fundraising event for the new school. Alex was utterly charming, of course.'

'Of course.' I seemed to be missing something entirely about Alex's irresistible charms.

'It was a very . . . convivial evening. And subsequently we . . .'

'Who?'

'Alex and I . . . got to know each other.' She blushed. 'Do you understand?'

'I think so, Mrs Dodds, yes.'

'And anyway, after we had known each other for some time Alex suggested . . .'

She took a sip of her coffee, which must have been cold. She shuddered rather as she sipped.

'Well, you know what he's like.' She glanced around nervously, as though Alex might at any moment appear out of the walls.

'I'm afraid that I don't, Mrs Dodds.'

'No. Well. He asked me if he could take some photographs.'

'I see.'

'I was flattered, you see. My husband is ... Well, you've met my husband.'

'Yes.'

'So there we are, Sefton. I don't think I need say any more. He took some photographs.'

'Right. What sort of photographs exactly?'

She raised her eyebrow. 'I don't think further elaboration is necessary, Sefton, do you?'

'No.'

'And a gentleman would not have asked.'

'Of course not. Sorry. I—'

'Suffice it to say they are photographs I'm not particularly keen for my husband to see.'

'Oh.'

'Anyway, I subsequently broke things off – but Alex was able, or has been able to ... persuade me to persuade my husband to make some rather generous endowments for the new school building.'

'I see.'

'Which is how they've ended up at Rousdon.'

So it was blackmail, plain and simple. He was building a little empire: the benefactors were his bankers and the boys his currency. I had suspected something about Alex – he was entirely too good to be true. But I was rather disappointed that the something was quite so prosaic and dull: a bigger and better school. I began to find the atmosphere in the Mocha Café oppressive: the uncomfortable continental-style seat was indeed cutting into my thighs; the lights were dim; and the walls themselves seemed to grow darker and to have closed in, as if somehow to echo our conversation; it was becoming night outside.

'Frankly, Sefton, I don't care what my husband does with his money,' continued Mrs Dodds. 'We have more than enough, we don't have children, and why not give it to the damned school? I don't even care about Alex and his stupid club.'

'His club?'

'He has some sort of club he wanted me to join,' she said dismissively.

'What sort of club?'

'He said he wanted me to become an adept.'

'An adept?'

'Yes.'

'You'll have to explain, I'm afraid.'

'I don't know what it was. He's interested in all this psychical research – is that what it's called? I didn't really understand.'

'I see.'

'He claims that his grandfather was a Red Indian, and that his mother was the mistress of the last tsar. That he has all these connections and this ... knowledge. What did he call himself? He said he was some kind of "mage".'

'A "mage"?'

'I think so, yes.'

'And you joined the club?'

'I certainly did not! I began to find him – and the whole situation – utterly tiresome and absurd. Men! They're like children. Anyway, we parted.'

'You'd had your fun and you got bored.' I recognised all the traits.

'Perhaps.' She fixed me with a cold stare and then took a teaspoon and stirred the remains of the cold coffee in her cup. 'Women do get bored also, Sefton. All I want is to get back the photographs.'

She reached out again across the table and put her hand on mine. Her fingernails were painted a deep red. Her rather elaborate Art Deco-style wedding and engagement rings shone brightly under the café's lights.

'So, that's my problem. And here is my proposition, Sefton. It's perfectly simple: will you help me?' She peeped up at me from beneath lowered eyelids.

I was beginning to think that it might have been her who had seduced Alex rather than he who had seduced her.

'You think the photographs are in the darkroom?' I asked.

'Yes.'

'Why?'

'The darkroom is where he likes to . . . It's where we . . .'

She opened her brown eyes wide – I could see her perfect dark pupils.

'I see.'

A couple came and sat at a table close by and Mrs Dodds's tone changed.

'Oh, I really don't know why I'm telling you all this, Sefton.' There seemed to be a suggestion that I was somehow an unsuitable person to confide in.

'Clearly you have your reasons,' I suggested.

'Well, there's no one else I could turn to. I didn't want to get the police involved and everyone here . . .' She nodded towards the couple at the other table.

'I understand,' I said, as reassuringly as possible.

'So you'd be prepared to try to find the . . . items for me?'

'I would, Mrs Dodds. I shall.'

She smiled and breathed a deep sigh of relief. 'I am so glad.' Her whole body seemed to relax. 'And I would like to offer you something in return, of course.' She squeezed my hand tightly. 'To show my appreciation.'

'Mrs Dodds, really, there's no need.'

'But I want to, Sefton.' Her voice was low. 'I need to.'

She took her hand away and reached down into her lap. She produced an envelope from her clutchbag.

'I thought I might offer a small payment, Sefton. It's not much, but—'

'Mrs Dodds, I couldn't.'

'Please.'

'No, Mrs Dodds, I can't.'

She pressed the envelope firmly into my hands.

'Take it, please. And you'll let me know as soon as you find anything?'

'Of course.'

'Tomorrow night here, perhaps?'

'Yes.'

'But don't be late.'

'I won't be late.'

I reluctantly took her money.

CHAPTER 19

SATOR AREPO

I RETURNED EXTREMELY LATE to the school, late enough
for it no longer to resemble a school, but almost to have
returned to its former status as a grand home. The corridors were profoundly quiet. All that could be heard in
the entrance hall was the ticking of the grandfather clock,
which only deepened the profundity. I stood for a moment
and enjoyed the steady rhythmic silence, imagining the
place as it once was and was intended to be: a home for
the wealthy and privileged rather than a home for the sons
of the wealthy and privileged, a home with a father, and a
mother, a place ruled by adults who were parents and not
merely *in loco parentis*; a place with a heart.

I considered going straight up to the farm and to bed,
but then I thought perhaps I should find Morley. I was rather
keen to use my new-found knowledge of Alex to my advan-
tage. If he had been blackmailing Mrs Dodds it seemed highly
likely that he might have tried the technique with others. I
had no intention of course of divulging the information Mrs
Dodds had shared with me, but I wondered if I might at least

be able to put a dent in Morley's uncritical admiration for the man.

I went to the school library. But Morley was not there. I went to the kitchen. And Morley was not there. I went to the staff common room. And he was not there. I thought perhaps he'd retired for the evening to his room, perhaps to read: his nightly habit of reading a book before sleep was one that he maintained throughout our time together, which meant that – on a rough calculation, and not including the books he reviewed, weekly, or the books he read for research, daily, or indeed of course the many books he wrote, numbering into the many hundreds – he had read a thousand books, at night, for pleasure, during our acquaintance. I read perhaps a dozen, dozily – and mostly by him.

I was about to give up. But then I heard a strange sound. It was the sound of laughter, and something else – a kind of clucking, or clicking, like something was stuck in the throat. I made my way uncertainly towards the noise.

It was coming from a room I had not entered before. The thick oak door was temptingly ajar, and I peeked in: dim lighting, a fire in the grate, and Morley and the headmaster side by side in their shirtsleeves, cues in hand. They were engrossed in a game of billiards.

'Ah, Sefton,' said Morley, spying me immediately.

'Billiards,' said the headmaster redundantly.

'Let us lean across the cloth of green and o'er the rigid cushion lean,' said Morley. Whether he was quoting something or making up verse on the hoof it was often difficult to tell; either way it was not perhaps his finest rhyme. Also, I hadn't expected to see him playing billiards.

'Billiards,' I said pointlessly, echoing the headmaster.

'Yes. And I do believe I have perfected my screw,' said the headmaster.

'Intent on some strategic stroke,' said Morley, slapping the headmaster on the back. 'He raised his cue and so he smote.'

'And now I shall pot the red,' announced the headmaster.

He leaned over, pulled back, took his stroke – and the red kissed the cushion and then ricocheted to kiss another red.

'Blast!' said the headmaster.

'I wish I could share your disappointment,' said Morley. 'But I must confess I am secretly delighted.' He began carefully chalking his cue. 'Now, Sefton, how was your evening? Good film?'

'Yes. It was . . .'

'What did you see?'

'*Dangerous Secrets*?' I said.

'We have had an interesting evening ourselves, haven't we, Headmaster?'

'We have indeed, Morley, we have indeed.'

'The police have charged a couple of boys with the theft of Mr Gooding's animals.'

'Really?'

'Very unfortunate,' said the headmaster. 'But we can't have that sort of thing going on in school.'

'Precisely,' said Morley.

'Couple of the younger boys. Unexpected. But they both confessed, apparently.'

'I see,' I said. 'And Michael Taylor?'

The headmaster turned pale at the mention of the poor boy's name.

'Yes,' said Morley. 'The police seem to think that he drove himself over the cliff – an accident.'

'Rather than a suicide?' I said.

'I don't think that's even a possibility, is it?' said Morley.

'*De omnibus dubitandum?*' I said, quoting one of Morley's favourite Latin phrases.

'Anyway,' said Morley. 'The headmaster has suggested a few more places we need to visit for the book, Sefton. Wistman's Wood, up on Dartmoor—'

'Grows straight out of the granite,' said the headmaster. 'All oak.'

'Exclusively oak,' agreed Morley, blowing excess chalk from the tip of his cue. 'And at least five hundred years old. A must-see, wouldn't you say, Sefton?'

'Possibly something BC,' added the headmaster.

'We shall have to investigate, Sefton. A sacred grove of the Druids—'

'So people say,' added the headmaster.

'Who would gather mistletoe from the aged oaks, one assumes. Also, according to folklore, the home of the Black Huntsman, is that right, Headmaster?'

'Indeed. Allegedly. And his pack of Wish-hounds.'

'Whose wild cries may be heard at night. Sounds wonderful, doesn't it, Sefton?'

'Marvellous,' I said.

'We'll tell you all about the other places after we finish this frame though, shall we?'

'Don't let me stop you,' I said.

❧ ❧

They played on, speaking between themselves as old friends do. I slumped in an old overstuffed leather armchair and lit a cigarette. I always had the idea of Morley as an isolated man, yet he was not an isolated man at this moment: he was a man entirely relaxed in another's company. That moment, that evening, the two old friends before the fire in the billiard room, it seemed to me, was a portrait of pure agape: a subject about which and upon which Morley wrote at length, in perhaps his most unfortunate and most misunderstood little pamphlet, *One Love* (1939), in which he calls for a brotherhood of mankind based on the principles of agape, taking as his text 1 John 4:18: 'There is no fear in love; but perfect love casteth out fear, because fear hath torment. He that feareth is not made perfect in love.' *One Love*, Morley always insisted, was not a plea for appeasement: the misunderstanding arose, according to Morley, because of people's failure to understand St Augustine's concept of 'ordinate loves'. I'm afraid I rather failed to understand it also. But on that night this was all a long way away.

After they had finished their frame – Morley winning with a final triumphant thwack – they placed their cues back in the racks.

'Now, a drink perhaps?' said the headmaster. 'I think we deserve one, don't you? I know you won't of course, Morley, but I wonder if your young friend here might?' He looked at me hopefully. 'You might like to see the cellar, in fact?' suggested the headmaster. 'Have you seen the cellar? It is wonderful. One of the advantages of the new school here: all this underground storage. Marvellous. We had nothing like it before. Also, we managed to pick up some excellent claret in

France a few years ago – ten shillings a dozen, I think it was. Absolute bargain. Would you like me to show you?'

'Well . . .'

Morley shrugged on his jacket. 'Gentlemen, I do not partake, as you know. And I am rather tired. I have an article to write for tomorrow.'

'Anything interesting?' asked the headmaster.

'Something about this Bodley Head book, *Ulysses*. Have you come across it?'

'I can't say I have, Morley, no.'

'Some Irish chap. Odd, but rather interesting. More Sefton's sort of thing. Eh, Sefton?'

I smiled weakly. I had in fact procured a smuggled edition of the original *Ulysses* some years ago – and sold it when I was short of cash, not having read a single page.

'Too long, too scatological, and too self-consciously strange, in my opinion.' He glanced at both his watches. 'But there is something to it . . . Can't quite make up my mind. But, *Time and Tide* wait for no man. So I will bid you goodnight.' He made towards the door.

I saw my chance.

'Headmaster,' I said, 'I would love to visit the cellar – and perhaps the darkroom I have heard so much about?'

'The darkroom?' said the headmaster. 'That's rather Alex's domain.'

'So I understand, but—'

'You know I'm rather thinking of getting something going along those lines back at St George's,' said Morley, on the verge of departure, but his endless curiosity obviously piqued. 'Didn't know you had a darkroom, Headmaster. I might join you gentlemen, if I may?'

'By all means,' said the headmaster. 'I've not seen inside it since we moved in. I'd be interested to see what he's done with the place.'

And so we all made our way downstairs.

'Actually, I wonder if I might have a word, Mr Morley,' I said quietly, as the headmaster led the way.

'A word about what, Sefton?'

'It's rather personal, actually.'

'Oh dear,' said Morley. 'Can it wait?'

'Don't mind me,' said the headmaster.

'These things can usually wait,' said Morley.

'Indeed,' said the headmaster.

'I'm not sure,' I said. 'I—'

'Now, the keys,' said the headmaster.

'Have been speaking to someone about Alex . . .'

The headmaster had produced a huge bunch of keys from his jacket pocket and began rattling them.

'Alex set it all up down here. Very keen to get the boys involved in new technology of all kinds. Tremendous amount of expense. He's also had a few typewriters brought in. Teaching the boys to type! Quite something.'

'Essential skill,' said Morley. 'Should be taught to all schoolchildren along with penmanship.' (For further – extensive – elaboration on this point see *Morley's Light Touch Typing for Boys and Girls*, 1937.)

'Now, which is which?' said the headmaster. He tried one key. And then another. And another. Until he had tried them all.

'You know, I thought I had the key.'

'Apparently not,' said Morley.

'I can go and look for them up in my office. Won't take long. They must be there somewhere.'

'I could probably save you the time, Headmaster, if you would like?' said Morley, feeling in his own jacket pocket.

'Really? What? Abandon the plan and head straight for the cellar?' He winked at me. 'Not a bad plan, eh, Sefton?'

'With your permission, Headmaster?' Morley had produced what appeared to be a small pocket knife and brandished it before him.

'Goodness me,' said the headmaster. 'You're going to . . . cut the door open?'

'Jemmy it, I think is the phrase, Headmaster,' said Morley, unfolding the knife to reveal what appeared to be a long paperclip. 'But no. Not exactly.'

'You're going to . . . pick the lock?'

'Possibly,' said Morley, who quickly proceeded to do exactly that.

'Extraordinary!' said the headmaster. 'Have you been taking lessons, Morley?'

'Not lessons, no,' said Morley. 'But there was an occasion in Tehran where I had to make a hasty exit from a locked room. Misunderstanding about an interpretation of the Qur'an.'

The door swung open into darkness. I have never been scared of the dark, but years later, when we had indeed established Morley's own darkroom at St George's, and I was free to come and go and to use it day or night – though it sounds absurd – I chose never to go there during the hours of darkness. It may sound ridiculous to admit it, but the darkness inside a darkroom is of a kind – a total kind, a negative kind – that induces in me a sort of dread. One might almost believe that in a darkroom at night the souls of photographs come out to haunt one. Ridiculous, of course. But true.

The room was no more than ten feet square. It was lit by a red safelight. Everything was red: we looked as though we had bathed in blood. Solid wooden shelving had been installed all the way up to the ceiling. There were buckets set on the floor. Trays. And on one low shelf was a collection of cameras. Morley could not resist them.

'Well, this is a little treasure-trove,' he said. 'Absolutely marvellous! Look at this, Sefton. Little folding Kodak. A Zeiss. A Zeiss! Baby Box.' He picked up one from the shelf and held it out in his palm. 'Look at this. A Kodak Vest Pocket, if I am not mistaken. I have always wanted to get my hands on one of these little beauties.' He held the camera up close to me. 'Just look at this.' I looked: it was a small camera. 'This is the future, Sefton, mark my words. Pocket cameras. In years to come everyone will be equipped with one of these things. We'll be able to record our every waking moment and display it to everyone and for everyone.'

'Sounds hellish,' said the headmaster. 'I can't think of anything worse.'

He was looking around.

'What do you think, Sefton?' said Morley.

'It's fascinating, Mr Morley.'

'Yes, I wonder if we might set up something similar back at St George's. What do you think?'

'I think it'd be a marvellous idea,' said the headmaster.

'Absolutely,' I agreed.

'Alex has it set up rather nicely,' continued the headmaster.

'Indeed,' said Morley. 'Home from home. We should probably take notes, Sefton: list of materials, etcetera?'

'Yes, of course,' I said. 'I wonder if I might . . . ?' I indicated
the drawers and cupboards. 'Just to see how it's all set up?'

'Of course,' said the headmaster. 'Absolutely fascinating
actually, isn't it?'

And so I began opening drawers and cupboards.

'Now what about these?' said the headmaster. On a shelf,
beside some jars of chemicals and powders, there were a
number of figurines.

'Interesting,' said Morley. 'Egyptian gods and goddesses?'

'Seem to be,' agreed the headmaster.

They passed the little objects between them, holding
them up close. I continued – calmly – rifling through drawers.
I was very keen to find Mrs Dodds's photographs.

'What have we here?' asked Morley.

'An ibis-headed Thoth?' said the headmaster.

'Indeed,' said Morley.

'Ivory, I think.'

'Rather lovely,' said Morley. 'Anything interesting,
Sefton?'

I had alas found nothing interesting – or rather, plenty
that was interesting, but nothing specifically of interest to
me or Mrs Dodds.

'And a Horus,' said the headmaster, picking up another
ornament.

'Of course a Horus,' said Morley. 'And a fine specimen. He
has good taste, I'll say that for him.'

'And a . . .' The headmaster drew a blank. 'Not sure. What
do you think?'

'A lion-headed Sekhmet, if I'm not mistaken,' said Morley. 'Any idea, Sefton?'

I glanced up from a drawer. 'No idea,' I said.

'But again very nice,' said the headmaster. 'Very nice indeed.'

'Quite so,' agreed Morley. 'Nice little set-up Alex has down here, eh?'

'Very nice,' said the headmaster.

'Very nice, Mr Morley,' I agreed.

Another drawer full of equipment: tongs, scissors, paper . . .

'You know Zola of course described himself as a martyr to photography?' said Morley.

'Did he?' said the headmaster.

'Oh yes, absolutely obsessed with it. One can see why. I do think the art of photography might in years to come be regarded as an art form like the novel: a combination of documentary realism and fiction.'

'I can quite believe it,' said the headmaster.

'Might be worth an article, Sefton, what do you think?'

I did not reply. Beneath a pile of paper I had found a large brown envelope. The two men continued talking, admiring the set-up, debating what various pieces of equipment might be used for while I reached into the envelope – and my hand touched some thick and glossy papers. I turned my back to Morley and the headmaster and began to draw the papers slowly out of the envelope.

'Ah, what have we here?' said Morley, looking over my shoulder. 'Photographs, eh, Sefton?'

'Possibly,' I said, guiltily.

[264]

'Well, let's have a look, shall we?' said Morley.

And he and the headmaster gathered round to look.

'Oh,' said the headmaster.

'Well, well,' said Morley. 'What *do* we have here?'

'What on earth are these?' said the headmaster.

'Tarot cards,' said Morley decisively, which they were indeed. Several packs in fact. 'Hmm,' he said, spreading them out on the bench. 'Marked and unmarked. Someone is clearly taking their Tarot seriously. Mr Eliot would doubtless approve.'

'Mr Eliot?' asked the headmaster.

'Sefton's friend,' said Morley. 'T.S.'

T.S. Eliot was not in fact my friend, or even an acquaintance, though Morley himself had met him on several occasions. 'Very smooth,' had been his verdict. 'Cold hands. Direct gaze. Manners of a saint.' It was not, I thought, an entirely whole-hearted endorsement.

'I don't know Mr Eliot, I'm afraid,' said the headmaster.

'Poet,' explained Morley. 'Former banker: not a recommendation. Currently I believe panjandrum-in-chief at Faber and Gwyer, is that right, Sefton?'

'Faber and Faber,' I corrected him.

'As I believe they are now known, yes.' He was extracting cards from the pack as he did so, examining their garish colours. 'Though there was only ever one Faber, Sefton. Geoffrey Faber? Do you know him?'

'I can't say—'

'Curious chap. Doubled-up his name for the sake of euphony after he and my friends the Gwyers went their separate ways.'

'Ah.'

'Anyway, Madame Sosostris I believe, isn't it, in *The Waste Land*? Sefton?'

'Yes, that's correct.'

'Lot of nonsense, of course.' He began laying out the cards on the bench in a pattern. 'What is it, "Madame Sosostris, famous clairvoyante, wisest woman in Europe with a wicked pack of cards."'

'Something like that,' I said.

He finished laying out the cards.

'"Wicked", would you say, Sefton? Or childish, rather?'

'I'm not sure.'

'No. Now, would you care to give us a reading, perhaps?' He pointed to the cards, one by one: 'High Priestess; Magician; 10 of Cups; Queen of Wands; the Devil; 8 of Wands; 2 of Cups; Wheel of Fortune; Judgement; and the Knight of Swords.'

I looked at them. It was just a random pattern.

'Any thoughts at all?' he asked.

'No.'

'No. Like your friend Mr Eliot you seem to have an ignorance of the exact constitution of the Tarot pack. Do you know if Alex is interested in the occult sciences at all, Headmaster? Or one of the boys perhaps?'

'Not as far as I'm aware,' said the headmaster. 'But you know what boys are like. They pick up these odd sorts of things and . . .'

'Quite,' said Morley.

These were indeed odd sorts of things but I still hadn't found the photographs I was looking for. I was now up on a stool, going through the uppermost shelves.

'Well, anything interesting up there?' asked Morley.

'Notebooks, mostly,' I said.

'Notebooks,' he said. 'Hmm. Well, come on, man, let's have a look.'

I brought down a clutch of innocent-looking school notebooks. Morley ran a finger over their covers, looking for dust.

'In regular use,' he said. 'And yet set up so high. One might almost suspect that they were not meant to be seen.'

To my eye, there seemed to be nothing remarkable about them: they were standard school notebooks. Except that where usually the cover might read 'History' or 'Mathematics' these read 'Formula for Personal Spiritual Development', and 'Astral Explorations of Past Lives'. 'Notes on Astrology'; 'The Twelve Tribes'; 'Clairvoyant Investigations'; 'Horoscopes'; 'Seances'; 'Psychic Experiments'.

'Fascinating,' said Morley. He flicked quickly through one, and then another. The headmaster examined some of them also, and I rifled through the pages of some others. All the books seemed to be written in code. And they all contained diagrams, sketches of gyres, phases of the moon, disorganised material generally.

'Interesting,' said Morley.

'Really?'

'It's code. Yes. Seems to be. Do you recognise the handwriting at all?'

The headmaster studied the books. 'I'm not sure. It *could* be one of the boys, I suppose.'

'Or a teacher?'

'Possibly. Should we be worried?'

'I think it all rather depends on whether our amateur

occultist sees themselves more as a psychic or as a mystic,' said Morley.

'Is there a difference?' asked the headmaster.

'Yes, there certainly is, Headmaster. There is indeed. A psychic receives messages, sometimes unwillingly, and certainly unbidden. A mystic, on the other hand, goes seeking the divine.'

'Bad as each other, then?'

'Not quite, no. Psychics, I find, are perfectly harmless, on the whole – rather entertaining, often. Cranks, but harmless cranks. Individualists. Eccentrics. Wonderful woman down in Clacton ... But mystics ... Mystics tend rather towards the malevolent, in my experience. And they like to band together to cause mischief. Not a lot to be said in their favour.'

Morley was now digging deeper into some of the cupboards and produced some bits and pieces of religious paraphernalia. A crucifix. A bottle of holy water.

'Anything missing from the chapel, Headmaster?' asked Morley.

'I have no idea.'

'Might be worth checking.'

'Mr Morley?' I said. I was up on the stool still: there was another shelf of books below the shelf containing the notebooks. 'Do you want to look at everything?'

'Yes, yes, let's have them all down, Sefton, if you please.'

There were paperbacks and some books in soft leather linings. I passed them down to Morley.

'What have we got here then, gentlemen? Montague Summers, eh, *The History of Witchcraft and Demonology*? Now we're getting somewhere! Montague Summers, indeed.

Excellent little guide.' Morley flicked through the pages of the book. 'Though the problem with Summers of course is that he actually seems to believe in the witch cults.'

'You do seem terribly familiar with all this material, Morley, if you don't mind my saying so,' said the headmaster.

'"Moses was learned in all the wisdom of the Egyptians,"' said Morley. 'The Book of Acts, is it? Occult knowledge: it is tempting, I suppose. For a moment. And I have read widely – or as widely as one might need – in the alchemists, the Gnostics, the Hermetists, Neoplatonists and what-not, but I can't honestly say I've found that much there that one might not find in Plato's *Timaeus*. Also, do you know Mr Watkins' bookshop on Cecil Court?'

'In London?'

'Off Shaftesbury Avenue,' said Morley. 'You know it, Headmaster?'

'Cecil Court, yes. I think I've taken Mother down there a few times. Not the bookshop though, I don't think.'

'It's rather "interesting", as Sefton might say. They hold these little soirées. I went along to a few, after my son ... Anyway. Tea, cake and theosophy. Makes for a pleasant enough sort of evening. I have struggled my way through the works of Eliphas Levi, and MacGregor Mathers. Max Müller's books on the sacred texts of the East. They're all after the same thing essentially.'

'Which is?'

'Power, of course. The idea of transforming oneself into a magus. Solomon the Mage, Simon Magus, Comte de Saint-Germain. Etcetera. No shortage of the blighters. The magus, the sorcerer, the alchemist: all of them seized with an obsession, a desire for greatness. Insight. Power.

Wisdom. They think by force of will they might somehow achieve that which is impossible. Short cuts to knowledge. We know that often men wish for knowledge because power attends it; they strive for knowledge not for its own sake, but in order to attain power. Seized with such a perverted desire, men become demented. I have seen it oftentimes among university professors. Politicians are prone to the same fantasy, of course. Total control. Command.' Morley paused. 'Hmm. Are there people in the school who you think might be susceptible to this dangerous sort of fantasy, Headmaster? The idea that they might rightfully rule?'

'I really don't know, Morley.'

'The spurned lover? A man overlooked for promotion or cheated of some sort of preferment? The man who sees himself as the rightful ... Is Alex the only person with keys to the darkroom?'

'Apart from me,' said the headmaster.

'And your keys have mysteriously disappeared?'

'Or been misplaced.'

Morley fell silent. The atmosphere in the room had changed. As Morley had been talking the headmaster had been absent-mindedly going through one of the notebooks, where he had found a set of negatives, which he was now holding up to the red safelight.

'Ah,' said Morley. 'Well spotted, Headmaster! At last! Some photographs. I was beginning to wonder what Alex used the room for!'

It became clear, at that moment, what Alex used the room for.

They were photographs, mostly of women – naked

Photographs, mostly of women

women. In the negatives of course their skin was jet black, and the hair – and pubic hair – a quite startling white.

'Well well,' said Morley.

'Oh dear,' said the headmaster.

Several of the negatives were indeed of Mrs Dodds. She was quite right: they were not photographs that her husband would have been pleased to view.

'Well . . . only to be expected perhaps,' said Morley. This was, I think, the only occasion during our time together that I saw him blush – though it may simply have been the red light. 'New technologies always lend themselves to – shall we say – fleshly uses. You know that many of the first pamphlets published after Gutenberg were nothing more than scurrilous . . .'

But there were also photographs of men. With other men.

'Is that the chaplain?' I said.

'I rather fear so,' said Morley. 'Headmaster?'

The headmaster seemed to have lost all his strength; he collapsed down upon himself, onto the stool on which I had been standing, collapsing like a boxer returning to his corner and throwing in his towel, a gesture of total defeat. Morley turned his back to me slightly and laid a hand upon the headmaster's shoulder – and in the same instant I laid my hand upon the negatives of Mrs Dodds and was about to put them into my pocket for safekeeping. But Morley had noticed me reaching out for them and grabbed my wrist with one hand, snatching the negatives with his other. His strength was quite astonishing.

'Sefton?'

'I . . .'

'What do you think you're doing, man?'

[272]

'I was just going to . . .'

'You were going to what?'

'I was just going to look after them.'

'And why do they need you looking after them?' asked Morley.

'They need destroying,' said the headmaster bitterly, his head in his hands.

'I'm afraid it may be too late for that, Headmaster,' said Morley. 'And I think you may have some explaining to do, Sefton. Do you want to tell us why you were interested in coming down here?'

I said nothing.

'Sefton?' repeated Morley. 'You'd better speak up, man.'

'I happened to have mentioned to someone that I was interested in the darkroom and they said that Alex had . . . asked them to become an adept.'

'Someone happened to mention to you that Alex had asked them to become an adept?'

'Yes.'

'And you didn't see fit to mention it?'

'No, I . . .'

'You may have wasted us precious time, Sefton.'

'But I thought . . . Alex was the hero of the hour and—'

'Who might this person be, might I ask?'

'An acquaintance,' I said.

'Sefton?'

I remained silent.

'Headmaster?'

Morley was holding up my negatives to the light.

'The face here looks familiar, but I can't quite think . . . Headmaster? This might be important. I need you to . . .'

The headmaster glanced up. He recognised her straight away. 'Mrs Dodds,' he said. 'It's Mrs Dodds, Morley.'

'And she is?'

'She's the wife of our benefactor. Mr Dodds, who has enabled us to buy the new school.'

'And the others are?'

'Mostly other benefactors.'

Morley was pacing up and down now. 'Oh dear, oh dear,' he said. 'Oh dear, oh dear.' He held up the negatives to the safelight. 'Sefton, what exactly did your Mrs Dodds say about Alex?'

'She said that he had asked her to become an adept.'

'And that's all?'

'And that Alex claimed he was some sort of . . . mage?'

'Come on, Sefton! And you didn't think to pass on this information?'

'I—'

'You can never trust a man who calls himself a mage,' he said.

'But you call yourself the People's Professor,' I said.

'Not a title I claim for myself, Sefton. It's merely a shorthand, for the newspapers.'

'Do you think he's a devil worshipper?' I asked. 'Alex?'

'You've clearly been watching far too many movies, Sefton. Only fools believe in devil worship. And only idiots believe in devil worshippers.'

'So—'

'I think it's more likely he's someone who believes in the perfectibility of man's soul. In developing full human potential. Do What Thou Wilt Shall be the Whole of the Law and etcetera. Love is the Law, Love under the Will.'

[274]

'Sorry?' I said.

'He was never the same after the war,' said the head-master, interrupting, lost in his own thoughts. 'He was always . . . looking for something.'

'Which is why you moved here?'

'Mother thought it would be a good idea to move the school here.'

'Because?'

'I think . . . I thought she just wanted a view of the sea. But Alex had these grand schemes and plans. He was able to persuade all these benefactors. I thought it was . . .'

'And you knew nothing about it?'

The headmaster was silent.

'Well,' said Morley, clearing his throat, 'let's just see if we can establish exactly what's going on here, shall we?' And then having peered at the photographs for a moment, he suddenly swung around and pointed over the doorframe.

Inscribed over the door, in the dark I could make out black-painted letters, SATOR AREPO, set out in a pattern:

SATOR
AREPO
TENET
OPERA
ROTAS

'That,' said Morley.

'What?'

'In a lot of the photographs. The Sator Arepo, from the testament of Solomon. Magic palindrome. Now, if we have the Sator Arepo, we're probably going to have . . .' He looked down at the floor. 'Move out of the way, Sefton.'

There were markings on the floor.

'Damn!' said Morley. 'Damn!'

'What is it?' asked the headmaster.

'This,' said Morley, indicating some markings on the floor, 'this is the Tree of Sephiroth, if I'm not much mistaken.'

'Which means?'

'It means that this is some sort of chamber.'

'What sort of chamber?'

'Wasn't there a notebook there, Sefton, that said something about the moon?'

'I don't know.'

'Just have a look. Ephemerides tables, that sort of thing? Saturn in the ascendant? Mercury triune to the ascendant? Saturn and Uranus triune to the moon? It's not a full moon by any chance tonight, is it?'

'It is, Mr Morley, yes. I think so.'

'Which means our occultist friends will be active exactly' – Morley checked his watch with the luminous dial – 'around now.'

'But there's nothing happening here,' I said. 'You couldn't swing a cat in here.'

'No. But a cockerel maybe,' said Morley.

'A cockerel?'

'Or a hen.' He pointed to stains on the floor. 'Mr Gooding's missing chickens?'

'What on earth are you suggesting, Morley? That—'

'They'd really need bigger premises,' continued Morley. 'Somewhere private. And if you were involving the boys . . .'

We began running upstairs to the dormitories.

CHAPTER 20

AN ARTIFICIAL PARADISE

MORLEY RAN SO FAST I thought he might actually take off. He took the steps two at a time, the headmaster not far behind him.

The dormitories stretched across the top floor of the building. The candles in their sconces illuminated the corridor: it was like walking into a bad dream. Morley had made it to the first dormitory before I had reached the top of the stairs. The headmaster followed him in. I followed them both.

I was momentarily shocked and disorientated. Glancing frantically around in the darkness trying to find my bearings, different objects seemed to loom from nowhere and become suddenly visible: the beds, of course, their metal glinting in the moonlight, and the lockers, a pile of books here, a few pebbles on the windowsill there, the clock on the wall, and row upon row of old school photographs. And then directly opposite the door – a dark black face, with one big round white eye staring at us, teeth bared. It was as if eternal night itself had fallen and the devil was making his appearance. I gasped and stumbled back.

'Ssshh!' commanded Morley. 'Silence, Sefton!'

The big white eye – pitted like a peach stone – continued staring, boring into me. Somehow Morley and the head-master ignored it and this was almost as shocking as the thing itself. My panic gave way to suspicion. I made myself look again and stare back, steadying my breathing. It was nothing more than a big Geographia classroom map of the moon and the stars: the phases of the moon were the teeth.

I felt like an utter fool.

And then in the dim light came the sound.

There is a very distinct and peculiar sound that is the sound of a group of boys sleeping. It is the sound of turbulent rest, of troubled dreams and secrets, an endless flow of shuffling and mumbling and stifled tears: a room of sleeping boys is never actually silent. The noise, the terrible cacophony of humans even at rest. It used to torment me when I was young and at school: there seemed nowhere to hide from it. The incessant sound of silence. It made me nervous and unsettled – the terrible sound of boys asleep.

And now there they lay, lit only by the moon filtering in through the windows, their eyes and mouths half open, like a row of mannequins in a bizarre shop display, hidden and yet visible, present and disappearing, abandoned to themselves and to the otherworld of dreams. The wonderful sound of boys asleep.

Morley and the headmaster went quickly and silently along the rows, taking a head-count.

Everyone was there. Everything was in order.

Once the headmaster was satisfied, we went across

to the other dormitory. It was the same thing. All present and correct. A chubby boy in the regulation blue and white striped pyjamas half woke at the sound of our footsteps and sat bolt upright in his bed, muttering, his eyes open, his cheeks damp with tears.

'No, sir! I didn't, sir! Sorry, sir. Yes.'

'It's all right, William. Just doing the evening rounds,' said the headmaster, patting him gently on the shoulder.

And the boy lay back down, turned over, and retreated again into his own private world of terrors.

Back out in the corridor we tried to gather our thoughts, whispering between ourselves.

'Well, thank goodness,' said the headmaster. 'We seem to have been mistaken, Morley.'

'Indeed,' said Morley.

'The boys are all safe.'

'Yes. Yes. They are.'

'So?' said the headmaster.

'It's not about the boys,' I said.

'Not about the boys?' repeated the headmaster.

'Yes!' said Morley. 'That's it, Sefton! There were no photographs of boys, were there?'

'I didn't see any, no.'

'We just assumed, that ... Headmaster, where are all the teachers?'

'Where are they all?'

'Where do they all live?'

'A few live in lodgings, and some of them in Sidmouth, but most of them live here on site, in this building, or in the houses: Alex and his wife have a house, and some of the other married staff. And—'

Morley had already started for the stairs.

We followed passageway after dark passageway to the back of the building and to the teachers' quarters: oak-panelled walls and heavy oak doors. We knocked on one. No answer. And then another – and again no answer came.

'Perhaps they've all gone into Sidmouth?' said the head-master. 'They sometimes organise outings.'

'It's nearly midnight,' said Morley.

'It is a little late, I—'

'Take us to the houses.'

Alex's house was part of the terraced row that led down towards the farmhouse where I had been staying. These were the grander kind of workers' cottages: roses growing round the door, mullioned windows. A picture-perfect picture of rural domestic England. We knocked on Alex's door. There was no answer. We peered through the mullioned windows and there seemed to be a light on somewhere at the back of the house. So we knocked again. We tried the door: it was locked. Morley checked the dial on his luminous watch. It was almost twenty to midnight.

'We could go round the back?' said the headmaster. 'We just have to go round by the school and then up past—'

'Kick it in, Sefton,' said Morley.

'I say, Morley!' objected the headmaster. 'Hardly neces-sary, is it? If we just go round the back and—'

'Too late, too late, shall be the cry,' said Morley. 'Kick it in, Sefton. Aim just below the door knob. Weakest point. Here.' He pointed exactly at the spot where he wanted me to kick.

'Come on, man. Hit with the sole. And push up from the heel of the other foot.'

He nodded, the headmaster shook his head and gave a kind of low moan, and I kicked. The sound of a blunt instrument – me – hitting an inanimate object echoed in the still dark night. It hurt.

'Any give at all?'

'A little,' I said.

'Again,' said Morley. 'Come on.'

'Morley!' said the headmaster. 'I really must object, I think this is—'

Morley nodded at me to go ahead.

I kicked again. And then again. And again, like a smithy at his forge. And then again – and it gave.

Morley raced through the front room of the house and out towards the back. Which was where we found her, sitting in the kitchen: Alex's wife. The kitchen was lit by a single lamp that cast a thin, wavering languid light. A low-beamed ceiling, bits and pieces of cheap crockery on an old dresser, a range that hadn't been blackened in some time, and the smell. That smell. The delicious disorientating smell either of something very wrong, or something very right. It was a smell I knew only too well. The smell I'd detected in the staff common room. There was absolutely no mystery about it: the table was filled with bottles, like those in a dispensary in a hospital, each containing different chemicals. Morley glanced at me.

Mrs Standish sat staring straight ahead. She was dressed entirely in black, as usual, her dark hair swept back, her cheeks flushed, as though having recently emerged from the cockpit of a plane. Around her neck hung a string of black pearls. Her eyes were rolled back in her head. She looked like a ruined rag doll. She was absent-mindedly stroking a lizard in her lap, her pale fingers and white nails pulling back and forth against the scaly green skin.

'Good God!' said the headmaster.

She looked straight at him then, her dark bright eyes jangling around, and she laughed. It was not the laugh of someone who was happy.

The headmaster seemed nonplussed.

'What is this?' he asked. He had no idea what he was witnessing.

I picked up a phial of liquid and sniffed it.

'What is it, Sefton?'

I suddenly felt a sympathetic longing for something – not having touched anything for . . . days.

'Sefton?' repeated Morley. 'What is it?'

It was laudanum.

'Drugs,' I said, simplifying rather for the sake of the headmaster.

'What?' Morley repeated.

'Drugs?' said the headmaster. 'Well, what sort of drugs? Here? In the school?'

'Lotos-dust,' said Morley to himself.

'What?' said the headmaster.

'She lies beside her nectar,' continued Morley.

'What is this?' insisted the headmaster.

I knew exactly what it was.

'It is a door to an artificial paradise,' I said.

'Michael Taylor – the boy who fell to his death from the clifftops?' said Morley. He was addressing Alex's wife now, kneeling down before her, his face up close to hers. 'Had he found out what was happening?'

'A school at the top of a cliff!' She laughed. 'A school at the top of a cliff!'

'Indeed,' said Morley. 'Where are they? Where are your husband and the other teachers?'

But Morley was wasting his time. Alex's wife had entered a place from where I knew it was impossible to return. She had passed the stage of speech: she had reached the stage of inner speech: she had taken so much of what she was making that she had become quite incapable.

The headmaster sat down on a low chair beside the range, incapable of comprehending what was happening. He looked tiny, like a boy waiting to meet some terrible punishment.

'Drugs?' he said. 'And . . . those pictures. And the occult? In the school?'

'Headmaster,' said Morley. 'You need to think. Is there somewhere they're likely to have gathered? Somewhere nearby? A big empty space? Somewhere they could meet and not be seen by others? Somewhere private?'

'Somewhere—' began the headmaster.

'Somewhere – hidden!' cried Morley. He began clicking his fingers, attempting to summon forth some idea, or to forge some connection. 'Hidden, hidden. That's it! What is it, Sefton?'

'I'm not entirely sure, Mr Morley.'

'And here . . . And here the sea-fogs lap and cling / And here, each warning each, / The sheep-bells and the ship-bells ring / Along the hidden . . . beach!' He bolted for the door, calling behind him. 'Headmaster. You stay here and notify the police. Do you understand?'

The headmaster sat as insensate as Mrs Standish.

'Headmaster?'

He nodded.

And Morley looked at me, and we began to run.

᷈ ᷈

The steep path down to the beach was rutted and rocky and the trees had cast the way in darkness. As we tumbled and tore our way along, Morley barked out instructions to me – not to do this, not to do that – and eventually we reached the place down by the water-pumping station where the steps were cut into the cliff. There was a light shining from behind the door of the water-pumping station.

'Odd?' said Morley. 'I wonder . . .' He glanced at his watch and then quickly entered the building. There was nothing odd about the place at all. It was an office – there were charts on the wall, a pile of ledgers. It was entirely innocuous. And then we went through a door that led into a corridor that led to another door. On the lintel above the door someone had scratched a word I couldn't quite make out. The first two letters seemed to be 'E' and 'D'.

'Eden?' I said.

'Edom,' said Morley.

'Edom?'

'Dogs and wildcats, screech owls and crows and other creatures hold a demonic Sabbath there: Isaiah 34. Prepare yourself, Sefton.'

The door opened onto a passageway lit by candles –

some kind of service tunnel. Morley glanced behind him, put a finger to his lips and went on ahead into the passageway. It was cut through rock, winding down and down, deeper and deeper, like the steps at Goodge Street Station, except that following the steps down we emerged not to a station platform but an underground cave.

I stared at the dark stone walls, which were lit by guttering black candles. There was a row of trunks lined up against a wall, and a long hanging rail for clothes. It was like a changing room in a school sports pavilion. It even smelled like the changing room in a school pavilion: linseed oil, sweat, old leather and mould.

'The robing room,' whispered Morley.

We entered a narrow passageway into another chamber.

This room was larger – perhaps twice the size – and there was a large round table in the middle of the room, with chairs set around it and books and papers spread across it.

'The round table, eh?' said Morley bitterly, shaking his head.

There were bookshelves against the walls, and a cabinet set with what appeared to be stationery supplies and arts and crafts equipment: quill pens, ink pots, knives and scissors. The place seemed to be designed as some sort of study area. There was even a sign hung below one of the candle sconces that had clearly been borrowed from the school library. It read, in time-honoured tradition: 'SILENCE, PLEASE'.

'Ah, yes,' said Morley quietly, beckoning me over, pointing at the books on the bookshelves. 'Here we are, Sefton. Dornford Yates. Of course.'

I raised a quizzical eyebrow.

SILENCE, PLEASE

'Occult guff. Knorr von Rosenroth. Same. Glanville: absolute total guff. And Bulwer-Lytton. Yes, of course. *The Coming Race.*'

'Wasn't that the chap old Mrs Standish was talking about?'

Morley picked up the book. 'Hmm. Story of a sub-terranean master race who have the power to heal and destroy humankind. Great favourite with the Rosicrucians, and all sorts of other crackpots . . .'

Morley became momentarily absorbed in flicking through the books. I turned to the table and picked up a card that had been laid out with a set of others; they were like the Tarot cards we had found in the darkroom, except that these were crude, home-made things, featuring weird hand-drawn symbols. They were arranged on the table in a pattern resembling a cross.

'Mr Morley,' I said quietly, holding the card up to him: it showed a dagger.

'Yes,' he said. 'Tattwa cards. I've never seen a set myself.' He studied the cards set out on the table. 'Wand. Pentacles. Stars. The dagger.'

'What does it mean?'

'I'm not sure,' he said. 'Divining instructions.'

'What sort of instructions?'

'Maybe related to this . . .' He picked up what appeared to be a parchment manuscript set beside the Tattwa cards. 'Oh dear,' he said. 'A grimoire?'

'Grimoire?'

'Repository of magical knowledge, Sefton. A sort of store of curious information and quaint ideas, scraps of folklore, old legends and superstitions.'

'Sounds familiar,' I said. It did not sound dissimilar to our own enterprise.

He carefully turned the pages of the book – each page covered in dense handwritten notes. 'A means of arming oneself against evil spirits and witches, though more usually it's a book that people turn to in order to fulfil their wanton desires.'

'I see.'

'How to seduce women, how to gain power over others. How to cause rain. You know the sort of thing, Sefton.'

'Yes,' I said. My eye had been caught by a photograph that lay with the Tattwa cards. I picked it up. It showed Miriam.

'It's like a book of spells,' continued Morley. 'Except the other thing about the grimoire' – he turned the book over and over in his hands, stroking the dark brown cover – 'is that the book itself is also magic.'

'The book itself?'

'Certain words within it have active properties. But more important is the paper and the ink . . .' Again he stroked the pages of the book. 'I'm afraid I recall reading somewhere that the most valuable grimoires are those made from a parchment made from the skin of the unborn.'

'The skin of the unborn?'

'An aborted animal foetus, for example, such as—'

'A cow?'

'I fear so, Sefton, yes.'

'Mr Morley,' I said, about to show him the photograph.

'Good God,' said the headmaster. He had followed us down from the school.

Morley swung around. 'Headmaster,' he said. 'I told you to stay and . . .'

But the headmaster – who seemed to be in some kind of daze – ignored us, walked past us towards another narrow passageway that led into yet another deserted chamber.

'Good God,' he repeated. 'God forgive us.'

Morley and I entered this final place together and we all stood together, staring, speechless.

There were crude, mysterious symbols painted on the stone walls with black paint. And in the centre of the room, a long refectory table that had effectively become an altar. The floor beneath this altar was awash with blood. And upon it was a slaughtered donkey.

'Mithraism,' said Morley decisively.

'What?' said the headmaster.

'Sacred cult.'

'Mithraism?' said the headmaster. 'But—'

'They worshipped in underground caverns. Brutal initiation rites. This certainly looks like a Mithraist sacrifice.' Morley approached the donkey on the altar. 'Should be a bull, of course, strictly speaking, but—'

'But this is . . . my school,' said the headmaster.

'Someone seems to have established another kind of school, Headmaster. The cave schools of magic at Toledo and Salamanca?'

'How on earth did they get it down here?' I said.

'Taurobolium,' said Morley. 'That's it! That's what it's called. Bull sacrifice in which the blood of the beast is shed and flows onto the worshipper, which then empowers them to—'

'There must be another entrance,' I said, glancing around.

'Good God!' said the headmaster again. 'In my school?'

'Headmaster,' said Morley, turning to face the headmaster,

his temper suddenly flaring. 'This is not your school. You have lost control. Do you understand?'

I had found another wide passageway behind the altar table, hidden behind a heavy damask curtain. The passageway led down and out.

'Here!' I cried. 'Mr Morley! Headmaster! There's a way out!'

I was right. There was a way out – and there wasn't.

CHAPTER 21

THE FULL MOON

THE PASSAGE LED straight onto the hidden beach below
the cliff.

At the best of times a beach at night can be a shudder-
some place – all the colour gone, and with it all charm and
beauty. A place of pleasure during the day can seem like the
most desolate spot on earth at night. And on this night the
beach at Rousdon seemed like hell itself.

The full moon lit the scene before us like a theatrical
set. Alex of course was centre stage. He wore a peculiar
headdress and what looked like a lace dressing gown with
no buttons down the front, the kind of garment that could
only have been made by the lacemakers of Honiton. In the
darkness his lips appeared to be tinged with blue and his
face – just as it was in the caves – was a burning phosphor-
escent yellow.

Above him was the full moon. Behind him, the endless
grey sea spitting pebbles up onto the beach. And before
him, a crowd of benefactors and teachers – and held
aloft between them, bound and gagged and tied to one of

Morley's surfboards, was Miriam. She was dressed in an outfit similar to Alex's. God only knows what they were planning.

Morley yelled. I yelled. We ran full pelt towards the gathered ghouls.

It is difficult to describe what occurred then in the chaos that ensued, but this an account as good as I can recall.

Most of the teachers and benefactors scattered, running for the cliffs. Morley made it to Miriam and began to untie her from the surfboard – and when he undid the gag around her mouth she sat up and let out a bloodcurdling scream worthy of Fay Wray herself.

I went straight for Alex and launched myself upon him. He grabbed me with both hands by the throat, but I struck him once, twice and three times with all my might, and then grabbed at his fingers and bent them back until I heard them snap – and he fell down on his knees in agony. In Spain I'd learned from a little Hungarian named Imre some basics of hand-to-hand combat: attack the most vulnerable parts of the body, the groin, the eyes, the neck, the fingers. And use any available object. As Alex lay stunned before me I grabbed a large pebble, a rock really, the size of my fist, and was about to dash it down on his stupid shining head when someone or something flew at me. It was Miriam.

'No!' she screamed with a demonic rage. 'Sefton, no!' She hung on my back and dug her nails into my face, scream-ing; we fought intensely for a moment, me trying to throw her off, until she began sobbing. 'You must not kill him! You mustn't! You mustn't! Don't do it!'

And I realised suddenly that she had attacked me for my own protection, not Alex's. It was me she was seeking to save from the consequences of my actions. Stunned, I released my grip on the rock and turned to her.

'Don't!' she cried. 'Please, Sefton! Don't!'

I looked at her – for the first time perhaps properly looked at her – and she looked back at me. But then there were shouts from behind, and I turned to see that the headmaster had now got to Alex, and that he had somehow dragged him down into the shallow waters and had his head under the waves, pressing down and down. I ran towards him as he stepped back as if in shock, his hands free, and Alex did not reappear. I dived under the surf and swam towards Alex's body.

With all my remaining strength I dragged him back towards the shore, and then Miriam joined me and helped me drag him up onto the pebbles and I attempted to give him the kiss of life, the man who only moments previously I had been about to murder.

It was no good. Miriam was sobbing, her head upon Alex's chest, and then suddenly she stopped, by instinct, and turned. She'd noticed something. It was Morley.

'Father!' she cried.

Morley was lying flat on the surfboard, fully clothed, frantically paddling out into the waves.

The headmaster, ahead of him, was swimming far out into the dark ocean.

They headed far out, too far to be reached.

And then there was only the sound of the water.

Alexander – Alex, X – Standish

CHAPTER 22

BACK TO THE LIGHT

WE STAYED FOR AS LONG as was necessary to help the police with their enquiries. During the day Morley would work on his articles and on the book, writing and writing – his usual salve. Miriam stayed mostly in her room, and away from me – ditto. The police arrested and then charged a number of teachers, and most of the school's benefactors. Dr Standish's favourite, the inquisitive Michael Taylor, it was thought, had discovered the underground cave and had been punished – whether by Alex or by someone else it was not clear. Dr Standish's body was found washed up near Budleigh Salterton. Mrs Dodds did not show her face. And as for the two Mrs Standishes? They simply disappeared. The Good-ings claimed that old Mrs Standish had visited a place called the Crazwell Pool, near Princetown and – as superstition had it – she had seen who would be the next person in the area to die, and she went, taking her lizard-loving daughter-in-law with her. Morley remembered where he had seen her before: at a soirée at Watkins occult bookshop in Cecil Court in London. Bernhard, who appeared to be entirely blameless, took over as temporary headmaster. And as for me, during the day I took photographs for the book, and assisted Morley, who was uncharacteristically subdued, and in the evenings I would sit and drink cider with the Goodings at their farmhouse. Shadrach, Meshach and Abednego turned out to be excellent companions. And then, on the third day, it was time to go.

～ ～

We left All Souls, as we had arrived, in darkness.

The Lagonda was packed – everything minus the surf-boards, which Morley had decided to donate to the school.

'We could always wait until tomorrow?' I suggested, as Miriam settled Morley into his seat in the back, and placed his typewriter on its plinth around him. I was rather keen still to see Mrs Dodds, in the hope that she might be keen to express her gratitude. But it was not to be.

Morley seemed to revive as soon as he was in the Lagonda.

'Motoring all through the night,' he said, 'is one of the fifty-seven things that every man should do at least once in his lifetime, don't you think, Sefton?'

'Fifty-seven?' asked Miriam. 'Why fifty-seven, Father?'

'No idea,' said Morley. 'It just came to me. Rather catchy though, isn't it? *The Fifty-Seven Things a Man Should Do in his Lifetime.*'

Might this be another book coming on? I rather hoped so.

'Take a note, Sefton,' said Morley.

It was good to hear those words again.

We bade farewell to Bernhard, and to the Goodings,

and to the pupils – many of them seemingly unaware of the events that had unfolded, and one can only hope that they really were unaware, and were ignorant, for in such a case as this ignorance truly is bliss – and so we began our journey home, swooping through valleys and up hills and through towns and villages.

'What are you looking forward to then, Sefton, about getting back to Norfolk?' asked Morley.

'I'm—'

'I'm looking forward to seeing the animals. And some good home-made marmalade. And a nice strong cup of Russian tea.'

'Let him answer, Father, for goodness sake!' cried Miriam.

After days of fresh air in Devon I was yearning for a delicious thick yellow London fog.

'It'll be nice to have a rest,' I said.

'Now, now, we have a lot of work to catch up on, I'm afraid,' said Morley. 'What is our motto?'

'No shirking,' I said.

'No shilly-shallying,' said Morley.

'No funking,' said Miriam.

Devon flew past, in darkness, and at great speed.

'Goodbye to Devon!' said Miriam. 'And good riddance!'

'We shouldn't judge the place too harshly,' said Morley. 'Just because of . . .' He was rarely lost for words, but this was one of those occasions.

'I know, Father.'

'I'll certainly miss some of them,' I said, perhaps not entirely appropriately. 'The Goodings, they were a—'

'I think Mrs Standish rather took a fancy to you, Father,' said Miriam.

[297]

'Old Mrs Standish?'

'Young Mrs Standish.'

'Alex's wife?' said Morley.

'Yes.'

'Don't be so ridiculous, Miriam.'

'Probably an effect of the drugs,' she added.

'I must say I would rather have liked to have given her a monkey,' said Morley.

'I beg your pardon?' said Miriam.

'A monkey?' I said.

'A capuchin, I think. Terribly intelligent. One can still easily pick them up from Jamrach and Cross. They might have kept it in the school during winter and allowed it to run about during the summer. Plenty of space there. All they need is a little rice and some carrots, a few meal-worms, some minced chicken. They really do make excellent house pets. I can't understand why more people don't keep them, actually.'

'Because a capuchin monkey is clearly not suitable as a house pet, Father!' said Miriam. 'That's why people don't keep them. It would be cruel and unnatural.'

'But we have Sir Toby at home,' said Morley.

'Sir Toby?' I said.

'The damned monkey Father keeps in the hall.'

'Ah.' I recalled Sir Toby from the menagerie at St George's.

'Monkeys are wild creatures, Father. They are not pets. They are not intended to be kept as pets.'

'But you're very fond of Sir Toby, aren't you?'

'That's beside the point, Father.'

'I do think some of these modern ideas are very unhelpful you know. I knew a chap once who kept a rhino as a pet. Excellent beast. Tame, affectionate, most engaging little creature – this was in East Africa, of course. And a lion, also perfectly reasonable.'

'This is England, Father, not East Africa.'

'Well, more's the pity,' said Morley. 'If it means we can't enjoy the company of God's creatures, as he clearly intended. Is that the North Star? Astronomically . . .'

The conversation seemed to be back to its usual form.

Miriam revved the engine and glanced across at me.

'Shouldn't we slow down?' I said.

'Nonsense!' cried Miriam.

'I think statistics show that most street accidents in London occur at speeds of less than 10 mph,' said Morley.

'But we're not in London,' I pointed out, as hedges and verges flew past.

'Precisely,' he said. 'Nothing to fear. Absolutely nothing.'

In all our years together we rarely spoke of Devon again, and never of the events that had unfolded at All Souls. I never asked Miriam about Alex, and I never asked Morley about Dr Standish. But there is a passage in *The County Guides: Devon* about the caves of Beer that speaks perhaps as clearly about Morley's feelings for his friend as any outpouring or encomium. 'One should take care in the caves not to lose one's bearings. It is easy to do so, and difficult to find one's way back to the light. For this reason one should never venture into the caves alone, but ensure that one always sets out with a trusted companion.'

Dr Standish – trusted companion

ACKNOWLEDGEMENTS

For previous acknowledgements see *The Truth About Babies* (Granta Books, 2002), *Ring Road* (Fourth Estate, 2004), *The Mobile Library: The Case of the Missing Books* (Harper Perennial, 2006), *The Mobile Library: Mr Dixon Disappears* (Harper Perennial, 2006), *The Mobile Library: The Delegates' Choice* (Harper Perennial, 2008), *The Mobile Library: The Bad Book Affair* (Harper Perennial, 2010), *Paper: An Elegy* (Fourth Estate, 2012) and *The Norfolk Mystery* (Fourth Estate, 2013). These stand, with exceptions. In addition I would like to thank the following. (The previous terms and conditions apply: some of them are dead; most of them are strangers; the famous are not friends; none of them bears any responsibility.)

3rd Bangor Boys' Brigade, Eric Akoto, Francesca Arcieri, the Association of British Counties, Seb Averill, Albert Bandura, Bangor Orthodontics, Tom Berry, Billy the painter, James Blunt's Twitter feed, the Boiler Room, Dan Boland, Andrew Bovingdon, Serena Bowman, Gwyneth Box, David Boyles, Charlie Bromley, Rob Brydon, Grace Cain, Grace Carlini, Jordan Charles, Cinemagic (Belfast), the Clandeboye Lodge Hotel, Tom Clayton, Claire Collins,

Company Pictures, Simon Critchley, Charles Dantzig, Bette Davis, Matthew Dodds, Martin Doyle, Edward Sharpe and the Magnetic Zeros, Farriers, Flybe, David Gallacher, Cathy Galvin, William H. Gass, Tom Gatti, Lauren Gibb, Antonello Guerrera, Jim Henson, Sebastian Horsley, Ibis (Coventry), Nicolas Jaar, Howard Jacobson, Charlotte Jones, Kevin Kohan, Francis Kolinsky, Robert Lacey, Alessio Lana, Lisa Landrum, Tim Leach, Hari Mackinnon, Conor Mahon, Mammal Disco, Stephen Maxam, Ross McConaughy, Patrick McGuinness, Conor McKay, Sean McSweeney, Melia White-house Hotel, Joe Milutis, James Minihane, David Moore, Stephanie Moore, Stephen Moore, Paul Moran, Casey Neistat, Will Nott, the staff of the No.1 Lounge (Birmingham Airport), Open House Festival Bangor, Lillie Parmar, Jill Partington, Liese Perrin, Steve Peters, Natalie Pollard, Propertynewsni. com, the staff of the Rabbit Rooms, Holly Race, Man Ray, Penny Rimbaud, Liz Rosenberg, Lucy Santos, Gianmarco Senatore, Stephen Shapiro, David Shields, Viktor Shklovsky, Alexander Smith, Octavia Stocker, Mariusz Szczygiel, Peter Tarnofsky, Mark Tavender, Jill Thomson, Chris Todd, John Truby, the staff of the Ulster Hospital A & E Department (again), Jana Viarta, Michael Watkinson, Lucas Whitaker, Andrew Williams, Peter Wilson, John Yorke, Alice Yousef.

In the third of *The County Guides*,
Westmorland is the destination . . .

SWANTON MORLEY, the People's Professor, sets off on the
Great North Road to the ancient county of Westmorland. But
tragedy strikes: a train crash, followed by the murder of a
young woman. Are the two incidents connected – and if so,
how? Does the answer to the mystery lie with the raggle-
taggle gypsies befriended by Morley? Or with the close-knit
community of railwaymen on the Settle–Carlisle line?

Morley's assistant Stephen Sefton finds himself increas-
ingly haunted by his past. And Morley's daughter Miriam
once again attracts an unsuitable suitor.

Join Swanton Morley, Miriam and Sefton in Westmorland
for a tale of railways, wrestling, and gypsy lore . . .

PICTURE CREDITS

THE NORFOLK MYSTERY

IAN SANSOM

The first of

THE COUNTY GUIDES

Spanish Civil War veteran Stephen Sefton is flat broke.
So when he sees a mysterious advertisement for a job
where 'intelligence is essential', he applies.

Thus begins Sefton's association with Professor Swanton
Morley, autodidact. Morley intends to write a history of
England, county by county. His assistant must be able
to tolerate his every eccentricity – and withstand the
attentions of his beguiling daughter, Miriam.

The trio begin the project in Norfolk, but when the vicar
of Blakeney is found hanging from his church's bell rope,
they find themselves drawn into a fiendish plot.
Did the Reverend really take his own life,
or was it – murder?

FOURTH ESTATE • *London*

TELL THE WORLD

THIS BOOK WAS

Good	Bad	So ·so